Eyes Like Sky and Coal and Moonlight

Stories by

Cat Rambo

Eyes Like Sky and Coal and Moonlight © 2009 by Cat Rambo
Introduction © 2009 by Michael Livingston

"The Accordion" first appeared in *Cafe Irreal*.
"I'll Gnaw Your Bones, the Manticore Said" first appeared in *Clarkesworld*.
"Heart in a Box" first appeared in *Strange Horizons* as "Foam on the Water."
"In the Lesser Southern Isles" first appeared in *Black Sails*.
"Up the Chimney" first appeared in *Postcards*.
"Events at Fort Plentitude" first appeared in *Weird Tales*.
"Dew Drop Coffee Lounge" first appeared in *Clockwork Phoenix*.
"Eagle-haunted Lake Sammamish" first appeared in *Shimmer*.
"Sugar" first appeared in *Fantasy Magazine Sampler*.
"A Key Decides Its Destiny" first appeared in *Say...What's the Combination*.
"The Towering Monarch of His Mighty Race" first appeared in *Intergalactic Medicine Show*.
"The Dead Girl's Wedding March" first appeared in *Fantasy Magazine*.
"Worm Within" first appeared in *Clarkesworld*.
"Magnificent Pigs" first appeared in *Strange Horizons*.

Published by Paper Golem LLC
1049 Union Meeting Road
Blue Bell, PA 19422 USA

http://www.papergolem.com

Cover Art by Carrie Ann Baade
Cover Design by Mary Robinette Kowal
Book Design by Lawrence M. Schoen

ISBNs:
Hard Cover	978-0-9795349-4-2	0-9795349-4-1
Soft Cover	978-0-9795349-5-9	0-9795349-5-X

Paper Golem

Eyes Like Sky and Coal and Moonlight

Stories by Cat Rambo

edited by

Michael Livingston and Lawrence M. Schoen

DEDICATION

For Wayne, always.

ACKNOWLEDGEMENTS

When I first went to Clarion West in 2005, I had no idea what an amazing journey it would launch, or how many friends and family-of-affinity members I would acquire along the way. I'd like to particularly acknowledge the following:

- My fellow members of Clarion West 2005, who saw several of these stories in embryo, and who have been sources of encouragement, inspiration, and the occasional kick in the ass. And our instructors: Octavia Butler, L. Timmel Duchamp, Andy Duncan, Michael Swanwick (who did not make us cry), Gordon van Gelder, and Connie Willis. And last but never least, Neile Graham and Leslie Howle, who kept us all sane.
- Members of the Codex Writers' Group as well as the Redmond Riters and Horrific Miscue, Seattle Branch.
- Lawrence M. Schoen, Michael Livingston, and Mary Robinette Kowal.
- Kris Dikeman, to whom I owe so very, very much
- Sean Wallace, who always tells me the good gossip.
- Jeff VanderMeer, who rocks my socks off.
- Ken and Sarah, most excellent proprietors of the Griffon Bookstore, which made adolescence bearable.
- And my mother, who started reading F&SF because I was writing "that kind of stuff."

CONTENTS

Eight Letters of Wonder

I'm not a gambling man. Never have been. But I bet the odds are good that I can guess what you, Dear Reader, are thinking as you hold this beautiful book in your hand. After all, almost everyone who encounters Cat Rambo's work undergoes the same two-step process of thinking. I went through it myself several years ago.

If this is your first exposure to Cat's work, you're wondering if that's her real name. There's no chance, you're thinking, that those two nouns actually came together in any natural way. One or both of the names just has to be fake, right? I thought the same thing once. But I was wrong. To quote the Seinfeldian response to a rather unrelated question of authenticity, "They're real, and they're spectacular."

If, on the other hand, you've read Cat's work before—*any* of it—then you're thinking you know damn well what a good book this is going to be. And I'm pleased to say here at the outset that you'll not be disappointed.

Cat's career has been on a space-lift trajectory of late, and Rambo-reading veterans have no doubt why: Cat's good. Really good. She moves smoothly in and out of genres and voices. Effortlessly, as if her work is the ether that binds them. Fantasy, science fiction, horror . . . Cat takes them on, two or three at a time, mixing and matching them with alchemically fantastic results. Jeff VanderMeer, introducing her as a recent Guest of Honor at ConFusion, called Cat's fiction "often lyrical but tough-minded, unabashedly mixing traditional tropes with unconventional approaches. You get a sense in her work of someone who has actually lived a life and experienced a lot. That's something you can't really fake in fiction."

As I said, she's really good.

So good, in fact, that as I sit here staring at the table of contents for the amazing collection of her work that you and I, Dear Reader, are fortunate enough to hold in our hands, I wonder if Cat's success was somehow fated, if somehow we have here, in the pages of this slender, precious volume, evidence of some fictional providence at work. Just look at that name again: *Cat Rambo*. It's too striking to be legit—what with the cute purring-ness and the rough Stallone-ness juxtaposed in a violently abrupt eight-letter collision of worlds—yet it is. And more than just being real, it's almost perfectly apt for the unique web that Cat's fiction weaves. We are, after all, about to embark on a journey that takes us from memories of magic in strange lands to encounters with pirates, zombie girlfriends, famed elephants, distracted wizards, slave centaurs, and one of the most sweetly heartrending stories with pigs since *Charlotte's Web*.

Cat Rambo. Colliding worlds in eight letters of wonder. It's magical enough that it is so, more wondrous still that we get to share it. So let's begin, shall we?

Michael Livingston
The Citadel

Her Eyes Like Sky, and Coal, and Moonlight

This story, written in the spring of 2008, is set in the world of the online game I work with. A war-torn desert planet where magic shapes people's lives, Zalanthas has provided the backdrop for a series of stories about the female soldiers and sorcerers involved in the endless struggle. "Her Eyes" is told by one of the peripheral figures, a woman who sees the war only when it touches her own daily life. She finds a figure there, Alkyone, which informs her own, equally harsh, existence.

The story was written after a workshop with John Crowley about time in fiction writing, and I tried to work out some of the things I'd learned in the piece. It functions in a space of being told, in which it is anchored by the storyteller's references to the moment of the telling. The storyteller is herself a character in the story, first as a child and later as adult, and her development serves as the subplot that is both shaped and which acts out the overall plot: how Alkyone is shaped by her decision to assist in the war. Its cost—the destruction of the city of Tuluk by elementals—is mirrored in Alkyone's own destruction.

The first time I saw Alkyone, her eyes were blue, the color of sky in a child's story. The second time, her eyes were terrible coals, long past their fire. And the third, the third time—her eyes were moonlight, silvery as Lirathu's benign gaze. That's the color I remember best.

Almost a King's Age ago, when I was just a girl, my parents ran an inn, the Blue Pipe. It sat just inside the city walls, serving travelers and merchants coming through Caravan Gate. Gone now, destroyed in the Rebuilding, but it stood through all the tumultuous years of my life: the night of the devastation, the battle between Kul and Isar, the long years of the Occupation.

Offering me some ale now to wet my throat? Very well. I like the dark brew, flavored with groundnuts. If you wish to hear of her, to know about the wind mage, Alkyone, it'll quicken the tongue.

Smell the storm brewing this evening—that edge of lightning riding the wind? That's how it smelled that first night they came. Everyone in the tavern was alive

and excited that night. Word had spread there was to be a secret meeting of those
who opposed Lord Isar.

The commons were packed to the gills with Tan Muark and Tuluki followers
of Kul. Everyone called him Kul, despite his rank, as high as that of Lord Isar.
Everyone thought of him as a distinguished friend, an elder brother. The one who
would defend us all.

In the back room, several of my siblings and cousins served a gathering too
important to be seen. History being made, my brother Amos said, puffing himself
up. The Muark leaders and Kurac merchants, come to discuss what was to be done
about the tyrant.

And elementalists were there. Does that shock you, nowadays when no one can
admit to practicing the elemental magics? Even then, most people didn't speak of it, as
though it were something disgraceful. Sometimes I wondered about my father. He had
a fiery temper, the way followers of Suk-Krath are rumored to, and once I thought I
saw him light the fire in the hearth with a gesture, but I was very small at the time.

Alkyone was an air-mage. A hawk-faced woman who wore her white hair in tiny
braids, each tied off with a stone bead, as though to weigh her down, keep her from
flying off. Her left cheek was tattooed—a triangle of blue dots, set just below her
paler-colored eye. I had never seen anyone like her before, and I pressed forward,
staring, until she looked up and caught my gaze.

She smiled at me and shared her honey cakes, crumbling them with long,
nervous fingers. Her accent was lilting as she told me she had never had honey cakes
when she was growing up.

"I come from a village where the thornlands give way to the hills, in the east,"
she said. "But most lately I am come from Allanak, child. Do you know it?"

Wonders came from the southern city of Allanak: obsidian bracelets, and
puppets with joints carved from bone. And sticky dried insects laced with honey that
came in big blocks so chunks could be pried off to be chopped and added to pastries.
I said this.

She looked around at the press of people. "There were these many people in
Allanak, and then some, but still I am unused to being among so many. I like the
desert. I like sleeping where I can feel the wind on my face and hear what it sings,
deep in the night."

I ate a little honey cake and told her that usually we were not so busy.

"Do you know why everyone has crowded here?" she asked.

To fight Lord Isar, I said.

"And why we are fighting him?"

Her teacher's manner made me impatient. I knew this lesson as well as she did.
Two of my cousins and my brother Lucius had been taken by Lord Isar for speaking
out against him, I told her.

She looked abashed. "Indeed. Down in Allanak I have been around those
that do not understand the need to fight him, and so I have fallen in the habit of
lecturing." She held out the rest of the honey cake. "Am I forgiven?"

I accepted the cake. She smiled and leaned forward to sort through the bag at her feet. The room was hazy with smoke, both from pipes and the fireplace along the wall, and the air was damp with the smell of brandy and beer. People were still gathering, being stopped outside to give the word of the day, the word that signaled they were not one of Lord Isar's spies. That night it was "the sun will shine again." I have always remembered that.

Alkyone took out a box made of blue glass beads inlaid in larger squares. "These came from Allanak as well," she said.

One of the men filling the room muscled his way through the crowd. He was blonde bearded, a northerner like me. As he approached, he scowled down at me, but spoke to her.

"What are you up to, Alkyone?" he said.

"Lightening my pack," she said. "It has been heavy lately."

"We can't afford to be giving away things all over the place," he said. "Come in the back room. They wish to know what our magics are capable of, and whether yours could carry someone outside the gate."

I opened the box, and he spoke as I saw what lay inside. "Those are your favorite earrings, Alk!"

She put her head down, looking at the floor planks between her boot toes. "I had those before we ever met, Phaedrin. My friend Jhiran gave them to me, and I may give them where I will."

That was the end of that. I said, "When you go back to your village—wouldn't someone there want them?"

Her face shuttered tight enough to keep out wind or emotion. "They are all gone. I will not be returning." She reached up to close my fingers over the earrings and smiled at me again. Then she stood and followed Phaedrin back to the crowded room filled with angry argument and low-voiced discussion.

I crept closer and listened. There was no chance of sleeping that night. I couldn't understand everything that was said. But through a crack in the door I watched her talking, worrying her lower lip between her teeth as she thought before answering questions. Phaedrin watched her as though annoyed by the conversation, but the Muark, who never trust those outside their tribe, treated her as a comrade. It was something about her, something that shone through and made you want to be a little bit better, somehow. To live up to her friendship.

Everyone left before the sun rose over the city. Alkyone's group rode away to the south-east, down to Luirs and the Tan Muark lands, vanishing into the darkness of the North Road. After they had gone away, my cousin Liselle tried to get the earrings and the box from me, but coax and threaten as she might, I would not give them up.

"Keep your traitor-gifts then," she said, taking a step back, face red with fury.

I didn't know what she meant, but I knew it was bad. I pushed her down, and I hid the box and earrings in the stable-loft, where she couldn't find them. Sometimes I took the earrings out and held them in my hand, and let them flash in the sun so the barn kittens could chase the bits of scattered light they threw across the ground.

Sometimes I pretended I was Alkyone, pretended so hard that it was as though I walked in a different skin. I would sit on the stone wall outside the inn and stare at the dust devils dancing in the road, willing them to move. My heart would leap when it would seem as though one had heard and answered. But then, inevitably, it would die away or move in a contradictory direction.

I wanted to be her, to have people listen to me instead of telling me what to do. I wanted them to smile at me as they did at her, with love and respect, and sometimes a trace of fear.

My ineffectual efforts at magic died out after a while and our lives continued. When I was twelve, there came rumors of magic outside the city. Travelers reported the undead walked the North Road at night, and no one dared journey beneath the moons. Day by day, the stories grew wilder. They said an ancient demon, the Lord of Ash, and his servants plagued Tuluk and that the Templarate could do nothing to stop him. Some said that the reason the Templarate did nothing was that they had given their power to Lord Isar.

My mother had been accustomed to using Isar's name to threaten us when we misbehaved. Now she dared not invoke his name in threats lest she somehow come to his notice. At night we shuttered the windows and barred the doors, for fear of the sorts of travelers that might enter after the sun had set.

When I had my first woman's blood, my mother said we would have a celebration, even though business was so bad. She braided my hair and pierced my ears and I wore Alkyone's earrings, despite Liselle's frowns.

The night winds were howling, and my mother lit thick cones of lanturin incense to keep away ghosts. In the middle of the meal—duskhorn steak, the wild-fed kind you can never get nowadays—the main door blew open, or so we thought at first. The youngest children were all screaming and things were confused. My mother glimpsed Alkyone's form huddled outside, a few feet away from the lintel. My brothers pulled her in, dragged her beside the hearth, pressed hot tea and soup on her. She kept her eyes turned down, her cloak's hood drawn up.

A few hours later, her friends arrived. They stood in the doorway. She did not look up. No one had wanted to go to bed after that, not with all the excitement, and my father had allowed us to heat watered wine and drink it, stretching out the sips to make our time awake as long as possible.

"Alk," the leader said, his voice half-cracked with pain. He was a plain, brown-faced Northerner, the Kuraci. "Tell me it's not true."

"That what's not true?" It was the first time she spoke that visit, and her voice was as sweet and intoxicating as the liquid in my mug. The wind outside changed pitch and tenor, softened, then became melodic for a moment, a heartbeat.

He took a step forward at the words, face brightening. "Then it's not true—the Lord of Ash has not touched you?"

She raised her face slowly—I can see that clear as day in my mind's eye, clearer than I see most things now—and the fabric fell away, revealing that her once-blue eyes were black as coals.

"See how he has touched me because I dared oppose him and his ally!" she said. "Like all his creatures, I'm marked. But is my spirit still my own? That I believe to be true, but I make no guarantees." And with a bitter, brittle laugh, she pulled the hood back up around her face.

She did not look at them, but they looked at her. Five men, all from the crowd that had gathered to discuss Isar so long ago: the brown man, and Phaedrin, and a stocky little fellow, one of the kinless half-blood, and another man, thin but with the bleary reddened vision of a spice-smoker, and another of the Tan Muark.

"His evil lives in you—you are his servant now!" Phaedrin said, but the Tan Muark had a blade against his throat and backed him off, step by step. My littlest sister gasped and hid her face in my mother's skirts.

"Could Kul cure her, perhaps?" the Muark asked.

"Perhaps, if he had the crown of Fel Karren—but no such luck yet."

"What about Arianis?"

"You have not heard? Arianis is dead."

Alkyone paled further. "Arianis gone? But he was the best of our leaders, our only guidance! No wonder the Lord of Ash stretched out his hand to take me so easily!"

She lowered her face into her hands and wept. And those men, they fell into silence and stood there looking at her in the way you would a stone that has become a scorpion, or a stick that writhes and becomes an adder.

When those black pits had been concealed by her long-fingered hands, I could move again. I put my mug down, and went forward to embrace her. I buried her head in my shoulder so I did not have to face that black gaze, but even so, I held her and did my best to conceal the terror that shook me, like an earthquake that sets the world ashiver.

For a frozen time—a dozen breaths?—she let me hold her, she clung to me.

Then a hand fell on my shoulder, and my mother pulled me away, begged their pardon, and took me off to shake me hard and tell me never to meddle in matters of magic.

It was half in me to demand what about my father. Wasn't he as steeped in magic as Alkyone, whether or not he hid it? But something in the way my mother looked made me hold my tongue.

"Is Alkyone the Lord of Ash's now?" I asked, and my mother shook me again, so hard my neck popped on its spine, which startled me, because she'd never been one to strike us in anger.

"Magicker business!"

No one spoke about Alkyone after she'd gone. No one said anything, even though I tried to ask. My mother hissed me into silence, and my father—when he was there—would not speak of it.

A half year later I was outside emptying slop buckets when I saw lights in the sky. Stars and comets, dancing lights, far to the south. I ran inside to fetch the others, but by the time my family came out into the yard, the lights were gone, and they only made fun of me.

Months later, though, I was vindicated when travelers spoke of the night the lights had flashed in the sky, marking the last battle with the Lord of Ash. They said Alkyone helped defeat him, but that it was a joint effort, really—the J'Karr and the Tan Muark, and a handful of magickers joined together. That their dead friend Arianis had come back as a gwoshi to help them defeat the Lord of Ash, that there had been a fierce fight nonetheless, and Kul had offered no aid—he'd been off in the North on his own expedition, searching for ways to defeat Isar.

They said down in the Salt Flats there was just a statue of the Lord of Ash, what he had been, turned into black stone—obsidian. My eldest once traveled down to see it, and said it was large and wicked, and that she dreamed of it for three nights running. The Muark still make the trip there once a year, to piss on its feet and curse it.

Phaedrin had turned out to be working with the Lord of Ash. He died on those sands as well and no statue marked his grave.

Time wore on, and my mother entrusted me with more and more of the inn's running. My father was taken away by Lord Isar's people under suspicion of being an unlicensed elementalist. Every week my mother went to ask news of him and every week there was none. They never said officially whether or not it was true. He was gone, either way, and he didn't come back. People disappeared in those days, just as they do now. That's always been Tuluk's way, no matter who sits in power.

I had my first boyfriend. Liselle stole him and broke him so when he came back to me, he wanted me as little as I wanted him. I listened to travelers' stories and the news that the bards passed along in their songs, the few bards that still existed under Lord Isar's hand. Poet's Circle, where they had once all lived, was boarded up and guarded.

I wore the earrings Alkyone had given me each year at Isar's Festival. One year I had a daughter with my broken boyfriend, and then two years later another with a man who wasn't broken, and who loved my first as his own.

Thoughts of Alkyone, somehow, pulled me through. I listened for news every night in the inn's common room. I heard she had died. I heard she had never died or that she had come back. I heard that she was sometimes an elemental and sometimes human, and sometimes something in between. Other rumors said Kul was in exile. He'd tried to kill Isar after retrieving some artifact, and had been driven to live with the Tan Muark. Some people said he'd married a Muark woman who'd fallen in battle a few days later. We did not see the tribe much after that, and you couldn't get blue silk ribbons for years. They were the only ones with the secret of the dye.

Then a few Muark appeared, began passing the word to watch out, that on the night of Isar's Festival, rebellion would break out. That something was happening, that the last of the rebel magickers were planning something. That we should hide that night, and be ready the next day to take the city.

No one knew what to expect. No one dreamed how bad it would be. But we hid like they told us, for all the good it did most of us.

That night, elementals walked through the city, beings from planes outside our own. The city shook with their passage all night long. My family and I hid in the cellar with four crates of Reynolte wine and a keg of spiced brandy. The Tan Muark had brought up a great wheel of cheese on their unexpected visit two days earlier, and we ate half of it that night because there wasn't anything else to do.

I wondered where Alkyone was. Surely she was part of this? Had the Lord of Ash returned, was she out there helping defeat him once again? Who had brought the elementals to destroy the city? Were her friends with her still, was exiled Kul there to defend his home? Did she remember giving me her honey cakes, back when I was as old as the child huddled against me?

And what color were her eyes now?

It was a long night. None of us slept. We sat awake listening to the cries and feeling the earth shake whenever some monstrous thing passed in the street outside, nibbling at our cheese as though it would quiet the nervous snakes in our stomachs.

In the morning, the city was gone.

Our inn still stood, but other buildings near us had been burned and flattened.

Survivors recounted stories of a great fire-winged hawk from the plane of Suk-Krath, and a stone tortoise from Ruk, and a girl made of water from Vivadu. Liselle was dead. They wouldn't let me see the body, but I heard the whispers. The water elemental had drowned her with a kiss.

No one knew what happened, but they knew Lord Isar was defeated. Kul and his soldiers marched through the streets with Lord Isar in chains before them, hunched over, looking small. The prisoners in his dungeons were freed, but my father wasn't among them.

Kul came to the Inn that night. I knew it was him. Hadn't I seen him during the march? Hadn't he waved to the crowds, perhaps even seen me there? For a moment when he entered, lean and rugged, flanked by two soldiers, I dreamed that he had noticed me, had come to claim me for his bride.

But his gaze was perfunctory. He went to the back room. On his head was a high crown made of wrought metal, green with verdigris. Others came—high ranked merchants, the Kuraci, the young general, Garas, who had helped with the defeat of Isar's troops.

Alkyone came in after most of them, two Tan Muark men with her. When she entered the back room, voices were raised. I maneuvered myself near the door, tried to overhear what was happening.

Kul was ordering every magicker out of Tuluk.

"How can I trust any of you, after this?" he demanded. "We are so weak that even now Allanak is readying itself to come and gnaw the spoils your folk have prepared for it!"

"We gave you your victory, gave you what you needed. We didn't know what the elementals would do!"

I picked up a tray and went in to retrieve glasses, counting on a servant's invisibility. Kul stood near the fireplace, his arms crossed, and gave Alkyone no smile. "You have a day to leave the city."

"She'll go with us, since you don't seem to acknowledge your debt to the Tan Muark either," one of the men said. Everyone else in the room scowled at him. Merchants dislike the Tan Muark, who have tricked every house in the Known World in their time—often more than once.

Kul stared the Muark down. "My city is destroyed. Press me no further." Alkyone stirred as though to speak, but Kul turned to cut her off with a gesture. "And tell your comrades in magic that they will get no favors from me either. I mean to put them entirely out of the city or see them dead. There is blood on all your hands, and you cannot wash them clean enough for me. And make no threats—this crown enables me to defeat any of you."

"I have made no threats. Indeed, wasn't I there to help you secure that crown, Kul?" she said. "I am tired and heartsick. Many of those I loved vanished in this as well. You give me a deadline, but I already have one. I gave my life to fuel the ceremony that opened the gate. I have but a day in this form before I am returned to the wind. Do not reproach me. I have given my life to this struggle and it has taken all that I am."

And with that, she walked away.

At the door, she stopped, seeing me. "I recognize those earrings. Is all well with you?" She waved her two Muark companions on ahead.

"The inn is still standing—we lost the stable and some livestock," I said. "And my little sister's barrakhan pen, which is why we have no eggs."

The words were inconsequential. I drank in the sight of her. Her eyes were no longer coal. They were the color of moonlight on the sands. They were sad, but they were so beautiful that they gave me hope.

For years afterwards, I could take my breath away just thinking of her eyes. It took me through some hard times—the occupation by the Allanaki, the night when my two youngest were killed by the Borsail lord they'd sent up to oversee things. We didn't know it then, that we'd be decades under their heel because of what the elementalists had done. But I never hated her, never thought that even when they were taking my children.

She had not stood back, she had gambled. None of us knew what had been won or lost at that point.

As she paused in the doorway, one of the men said, "Come on, Alkyone." But she shook her head.

"I believe I'll walk in the desert by myself for a little while," she said. The other held out his hand, and she sidestepped it with a wry twist to her shoulders that had them both laughing as though to keep from crying.

"This is goodbye, then," the Muark said.

"I've walked by myself most of my life," she said. "That's how I intend to end it." She smiled at me.

I'll always remember her eyes. All through my life, through the betrayals and petty rivalries, the moments that were large and small and everything in between, the thought of her eyes has gotten me through the hard times. She walked by herself, and gave me the strength to do it too, by remembering her eyes. Not as they were at first—that storybook blue, the color of the ancient days when it rained—and certainly not when they burned with that black, fierce light.

But rather as they were that final night, when she walked out in the company of the gentle evening wind, a fearless woman who had given all she could in the fight and would never be seen again. Her remarkable eyes, silver as the moonlight, and twice as kind, and a thousand times as brave and alone.

The Accordion

I wrote "The Accordion" in the summer of 1990 before attending the graduate Writing Seminars at Johns Hopkins. It was the first piece I workshopped there. Because it was short and included in a batch of three short-short pieces, which puzzled everyone, because they were looking for connections between the stories when there were none. The others involved Death doing crossword puzzles on a train and life on Planet Crabby. After that I calmed down and produced one story at a time.

In trying to figure out the elements of the story, I remember I was living in Charles Village and daily passed a house where there was not just one accordion player, but two on different floors. I don't know where the chickens came from, but I was reading a lot of Donald Barthelme at the time. This story originally appeared in The Walden Review *and later was reprinted online at* Café Irreal.

If I play my accordion too loudly while you're painting, you complain. You stamp about in your room under mine. You fetch the broom from the closet and use it to thump vehemently on the ceiling. I feel the vibrations through my feet.

"I'm trying to work down here!" you shout furiously from your window.

I put the accordion down on the sofa. The air slowly squeezes out, making it wheeze like a beast perishing for love. I go to the window, but you have already pulled in your head, and are engaging your canvas once again. There is only the lit trapezoid of your window.

I lower myself in the window washer's abandoned apparatus, ropes squeaking, bump bump bumping against the bricks. I come to your window and peer in. There are pockmarks in the plaster of your ceiling. Your coveralls are streaked with drips of black and white and red.

You're painting still, a picture of hearts and flowers and maidens with mournful eyes. Are you thinking of me too? My breath makes a foggy patch on the glass. But when you turn around and see me, I am suddenly shy. I pull the window washer's cap down over my eyes and pretend to be squee-geeing.

You go back to your painting. Sadly, I hoist myself back up.

I hire jugglers to ambush you in the hallway, street mimes to gesture out my devotion to you, mariachi bands to stroll beneath your window in the little garden ten stories below.

But you ignore the jugglers, pay the treacherous mimes to go away, absent-mindedly empty the turpentine you've used to clean your brushes out the window. Several members of the band who were smoking cigarettes are badly burned.

I play my accordion again, and this time I hear no thumps. Can you be listening?

I look out my window and see yours dark and empty. You have gone away for the weekend.

The witch doctor down the hall offers to cast a love spell on you, if I give him twenty dollars and three live chickens.

I buy the chickens and bring them home, but in the car they look so reproachfully at me that I cannot bear to give them to him. Instead I install them in my room and feed them popcorn. They sit on the radiator, clucking peacefully. I play lullabies to them on my accordion.

I hear a door slam and then the thumping begins again. You are back!

Spring wears into summer, and now you don't even thump any more, because the drone of your air conditioner drowns out my accordion. I leave my window open. The chickens seem to enjoy the heat.

One day I despair. How will I ever reach you? I pace my room, at each turn banging my head against the unpainted walls, raising puffs of white dust which coat my eyebrows. The neighbors on each side complain, and rightly so. I stop banging but still pace, thinking feverishly. The accordion lies abandoned on the sofa. The chickens watch me with sad eyes.

I buy a bassoon, a cowhorn, a dulcimer, an euphonium, a flugelhorn, a glockenspiel, a harmonica, a jaw harp, a kettledrum, a lute, a marimba, a nail fiddle, an oboe d'amore, a pan pipe, a recorder, a samisen, a tambura, a ukelele, a violin, a wood block, a xylophone, a yang kin, and a zither. No use! I can't produce a single recognizable note. I can't step anywhere in my room without tripping over one of the instruments.

I go out for a walk. I leave the door unlocked behind me, hoping that someone will come in and steal the bassoon, the cowhorn, the dulcimer, the euphonium, the flugelhorn, the glockenspiel, the harmonica, the jaw harp, the kettledrum, the lute, the marimba, the nail fiddle, the oboe d'amore, the pan pipe, the recorder, the samisen, the tambura, the ukelele, the violin, the wood block, the xylophone, the yang kin, the zither, or perhaps even the chickens. Anything but my accordion.

When I return, there you are! Sitting on the sofa, next to the accordion. I can only gape in astonishment. You blush.

"I came to thank you for the eggs."

"Eggs?" I say. Perhaps artist's jargon for songs. I don't think so.

"Yes, the fresh eggs you've been sending down via the window washer's lift. I find them outside my window every morning. Aren't they from you?"

The chickens have a smug look. "Oh yes," I say. "From me."

"And the notes?" What could they have written?

But I nod. "Of course."

That night I play my accordion again. You and the chickens listen, sitting together framed by the perfect rectangle of the window, eating popcorn. When I finish, you applaud. Then you take the zither, and we play together.

I'll Gnaw Your Bones,
the Manticore Said

This story was written in late 2007, and it began entirely with the title, which I loved. I knew I had to create a narrative that justified it and I knew it involved a traveling circus and a manticore, but it took a while to figure out the whats and hows.

My favorite moment of the story is the attack of the zombie rabbits, mainly because I have no idea where that image came from. A close second is the final moment. I don't know why it works so satisfyingly for me, but it does, perhaps because it sheds some light on the relationship between Tara and Bumpus, which I intend to explore further, somewhere down the line.

Originally the piece had been accepted for Fantasy Magazine, *before I became an editor there. Sean Wallace ended up moving it to* Clarkesworld *because he had a slot he wanted to fill, and it appeared there in March, 2008.*

Even Duga the Prestidigitator, who never pays much attention to anything outside his own hands, raised an eyebrow when I announced I'd be hooking the manticore up to my wagon.

"Isn't that dangerous?" my husband Rik said. He steepled his fingers, regarding me.

"The more we have pulling, the faster we get there," I pointed out. "And Bupus has been getting fat and lazy as a tabby cat. No one pays to see a fat manticore."

"More dangerous than any tabby cat," Rik said.

I knew what he meant, but I kept a lightning rod at hand in the wagon seat in case of trouble. Bupus knew I'd scorch his greasy whiskers if he crossed me.

There is a tacit understanding between a beast trainer and her charges, whether it be great cats, cunning dragons, or apes and other man-like creatures. They know, and the trainer knows, that as long as certain lines aren't crossed, that if expectations are met, everything will be fine and no one will get hurt.

That's not to say I didn't keep an eye on Bupus, watching for a certain twitch to his tail, the way one bulbous eye would go askew when anger was brewing. A beast's a beast, after all, and not responsible for what they do when circumstances push them too far. Beasts still, no matter how they speak or smile or woo.

At any rate, Bupus felt obliged to maintain his reputation whenever another wagon or traveler was in earshot.

"Gnaw your bones," he rumbled, rolling a vast oversized eyeball back at me. The woman he was trying to impress shrieked and dropped her chickens, which vanished in a white flutter among the blackberry vines and ferns that began where the road's stone gave way to forest. A blue-headed jay screamed in alarm from a pine.

"Behave yourself," I said.

He rumbled again, but nothing coherent, just a low, animal sound.

We were coming up on Piperville, which sits on a trade hub. Steel figured we'd pitch there for a week, get a little silver sparkling in our coffers, eat well a few nights.

It had been a lean winter and times were hard all over—traveling up from Ponce's Spring, we'd found slim pickings and indifferent audiences too worried about the dust storms to pay any attention to even our best: Laxmi the elephant dancing in pink spangles to "Waltzing Genevieve," the pyramid of crocodiles that we froze and unfroze each performance via a lens-and-clockwork basilisk, the Unicorn Maiden, and of course, my manticore.

Rik was driving a wagon full of machinery, packed and protected from the dust with layers of waxed canvas. He pulled up near me, so we were riding in tandem for a bit. No one was coming the opposite way for now. We'd hit some road traffic coming out of Ponce's, but now it was only occasional, a twice an hour thing at most.

"You know what I'm looking forward to?" I called over to him.

He considered. I watched him thinking in the sunlight, my broad-shouldered and beautiful husband and just the look of him, his long scholar's nose and silky beard, made me smile.

"Beer," he said finally. "And clean sheets. Cleeaaaan sheets." He drawled out the last words, smiling over at me.

"A bath," I said.

A heartfelt groan so deep it might have come from the bottom of his soul escaped him. "Oh, a bath. With towels. Thick towels."

I was equally enraptured by the thought, so much so that I didn't notice the wheel working loose. And Bupus, concerned with looking for people to impress, didn't warn me. With a sideways lurch, the wagon tilted, and the wheel kept going, rolling down the roadway, neat as you please, until it passed Laxmi and she put out her trunk and snagged it.

I donned my shoes and hopped down to examine the damage. Steel heard the commotion and came back from the front of the train. He rode Beulah, the big white horse that accompanies him in the ring each performance. Sometimes we laugh about how attached he is to that horse, but never where he can hear us.

The carts and caravans kept passing us. A few waved and Rik waved back. The august clowns were practicing their routine, somersaulting into the dust behind their wagon, then running to catch up with it again. Duga was practicing card tricks while his assistant drove, dividing her attention between the reins and watching him. Duga was notoriously close-mouthed about his methods; I suspected watching might be her only way to learn.

"Whaddya need?" Steel growled as he reached me.

"Looks like a linch pin fell out. Could have been a while back. Sparky'll have a new one, I'm sure."

His blue gaze slid skyward, sideways, anywhere to avoid meeting my eyes. "Sparky's gone."

It is an unfortunate fact that circuses are usually made of Family and outsiders—jossers, they call us. Steel treated Family well but was unwilling to extend that courtesy outside the circle. I'd married in, and he was forced to acknowledge me, but Sparky had been a full outsider, and Steel had made his life a misery, maintaining our cranky and antiquidated machines: the fortune teller, the tent-lifter, and Steel's pride and joy, the spinning cups, packed now on the largest wagon and pulled by Laxmi and three oxen.

The position of circus smith had been vacant of Family for a while now, ever since Big Joy fell in love with a fire-eater and left us for the Whistling Piskie—a small, one-ring outfit that worked the coast.

So we'd lost Sparky because Steel had scrimped and shorted his wages, not to mention refusing to pay prentice fees when he wanted to take one on. More importantly, we'd lost his little traveling cart, full of tools and scrap and spare linchpins.

"So what am I going to do?" I snapped. Bupus had sat down on the road and was eying the passing caravans, more out of curiosity than hunger or desire to menace. "I'll gnaw your bones," he said almost conversationally, but it frightened no one in earshot. He sighed and settled his head between his paws, a green snot dribble bubbling from one kitten-sized nostril.

The Unicorn Girl pulled up her caravan. She'd been trying to repaint it the night before and bleary green and lavender paint splotched its side.

"What's going on?' she said loudly. "Driving badly again, Tara?"

The Unicorn Girl was one of those souls with no volume control. Sitting next to her in tavern or while driving was painful. She'd bray the same stories over and over again, and was tactless and unkind. I tried to avoid her when I could.

But, oh, she pulled them in. That long, narrow, angelic face, the pearly horn emerging from her forehead, and two lush lips, peach-ripe, set like emerging sins beneath the springs of her innocent doe-like eyes.

Even now, she resembled an angel, but I knew she was just looking for gossip, something she might be able to use to buy favor or twist like a knife when necessary.

Steel glanced back and forth. "Broken wagon, Lily," he said. "You can move along."

She dimpled, pursing her lips at him but took up her reins. The two white mares pulling her wagon were daughters of the one he rode, twins with a bad case of the wobbles but which should be good for years more, if you ignored the faint, constant trembling of their front legs. Most people didn't notice it.

"She needs to learn to mind her tongue," I said.

"Rik needs to come in with us," Steel said, ignoring my comment. "He's the smartest, he knows how to bargain. These little towns have their own customs and laws and it's too easy to set a foot awry and land ourselves in trouble."

Much as I hated to admit, Steel was right. Rik is the smartest of the lot, and he knows trade law like the back of his hand.

"I'll find someone to leave with you, and Rik will ride back with the pin, soon as he can," Steel said.

"All right," I said. Then, as he started to wheel Beulah around. "Someone I won't mind, Steel. Got me?"

"Got it," he said, and rode away.

"I don't like leaving you," Rik said guiltily. It was a year old story, and its once upon a time had begun on our honeymoon night, with him riding out to help with the funeral of his grandfather, who had been driven into a fatal apoplectic fit by news of Rik's marriage to someone who'd never known circus life.

"Can't be helped," I said crisply. He sighed.

"Tara…"

"Can't be helped." I flapped an arm at him. "Go on, get along, faster you are to town, faster you're back to me."

He got out of his wagon long enough to kiss me and ruffle my hair.

"Not long," he said. "I won't be long."

"We'll leave Preddi with you," Steel said, a quarter hour after I'd watched Rik's caravan recede into the distance. It had taken a while for the rest of the circus to pass me, wagon after wagon. Even for such a small outfit, we had a lot of wagons.

Preddi was Rik's father, a small, stooped man given to carelessness with his dress. He was a kindly man, I think, but difficult to get to know because his deafness distanced him.

We pulled the wagon over to the side of the road, in a margined sward thick with yellow loosestrife and dandelions. A narrow deer path led through blackberry tangles and further into the pines, a stream coming through the thick pine needles to chuckle along the rocks. I tied Bupus to the wagon, and brought out a sack of hams and loaves of bread before making several trips to bring him buckets of water.

Preddi settled himself on the grass and extracted a deck of greasy cards from the front pocket of his flannel shirt. While I worked, he laid out hand after hand, playing poker with himself.

The day wore on.

And on. I cleaned the wagon tack, and repacked the bundles in it, mainly my training gear. Someone else would be tending my cages of beasts when they pitched camp, and truth be told, anyone could, but I still preferred to be the one who fed the crocodiles, for example, and watched for mouth rot or the white lesions that signal pox virus and cleaned their cage thoroughly enough to make sure no infection could creep in under their scales or into the tender areas around their vents.

Bupus gorged himself and then slept, but roused enough to want to play. I threw the heavy leather ball and each time his tail whipped out with frightening speed and batted it aside. Fat and lazy he may be, but Bupus has many years left in him. Manticores live four or five decades, and I'd raised him from the shell ten years earlier, before I'd even bought the flimsy paper ticket that led me to meet Rik.

I hadn't known what I had at first. A sailor swapped me the egg in return for me covering his bar tab, and who knows who got the best of that bargain? I was a beast trainer for the Duke, and mainly I worked with little animals, trained squirrels and ferrets and marmosets. They juggled and danced, shot tiny plaster pistols, and engaged in duels as exquisite as any courtier's.

The egg was bigger than my doubled fists laid knuckle and palm to knuckle and palm. It was coarse to the touch, as though threads or hairy roots had been laid over the shell and grown into it, and it was a deep yellow, the same yellow that Bupus's eyes would open into, honied depths around clover-petaled pupils.

I kept it warm, near the hearth, but could not figure out what it might contain. Months later it hatched—lucky that I was there that day to feed the mewling, squawling hatchling chopped meat and warm milk. I wrapped the sting in padding and leather. Even then it struck out with surprising speed and strength. A manticore is a vulnerable creature, lacking human hands to defend the softness of its face, and the sting compensates for that vulnerability.

He talked a moon, perhaps a moon and a half, later. I took him with me at first, when I was training the Duke's creatures, but a marmoset decided to investigate, and I learned then that a manticore's bite is a death grip, particularly with a marmoset's delicate bones between its teeth.

Some beast trainers dull their more intelligent beasts. It's an easy enough procedure, if you can drug or spell them unconscious. The knife is thin, more like a flattened awl than a blade, and you insert it at the corner of the eye, going behind the eyeball itself. Once you've pushed it in to the right depth, perforating the plate of the skull lying behind the eye, you swing back and forth holding it between thumb and forefinger, two cutting arcs. It bruises the eye, leaves it black and tender in the socket for days afterward, but it heals in time.

It doesn't kill their intelligence entirely, but they become simpler. More docile, easier to manage. They don't scheme or plot escape, and they're less likely to lash out. Done right, even a dragon can be made clement. And those beasts prone to over-talkativeness—dryads and mermaids, for the most part—can be rendered speechless or close to it.

I've never done that, though my father taught me the technique. I like my talking beasts, most of the time, and on occasion I've had conversations with sphinx or lamia that were as close to talking with a person as could be.

After the marmoset incident, I left Bupus at home, the establishment the Duke allowed me, a fine place with stable and mews and even a heat-room, which the Ducal coal stores kept supplied all winter long and into the chilly Tabatian spring. I housed him in a stall that had been reinforced, and there were other animals to keep him company.

I'd gone to the circus to see their creatures. They had the crocodiles, which were nothing out of the ordinary, and the elephant, which was also unremarkable, since the Duchess kept two pygmy elephants in her menagerie. And an aging hippogriff, a splendid creature even though its primaries had gone gray with age long ago. I was surprised to find his beak overgrown, as though no one had coped it in months.

"Look here," I said to the man standing to watch the cages and make sure no one poked a finger through the bars and lost it. "Your hippogriff is badly tended. See how he rubs his beak along the ground, how he feaks? Your tender is careless, sir."

I was full of youth and indignation, but I softened when he perked up and said, "Can you tend them? We lost our fellow. How much would you charge?"

"No charge," I said. "If you let me look over the hippogriff as thoroughly as I'd like to. I haven't ever had the chance to get my hands on a live one."

"Can you come back later, when we close up?" He looked apologetic. He was a pretty man, and his uniform made him even prettier.

"I can." It'd mean a late night, but there was nothing going on that next morning—I could sleep in, and go to check the marmosets in the afternoon, or let the regular assistant do it, even, if I was feeling lazy.

So I came back late that night and pushed my way through the crowds eddying out, like a duck swimming against the current. He was waiting for me near the cages. I'd brought my bag of tools, and so we went from cage to cage.

He settled the hippogriff when it bated at the sight of me, flapping its wings and rearing upward. It was easily calmed, and he ran his fingers through the silky feathers around its eyes, rubbing softly over the scaly cere, until its eyes half-lidded and it chirped with pleasure, nuzzling its head along his side.

I trimmed its beak and claws and checked it over before moving on to the other animals. It took me three hours, and even so, much of that was simply telling Rik what would need to be done later on—to stop giving the crocodiles sardines, for example, before they got sick from the oiliness.

I refused pay, and he insisted that he should buy me a cup of wine, at least. How inevitable was it that I would take this beautiful man home with me?

In the morning, I showed my household to my lover. The dueling marmosets, the brace of piskies, the cockatrice kept by itself, lest it strike out in its bad temper. And Bupus, sprawled out across the courtyard. Rik was enchanted.

"A manticore!" he said. "I've never seen a tamed one. Or a wild one, for that matter. They come from the deserts in the land to the south, you know."

A year later, diffidently, while the caravan was spending a month in Tabat, he mentioned to me that the hippogriff had finally succumbed to old age and the caravan would like to buy Bupus.

I refused to sell, but when I married him, the manticore came with me.

When the sun touched down on the horizon and lingered there, like a marble being rolled back and forth beneath one's palm, we realized that there was some delay. If not tonight, though, they'd come tomorrow. Preddi and I discussed it all with shrugs and miming, agreeing to build a fire before the last of the sunlight vanished.

The woods that run beside the road there are dark and dangerous, which is why travelers stick to the road. As night had approached, there were no more passersby—everyone had found shelter where they could. Preddi and I would spread bedrolls beside the fire and keep watch in turns, but I wasn't worried much. The smell of a manticore keeps off most predators.

But as I picked through the limbs that lay like sutures across the ground's interwoven needles, a crackling through the dry leaves at the clearing's edge alerted me. Preddi was near the road, gathering more wood.

As I watched I saw stealthy movement. First one, then more, as though the shadows themselves were crawling towards me. As they emerged from the crevices beneath logs and the hollows of the trees, I saw a host of leprous, rotting rabbits, their fur blackened with drying blood, their eyes alight with foxfire. I did not know what malign force animated them, but it was clear it meant me no good.

Out of sight but not earshot, Bupus let out a simultaneous snore and long sonorous fart. Under other circumstances, it would have been funny, but now it only echoed flat and helpless as the rabbits, crouched as low to the ground as though they were snakes, writhed through the dry grasses towards me, their eyes gleaming with moon-touched luminescence.

The novelty of the sensation might have been what had me frozen. It was as though my belly were trying to crawl sideways, as though my bones had been stolen without my notice.

They were nearly to me, crawling in a sinuous motion, as though their flesh were liquid. Preddi wouldn't hear me shout. Neither would the snoring Bupus. I strained to scream nonetheless. It seemed unreasonable not to.

And then behind me there was a noise.

A woman was coming towards me along the deer path, dressed in the onion-skin colored gown of a Palmer, carrying an ancient throwlight. It was made of bronze, and aluminum capped one end, while the other bulged with a glass lens.

She thumbed its side and it shed its cold and mechanical light across the leprous rabbits, which recoiled as though a single mass. They smoldered under the unnatural light, withered away into ringlets of oily smoke.

"I saw your fire from the road," she said, letting the light play over the last of the rabbits. "This area is curse-ridden, and I thought you might not know to look out. Light kills them, though."

"Thank you," I said shakily. "Will you share our fire?"

"Yes," she said, as though expecting the invitation. She was a small woman with a head of short, brown-curled hair—slight but with enough weight to give her substance. No jewelry was evident, only the simplicity of her robe and the worn leather pack on her back, which she tucked her light back into.

"That's a useful thing," I said. "Where did you get it?"

"I found it," she said before changing the subject. "Are you unharmed? A bite from a curse creature can fester."

I shook my head. "They didn't get close enough," I said. "Good timing on your part."

Back at the fire, I tried to convey to Preddi that there was danger in the woods. I don't know if it got through or not. We built the fire up, and stacked the extra wood nearby, settling down to toast bread and cheese on sticks over the fire. Bupus whined for cheese, but it makes him ill, so I gave him chunks of almost-burned toasted bread instead. Coal's good for his digestion. He looked reproachful, but crunched them down.

The Palmer, whose name turned out to be Lupe, and I talked, Preddi's gaze moving between us as though he were listening, although when I tried to include him in the conversation, he gave me a blank look. I learned she was traveling from Port Wasp to Piperville, although she did not reveal the purpose of her pilgrimage. Well, that's a personal thing, and not one everyone shares, so I didn't push the question.

"You're a beast trainer," she said, eying me.

"I am—and my father before me, and his mother before him."

"A tradition in your family." Her eyes glittered in the firelight, malicious jet beads.

"Yes."

"Do you pass down lists of what are beasts and what are people?"

I sighed. One of those. "Look," I said. "We know which are beasts and which people. Beasts cannot overcome their natures and are not responsible for their actions. People can and are. There are four races of people: human, the Snake folk, the Dead beneath Tabat, and Angels, although no one has seen the last in centuries."

"But although beasts are helpless before their natures, should one kill a person, they are killed in turn."

"Of course," I said. "Any farmer knows that a dog that bites once will bite again. They cannot help it. People can learn, so they can be punished and learn from the experience."

She snorted and spat something fat and wet into the fire. "It's no use talking to you," she said. She turned to Preddi. "And what about you?" she said.

He looked at her blankly.

"He's a little deaf," I said.

"Ah." She leaned forward and shouted into his ear, putting a hand on his arm to steady herself.

It surprised him. Few of us talked to Preddi—too difficult to stand there loudly repeating a phrase until it penetrated the muffling of his hearing.

I stood up and went to see to Bupus.

He was lying on his back, sprawled out like a tomcat in hot weather. Spittle roped from his gaping mouth and his knobby, chitinous tail twitched in his sleep, its tip glistening with green ichor.

I checked him over for ticks, parasites, thorns and the like. He grumbled in his sleep, turning over when I thumped him, great flanks shivering as though bitten by invisible flies.

"Gnaw your bones," he muttered.

When I turned back to the fireside, I froze as deeply as I had with the rabbits. Off in the shadows beneath a sheltering pair of cedars, Preddi and the pilgrim woman were huddled together in his bedroll, moving in rhythm.

I was appalled on several levels. For one, you don't want to think about your husband's father like that. You know what I mean. Plus this woman didn't seem very pleasant. And this was awfully sudden, so I felt as though I should make sure she didn't chew off his face or turn out to be some sort of shifter. But above it all, I was irritated at their lack of manners. Was I supposed to act as though they weren't there on the other side of the fire? I could understand why they hadn't gone further, worried about the rabbits. But still. Still.

After they settled down, Preddi emerged and signaled he was ready to take his watch. He didn't look me in the face, nor was I sure what to say. I looked him over and if he'd been enchanted in some way, I couldn't tell, nor was I sure what the signs of such enchantment might be. So I tried to sleep, but mainly lay awake, wondering what Rik would say when he found out.

In the morning, Steel was there.

"Where's Rik?" I said, before any other business.

"There's been a little trouble," Steel said.

"What trouble?"

He flapped an irritated hand at me. "Get your manticore ready while I fix the axle." He gave Preddi and the pilgrim a glance.

"That's Lupe, a pilgrim," I said. "She saved my life last night."

He grunted and turned to the axle. I roused Bupus to get him into harness, grumbling under my breath.

Preddi and Lupe walked on one side of the wagon while Steel rode on the other. I drove. Lupe leaned on Preddi as they walked, and I noticed the slight hitch to her gait, as though one leg were shorter than the other.

"You can ride with me," I said, wondering if she'd be able to keep up otherwise. She shook her head, smiling at Preddi. It was a gesture that warmed me to her, despite my fears.

"What happened was this," Steel said. "Lily got two farmers all riled up and throwing insults at each other. They started swinging and then we got fined for disturbing the peace."

"Fined? How much?"

He winced.

"That much?" I said. "We don't have any cash to spare." Rik keeps the books for the circus, and I knew just how thin the financial razor's edge we danced on was.

"Yes," Steel said. "They let me out but kept the others in there. I'm supposed to raise the money. How, I don't know. Meanwhile, they're all sitting in jail eating their heads off and adding each day's room and board to the total."

"We have no extra money," I said.

"I know."

"I do," Lupe said from somewhere behind us. "I could help you."

We both turned to look at her, but Steel said the obvious thing first. "And what would you want in return?"

"A friend's wagon went into a gorge, two miles ahead. I need someone to go into it and bring out a box of tools that he needs. He'll come back later to retrieve the wagon itself, but he's gone ahead to Piperville. I stayed behind to see if I could get help in getting the wagon out, but had no luck. Now I just want to bring him his tools, but I am forbidden to go within walls during my journey."

It was flimsy; it was suspicious. But Palmers are on pilgrimage, and sometimes they act according to their geas. Steel and I exchanged glances, saying the same thing. Not much choice here.

"Very well," he said.

We trudged along in silence for the next mile, except for Lupe, who chattered away to Preddi. She had a trick of touching his arm to let him know she was speaking, to look at her, and he seemed happier than his usual self. I felt guilty—had Preddi been waiting all this time for someone just to talk to? I knew Rik's mother had died birthing him—that would have been over a quarter of a century ago.

I kept hearing her voice as we rode, high pitched inconsequentialities, the rush of words that comes from someone who has wanted to speak for a long time.

It was easy enough to see where the wagon had gone into the gorge. It was a bad place where the road narrowed—Lupe said her friend had been trying to make room for a larger wagon to pass. The blackberries were torn with its passage down the sloping, rocky side.

And when I climbed down through the brambles, since it was clear Steel had no intention of it, I saw a familiar sight: Sparky's little wagon, tilted askew.

He was not in sight, but I found blood and tracks near the front, confused and scattered, as though being pursued.

How to play this hand? What was Lupe's game? I opened the back door of the wagon and peered inside.

Sparky had collected scrap. Iron chains draped the walls, along with lengths of iron and lesser metals: soft copper tubing, a tarnished piece of silver netting. And in the center, his tools in their box. I opened it, trying to figure out why Lupe wanted them. Ordinary tools: screwdrivers, picks, hammers. His father had made them and carved the wooden handles himself, Sparky had told me once.

Wooden handles. I looked down at the tools again, and then at the chain draped walls. Finally I understood. I imagined Sparky being driven from his wagon seat in a cloud of elf-shot, wicked stings that burned, wicked stings that drove him in a mad rush to where he could be safely killed.

Taking a length of chain from the wall and draping it around my neck, I took the box and clambered up the side of the gorge with its awkward weight below my arm.

Lupe's fingers twitched with eagerness as she saw it. She and Preddi stood side by side, while Steel watched the road, ready to lead Bupus on a little further if some wagon should need to pass. I went over to him and laid the box between Bupus's front paws. Touching the manticore's shoulder, I leaned to whisper in his ear. He looked at me, his eyes unreadable, while Steel glanced sideways, eyebrows forming a puzzled wrinkle.

"Give it to me," Lupe said. Her voice had an odd, droning quality.

"Not until we have the money," I said.

She laughed harshly and I knew deep in my bones I'd been right. I stepped aside, putting my hand on Bupus's mane. Steel looked between us, bewildered.

"It's Sparky's wagon," I said. "Looks like he was driven away to be killed."

"You must be confused," she said. "That wagon belongs to my friend. I don't know who this Sparky is."

I continued, "And then she found she couldn't go in his wagon because of the iron, and yet there they were, wooden handled tools that she could use. You're some sort of Fay, aren't you, Lupe?"

Her black eyes glittered with rage as she stared at me, searching for reply. Preddi looked between us, his face confused. I had no idea what he was making of the conversation, or if he'd actually caught any of it.

Steel stepped forward, hand on his knife.

"Stay away!" she spat. Her form quivered as she shrank in on herself, her skin wrinkling, folding, until she resembled nothing so much as an immense, papery wasp's nest, tiny wicked fairies swarming around her. A desiccated tuft of brown curls behatted her and she rushed at me and the box in a cloud of fairies.

Bupus's tail batted her out of the air, neat and quick, and I laid the chain across her throat.

It immobilized her. The tiny fairies still darted in and out of her papery form, but they made no move to harm me. Cold iron is deadly to the Fays, even beyond its hampering of their powers.

I had my own tools in the wagon.

Another traveling show paid well for Lupe, enough to get all of our members out of jail. She huddled in the iron cage, quenched and calmed, and the malicious spark had vanished from her eyes. I hoped the dulling had left her with some language. I had not performed the operation in a long time.

Surprisingly, Preddi chose to go with her. All he said was, "She's a good companion." There was no reproach in the words. Rik did not entirely understand why his father was leaving, but he took it well enough.

In the evening, I took Bupus down to the stream near our camp for a drink. The full moon rolled overhead like a tipsy yellow balloon. He paced beside me, slow steady footfalls, and as he drank, I combed out his hair with a wooden-toothed comb, removing the road dust. When he had drunk his fill, I wiped his face for him.

There in the moonlight, he took my wrist in his mouth, pinned between enormous molars as big as pill-bottles. I froze, imagining the teeth crushing down, the bones splintering as he ground at them. Sweat soured my arm-pits but I stood stock still.

His lips released my wrist and he nosed at my side, snuggling his head in under my arm. I let go of the breath I had been holding. Tears sprang to my ears.

He rumbled something interrogative, muffled against the skin of my hip. I wound my fingers through his lank, greasy hair.

"No," I said. "You didn't hurt me."

"Good," he said.

I stood for a long time, looking up at the moon. Its face was washed clean by clouds, and stars came out to play around it. After a while, Bupus began to snore.

Heart in a Box

"Heart in a Box" was the story I workshopped my first week at Clarion West. I had arrived at the idea of doing something with the Little Mermaid that summer and had brought the first couple of paragraphs, the opening scene by the river, with me in my idea file. I set the story in Phuket, Thailand, where I had spent a Thanksgiving with some friends several years earlier.

The story is partially about feminism and the idea of sacrifice that sometimes gets woven into love stories, but it's also about guilt and being complicit in a system that consumes such sacrifices. It also expresses a certain irritation with the roles for women available in fairy tales. It appeared in Strange Horizons *in 2006 under the title "Foam on the Water," since the editors were concerned about the similarity of the original title to* Saturday Night Live's *"Thing in a Box" skit, which had recently appeared.*

Trevor, Ivory, and I were sitting by the river, the grass awning that had shaded us from the fierce Thai sunlight now blocking out the clustered evening stars. The bug screen was working overtime. You'd hear the almost subsonic whine whenever an insect hit it, making a shrill counterpoint to the jungle noises: birds squawking, the trees' hollow rattle, the drip and drop of moisture from the leaves.

Trevor had scored a lump of hash as big as my thumb; a curl of gold leaf marked its side, and we were working on making it smaller. A hookah sat on the rattan table, and we used my pocket knife to shave bits from the surface and pack the bowl. The smoke was sweet and rich as homemade cake batter, and I had a solid buzz going.

Trevor's lighter sparked in the evening darkness. The candle lamp on the table was nearly dead. We were killing time, all three of us. The waning moon was high and misshapen, and its blaze danced like the guttering candle on the cups of the waves, a foamy gleam barely visible.

We were still and stoned. Hash, good hash, doesn't make you feel stupid or sleepy. Just remote. Remote from the world, deaf to the cries of the vendors, the blare and growl of traffic, and the distant thump-a-thump of the Banana Disco.

From the river came a sound of splashing as though something enormous were thrashing in the water.

"What's that?" Ivory said.

We stared down through the darkness. There was no one else around; it was off-season and our waiter had deserted us before the sun had set.

Trevor stood, glancing at me. "I'm going to check it out."

"Could be a crocodile. You never know what you'll find in Thailand." Ivory didn't move but her voice was unalarmed. "Feel free, boys. I'll be right here."

"Where's your sense of adventure?" He grinned at her, flashing perfect white teeth.

"Left behind in an LA hotel room," she said.

So Trevor and I went together with cautious steps. There was a steep grade to the side of the river and thorny vines tore at us as we half-fell down it before encountering the sticky grasp of red clay mud threatening to pull our Tevas off.

She lay naked on the river bank like a fallen swan. Her skin white as snow, her hair midnight black. Her feet were thin and fragile as newly pedicured mourning doves, not a smudge or callous except for the mud that covered her.

As we slid towards her, she opened her eyes. Gray-blue, like the sea at evening, looking at us with a feverish terror. Another expression overtook the fear, unclenching the muscles, as she regarded me, a little startled but as though by an old friend.

We stopped a few feet away. I held out my hands and felt an absurd desire to say, "We come in peace." Instead I said, low and reassuring, "It's okay. It's okay."

Trevor shrugged his way out of his lemon rayon shirt and draped it over her as she sat up. She fingered the material uneasily and leaned to sniff it, her nose wrinkling.

"Not this year's style, but a classic is a classic, my mother says," he told her with a nervous little grin. She didn't smile, just cocked her head interrogatively, glancing between us.

Every time she looked at me, it was like a drink of water, or better, some intoxicating spirit. I found I could not look away and I know Ivory noticed that when we brought the girl back towards our table. I caught her cool speculative stare.

"Do you speak English?" Trevor said, and the girl gave him an inquisitive look.

She wasn't one of the natives, though slim and small as one. At first I thought her an albino Thai with dyed hair. But her eyes were gray and blue against the inhuman fairness of her skin.

Phuket Enclave was stylish a few summers ago, but now was just evidence of the aftermath of being stylish. All the little shops were starting to dwindle and consolidate. The vendors, once insistent, had grown dispirited and lackluster, no longer offering polished gemstones, statues carved of opal or mahogany, wonders worthy of an Arabian treasure cave. Instead they carried the detritus of tourism: cut-rate t-shirts, video clips of dancing elephants, rayon costumery—"Genuine Thai kick boxer suit, very cheap, very nice."

I'd been to see one of the painting elephants, Khwaam, the day before we found the girl. Standing in its clearing, I watched its keeper fill buckets of paint before the elephant curled its trunk around the brush and stepped up to the paper. He painted a picture of blue and green water, an intimation of a face below the surface. I paid the keeper 500 bhat and pinned the picture to my hotel room wall. My maternal grandmother invests heavily in animal art; I'd give her this one and see if she could help the elephant make a name for itself.

Though I get bored with places easily, after two weeks, I still liked Phuket. The evening of the Loy Kratong Festival, I'd stood alone by the bridge, watching little boats filled with candles and the glowing tips of incense slip past on the dark surface of the water, following the undulating trails of the full moon's light. Underneath the bridge, there was a splash and a flash of scales as a large fish roiled the water, scattering the boats.

In Thai tradition, putting a coin and a few hairs on one of the little boats allows you to wash away sins and bless love affairs. I had no love affairs to bless, but launched mine anyway, laden with a five bhat coin and a quick snip from one sideburn. I was in one of those transitional periods of life, where you feel yourself changing, but I wasn't sure what I was transitioning to, so any kind of luck was welcome. My family (you'd recognize the name) was eager for me to go into politics, back home in the US, but it seemed like a lot of work, and I'd just gotten done with four years of that at Yale. I was the family's odd duck, like my father before me. He escaped family expectations and became a novelist. Nowadays the elders of the family were waiting to see what path I'd choose. And I wasn't sure, to be truthful.

Ivory used to be a rock star—that was how we'd met her. Trevor, who was a wannabe rocker and my roommate in college, had sought her out when he'd found she was staying in our hotel. Her jagged, gravelly voice, her edged and world-weary lyrics, had created an enduring aura of glamour. For an older woman—Google revealed she was pushing sixty—she was well-preserved. But her breasts, silicone augmented and perpetually perky, gave her an odd appearance. Like lipstick on a chimp, Trevor confided the day after we'd met her. Sexy but it shouldn't be.

She'd stuck with us, maybe for the quality drugs Trevor scored, maybe for his looks. I wasn't sure—although I knew they slept together whenever she felt like it.

Her real name wasn't Ivory, of course, but I don't know where the nickname came from. Perhaps her appearance: blonde and thin as a piece of bone, and as classically beautiful. Dry. Dry as salt, with a sense of humor to match and a mystic streak that only surfaced occasionally in conversation.

Somehow Trevor talked Ivory into taking the girl. I would have volunteered, but I was too unsettled by her blue eyes regarding me, the half smile whenever I returned the look. By the next day, Ivory had her outfitted like any American tourist: faded jeans, ratty t-shirt. And a pair of Converse that must have been red once and now were faded to a shade of rust, loose on her tiny, perfect feet.

Her ears were unpierced; she had no tattoos anywhere. "Odd, in this day and age," Ivory said, one white eyebrow arching. "No plucked eyebrows, no razor stubble, no cosmetic surgery. Like a princess from a bedtime story."

The girl watched me with a steady gaze. She smiled at me.

"Name?" I asked her, but she shook her head, looking confused.

"What you call a naked woman that you find on a river bank?" Trevor said. "It sounds like a bad joke. She's not a Heather or Brittany or Tiffany."

"Mara. Marina," Ivory said, leaning forward. The girl did not respond. "Minnie."

And Minnie with its mouselike connotations stuck.

I found my reaction to her unsettling. I've worked hard at eliminating reactions to women. Too much potential trouble. Too much potential scandal. Here in Thailand it wouldn't matter perhaps. Back home it would. Children in my family are raised by nannies, governesses, tutors. Strictly vetted of course but a few oddities slip through here and there. Mine was Ms. Andersen. Tall, blonde, Danish. She had certain similarities to Ivory but was more magazine beautiful. She started teaching me when I was twelve, and that was the year I learned my cock had a mind of its own. There she'd be, talking about basic algebra, and under my desk my cock was shouting LISTEN TO ME while I sat there trying to will it down. After a while I started carrying a book bag around that I could swing in front of my crotch as a concealing shield when necessary.

This would have been all right, I think, except for her sadistic tendencies. Some sort of quirk. I found her out in the back yard killing mice in the humane trap that my tender-hearted aunt had insisted we use. It was early morning and she didn't think anyone else was around. She'd reach her hand in, take out a mouse, and then squeeze, her face expressionless. I watched her kill six of them that way, my cock as hard and rigid as a ruler. And when she raised her hand to her mouth to lick off a smear of blood, I came, right there in my pants. First orgasm.

That experience left its traces. It's why I don't date much. My family would kill me if I caused a scandal. But I know that I've got a taste for it. A taste for pain, courtesy of ice princess Andersen. I just keep it hidden away, like a sorcerer keeping his heart in a box, safe from threat.

Minnie was so passive. Ivory treated her like a doll, dressed her, brought her to meals, dragged her with us to sit in the shade and watch the ocean. "She keeps away the vendors," she said. "Have you noticed?"

And it was true. None of them came near her. Usually sitting there we'd be besieged by fruit sellers, masseuses, men carrying monkeys, hawks, and snakes, asking if we wanted our pictures taken with the animals. Instead we sat at the bar, drinking shots of lao kao and playing Connect 4 on the battered plastic sets that seem the staple of every Thai beach bar.

"You've been here, what, a month?" Ivory asked me.

"Two, three weeks," I said.

"What tourist things have you done?"

I shrugged. "Went down to Lampang and saw an elephant paint. That's about it."

"We should do tourist things," she said. The lao kao mixed with whatever else she was on had taken hold. Her eyes glittered with a frantic edge. "See the kick boxers, the dancers. Show your little friend around."

"She's not my little friend," I said. I didn't look at Minnie because I knew she'd be staring at me. "And she's a local, anyhow."

Ivory tilted her head to drain her shot glass to the dregs and slammed it down hard enough to crack it. "No," she said. "She's not a local."

The kick boxers are all show or so an Australian man once told me. He said the displays put on for the tourists, it's just costumes and a few flashy, inauthentic moves. But they looked real enough to me, moved faster, quicker than my clumsy American self ever will. They were followed by the dancers, who wore clothing that looked too tight to dance in and six-inch gilded fingernails. Their faces were heavily made up, painted masks.

Minnie danced with them. The women eyed her but made way as she stepped down from where she had been sitting with us. She moved with them, keeping her body as straight and upright as theirs, bending only with the knees. So graceful. So assured. Her eyes fixed on mine. With every step there was a flicker of pain deep within the blueness, and somewhere deep inside me something stirred, unwilling.

We walked all over that day, Ivory dragging us behind her like a covey of quail. A tuk-tuk carried us over to Patong and the Butterfly Gardens there. I kept watching Minnie as we walked among the butterflies, colored leaves drifting on the breeze, to see if my suspicions were right. And it seemed as though, as the day wore on, the shadows crossed her eyes more and more. As though she were walking on knives, or broken glass, but was too proud or too stupid to make a sound.

My heart, enclosed in its box, twitched at the thought.

We even went back to Lampang and the elephant. Ivory had never seen one paint. We all watched as Khwaam dipped his trunk to create wavy lines of blue. And then red paint to make smears like footprints crossing them. Minnie turned away as though uninterested but Ivory paid for the picture.

"Have you ever thought," she said on the way home, "of all the ways women mutilate themselves for love?"

"Women do it for themselves," Trevor said. "They like to look pretty. Ever seen a bunch of women turn on an ugly one? It's what sororities are made of."

"Sexist bullshit," Ivory said. "You don't deserve any of the things women do. The world would be happier without men."

"But would you?" he said, leering and putting a significant hand on his crotch.

"I don't know," she said, and the smile fell away from his face, replaced by confusion at the neutrality of her tone. But she wasn't even looking at him. Just staring out the window, her palm laid on her chest.

On a hunch, I said, "Do you regret the surgery?"

She laughed harshly. "Regret it? I'll have perfect tits until the day I die. What woman could regret such a thing?"

"Why did you do it then?" Trevor asked. "Not that I'm complaining."

"Because you can't sell things unless you look good," Ivory said. "At least, a woman can't. Men can always rely on *character*."

Minnie looked between us, uncomprehending but hearing the hostility in Ivory's tone.

If I'd known what to say, I would have. Instead I leaned over and took Minnie's hand. It was the first time I'd touched her. Her flesh was chilly and moist despite the day's heat. She smiled at me.

Ivory stared out the window, watching the spirit houses on the side of the road, the rolled up painting in her hand.

"Ivory's a little crazy," Trevor said apologetically that night in the lobby.
"You're telling me?"
"She thinks Minnie's a fairy tale."
"What?"
"She thinks Minnie's the Little Mermaid."
"The one with seashells over her boobs and singing fish for pals?"
"No, that's the Disney version. She means the original."
"What's the difference?"
"The ending's not happy in the original," Ivory said from behind us. I hadn't heard her coming. "You know the story? She's the youngest daughter of the Sea King and on her fifteenth birthday she's allowed up to the surface. She sees a ship with a handsome prince on it, and she falls in love with him. So she goes to the Sea Witch, who agrees to give her the power to walk on land and pursue his love, in return for her voice. She does, but the magic's imperfect, and it hurts her to walk. But she does it, for love of the prince. He falls in love with someone else, of course. In the end, she turns into foam and dies, because she has no soul."

I looked at her in disbelief. "And this is what you think is happening?"

"Oh, you're not a prince," Ivory said. "But you're close enough in her eyes. So what are you going to do? Buy her fake papers, take her home with you? I don't know if you'd like a steady diet of tuna, but I guess you'll get used to it."

"You're full of crap," I said.

"I've never seen you look at a woman before. I thought it was a challenge at first, but then I just figured you and I would share Trevor. But you're not even interested in that. So what is it with you, Prince Charming? You've never given your heart away, have you? How about to a nice little mute girl?"

I pushed her back against the wall as I shoved past.

In my room I fired up my laptop. You can find anything on the Internet if you've got a credit card handy. Anything. I lost myself in blood and bondage and pictures of pleading eyes and tried to avoid superimposing Minnie's face over any of it while my hand moved on my cock, demanding release.

No. I'm not a prince. But I never claimed to be.

We were at the Patong aquarium, lost in mazes of murky, green-lit glass. I stood by a case and watched a diver feeding black tip and leopard sharks, spots riding their backs like miniature saddles. Their eyes were flat and black and expressionless. I watched them tear the fish to bits, toss their heads like dogs with their teeth buried in something. Rending. Ripping. My heart pounded in my chest.

Minnie came up beside me but I wouldn't look at her. Out of the corner of my eye I could see her watching too, her face inanimate and nonjudgmental. To her the sharks, their teeth, the blood in the water, were just another fact of life.

I took her back to my room and closed the door.

It was early morning, and my head hurt from lack of sleep. I sat by the river again, but all the hash was gone. The coffee was bitter, and no matter how much creamer or sugar I added, it stayed that way.

Trevor and Ivory were still asleep, but Minnie had followed me out of bed like a silent shadow.

She leaned over and took my hand in hers, her eyes blue and enormous. She laid her fingers, her fragile, boney fingers, in my hand. Then she closed my fingers over them with her other hand and squeezed. She was much stronger than me. Her grip was painful but she didn't let go even though she must have been crushing her hand. She kept watching my face.

Arousal at the pain in her face surged through me like a crashing wave. It would have been easy to give in. But I'm not a prince.

I shoved her away and she fell backwards, still looking at me. Then she stood.

"Where are you going?" I said with a flash of panic. My thoughts boiled. Maybe I could take her home after all. No. No.

She ran down the riverbank and didn't look back, discarding clothing as she went. First the shirt, then the skirt, followed by the wisps of underwear. The rust-red shoes were still on her feet. I followed, slipping and foundering in the mud. I don't know why. Half of me had changed my mind, half of me was pursuing her.

She arched and leapt into the water of the swirling brown river in a single motion. And then there was only foam, dirty foam like polluted soapsuds, and my heart was still safe.

In the Lesser Southern Isles

In 2006, there was a craze for fantasy pirate stories. Shimmer Magazine *did a pirate issue, and there were at least two anthologies as well, including one edited by Ann and Jeff VanderMeer. By then I was starting to think writing on spec for theme issues was usually a bad idea, but a couple of stories did get sparked by thinking about pirates.*

This story started with the title and the idea of an expedition to recover a magical artifact— one of the classic fantasy plotlines. It's also the story of Lucy trying to figure out her sexual identity—drawn to both the non-threatening youth (who turns out to be very threatening) and the sexy pirate captain.

It was one of those Tabatian evenings when the sky is dark, pulsing blue. The shadows swelled and the sunlight, darkening to orange, took on an expectant, waiting look.

Lucy had been admiring new silks down on Thimble Street. One had been the same cobalt as the sky. She'd never get the silk—the youngest of four got second and third-me-downs. But she could dream a blue dress piped with black lace bands as much as she wanted to.

She heard the footsteps behind her as she turned into Stumble Lane but didn't take much notice.

A few blocks ahead, a lamplighter's distant golden flicker moved from pole to pole. The shuttered houses here were set close together in precise, two-storied arrays. Only a few lights gleamed, scattered in arched lower windows. To the left loomed the high iron fence surrounding Piskie Wood, caging tree trunks damp with the same rain that slick-misted the cobblestones underfoot. She slowed to look upward, arrested by the contrast of black leaves against the sunset's last efforts.

The footsteps approached in a rush and two men grabbed her from both sides, each taking an upper arm and rushing her along, continuing her movement down the street. They had no trouble lifting her. Even for a fifteen year old, she was small.

"Not a word, you, if you know what's good for yeh," one growled, his voice husky with tobacco and spirits. He shifted his grip and something sharp prodded her ribs.

"Hey!" a voice shouted behind them.

"Egga's wounds!" the other man said. "Didntcha have a lookout earlier?"

They were running. She half-lurched, half-flew, gasping for breath whenever her feet touched the ground. As they passed a house, curtains twitched aside and a woman looked out. For one horrified moment, their eyes met before Lucy was dragged on. Their pursuer was still running after them, yelling.

"In here!" She was pulled into an alleyway, pushed into one man's arms while his partner turned to meet the chaser, raising his arm and the club it held.

She would have paid more attention to his actions if it hadn't been for her own problems. With expert quickness, the other man thrust a wadded rag into her mouth despite her struggles. He tied it in place before dropping a sack, smelling of burlap and horse manure, over her and hoisting her over his shoulder.

"Got her."

"Yeah, what should I do with this 'un?"

"Grab it, Cap's always wanting more canaries."

A house alarm's vigorous clang came from somewhere and a woman shouted, "Guards, guards!"

"Frith's fingerlashings! Come on, this way."

She couldn't free her arms, bound painfully to her sides, so tightly she could hardly breathe. She jounced on her captor's bony shoulder, trying to work her jaws free.

The shouting quieted behind them.

She was thrown onto something. Helpless, impotent, she kicked out, colliding with a wooden wall. Straw itch overtook her and she sneezed despite the gag, half-retching as she fought the cloth in her mouth. There was a jolt as something else was thrown in beside her and the world rumbled into action.

The ride was uncomfortable but brief. She could tell they were heading downhill towards the docks. Inside the musty sack, she could see nothing, but when the cart rattled to a stop and she was pulled out, the cold breeze through the burlap confirmed her deduction.

"Please," she tried to shout despite the gag but to no avail. Hands grabbed and spun her. She was hoisted again on a shoulder, this time broader and more padded. It stepped forward and she felt the giddy sway underfoot.

A boat, she thought, we're on a boat.

She strained her ears but the bag's material muffled sound. There was clumping, and then she was out of the colder air and someplace warmer.

Her legs almost buckled as she was set on her feet and the bag pulled away with a rasp of rough cloth. A knife flashed and the gag fell away. She licked her dry lips and swallowed.

She found herself in a small cabin lit by guttering gilt lanterns set in pairs beside the doorway and reflected in the rounded mirrors on the opposite wall. The plushy carpet's color was peacock feather brilliant.

Space was at a premium here but every inch had been used. A desktop folded down from the wall on brass chains, its shelf rimmed to prevent objects from rolling off in rough seas and a bookcase had been set into one wall, jammed with worn volumes in motley assemblage beside a map holder whose round holes were filled with paper and parchment rolls. The only excess was the bed, which was wide enough for two and spilled with bead-bright, lozenge-shaped cushions. Like the desk and shelves, it had a railing edging it, presumably to keep the occupants contained during storms.

A carved wooden chair sat in the middle, a man perched on it. He leaned forward to glare at her, arms folded.

"This," he said in dubious tones, "is the Pot King's son, the College of Mages' prize?"

"He's in disguise, we thinks, Cap'n," one man said. "At the taverns we asked at, they said he likes to disguise hisself."

Lucy stole a glance over her shoulder. Her captors stood on either side of the door. Movement drew her eye downward: legs in unremarkable gray trousers and worn boots that twitched as though her stare had awakened them lay protruding from another burlap bag.

A cough returned her attention to the man before her.

"I am Captain Jusef Miryam, of the Emerald Queen," he said.

He was small in stature, perhaps a shade shorter than Lucy, who was used to having everyone tower over her. His beard and hair were a bristling black, combed and well-groomed. His skin was leathery and bronzed and his eyes were a perilous poet's green. When he flexed his hands impatiently, she noted their well-kept nails and the bright red stone framed in gold on his left hand. His clothes were gaudy although wrinkled and not much washed.

"Well?"

"I don't know why I'm here."

He frowned. "Let me cut right to the bone, lad. I will not put up with prevarication and the tongue twisting that wizards are known for." He nodded down at the bundle of burlap and legs. "What's that then, my fine fellows?"

"Tried to stop us from nicking her…er, him," one said. He jerked the sack away and a pale, freckle-faced boy blinked upwards from the floor. "Figgered we always needed canaries."

There was a knock on the door. "Cap'n, 'at finger-wiggler ya wanted tah speak to is 'ere."

"Throw them both in the hold for now," Captain Miryam said. "Give him a taste of what no cooperation would be like." He smiled faintly at Lucy. "Not that your present form isn't charming enough, but you might consider releasing it."

"Put them in cold iron chains," he said to the men. "Keep the candles I gave you burning in there, that'll keep him woozy enough to cast no spells. Check on them every turn of the glass."

They were hauled away.

The hold, Lucy found, was deep in the ship's belly, damp and cold. The timbers creaked and groaned around them and every time a wave slammed into the ship, Lucy felt the blow through the wall to which she had been chained. The older of the two sailors brought out a fat black candle and stooped to set it in a brass holder bolted to the floor. The younger stood staring at Lucy. He was a scrawny, scowling boy, his head shaved to gray-brown fuzz.

The other was old enough to be his grandfather. After setting the wick a-kindle, he took the boy by the shoulder with an admonitory shake and jerked him from the room.

The door slammed behind them and there was a clunk as it was barred. Lucy raised her head to look across at her companion.

He was pale and jug-eared in the flickering candle light, although a thatch of red hair hid part of the mushroom-white flaps set along his head. Freckles splattered across his cheekbones. His eyes were the color of Lucy's, a watery blue.

In turn, he saw a small, blond girl, dressed in a neatly patched cloak. Her face was narrow and triangular, and her mouth was rosebud prim, though not as pretty as that phrase implies.

"Well," he said. "Here we are, I guess."

"Who are you?"

"My name's Devon."

"Lucy."

"Pleased to make your acquaintance." His tone was cordial and she wondered at the power of manners that could somehow provide a script for this dreadful, chaotic situation.

"What are we doing here?"

"As far as I can tell," Devon said. "The pirates thought they were kidnapping someone from the College of Mages and got you instead. I was behind a ways and saw you getting grabbed, so I ran after you and was snatched in turn. I'm here to be a canary, whatever that is. There you have my knowledge's sum and total."

"Why did they think I'm a man, though?"

"Mages can go about in many disguises," Devon said. "Some actually change their shapes, while others rely on glamourie, illusion-casting. Lots like to walk around town that way so they're not spotted as mages. Everyone assumes mages can conjure gold and they jack up the prices like you wouldn't believe."

"How do you know so much about it?"

"I'm also a student of the College of Mages."

"Are you the person they were looking for?"

"Oh, no," he said hurriedly. "No, I'm not. But listen, I'm thinking that if they think you're him, that's the only thing keeping you from being used as a canary. And while I don't know what being a canary means, I'm willing to bet that since they have to kidnap people to be them, it's not a great thing."

Lucy mulled this over. "You're probably right."

"You can at least find out what they want," Devon said.

"What if he asks me to drop the disguise again?"

"Tell him it was a shape shifting spell that went awry and you were heading back to the College to have a Master Mage remove it. That happens all the time."

"It does?"

"You'd be surprised how often."

"I can't do it," she said, turning back to the question. "He'll glare at me and I'll start crying."

He frowned over at her. "Just put your chin up," he said. "Think about him naked."

She blushed, even more frightened. She still couldn't figure out how she, Lucy the Mouse, had ended up on a boat with pirates. It was like something from a ballad but much less glamorous somehow. She hadn't realized how frightening adventures could be.

They heard footsteps and the door being unbarred. The younger pirate stuck his head in and looked between them, then at the candle. Before either could react, he withdrew his head with a rapid snakelike motion and slammed the door.

"Not much chance for conversation," Devon said.

"How long do you think they'll keep us here?"

"Your guess is as good as mine. Look, Lucy, you've got to bluff your way through this. Pretend you're someone else. Perhaps some character from a play you've seen?"

"I haven't seen any plays since I was very little," she said, dismayed.

"Well, what about one that you liked as a child?"

She thought. She remembered the stories that she loved listening to at night, all four children crouched around her mother's skirts. Lucy had been so small she could barely remember the stories, but they came back to her now: The Rabbit that Stole the Moon, and Mary Silverhands and Sister Wind and the Golden Bridle, Whitepetal and Blackleaf, and the Princess with the Copper Scales.

There had been a street puppet theater, a cloth screen stretched over a wooden framework, so different on one side from the other. In front, the puppets moved, but past the curtains had been the dancing puppeteers, pitching their voices upward, avoiding each other as they maneuvered the wooden sticks manipulating the forms above them.

She remembered Mary Silverhands, her glowing hands held before her, turning everything she touched to metal: the food on her plate, the drink in her glass. And the blonde-haired puppet's dignity, its upright stance, the patient grace conveyed by its inanimate face.

She closed her eyes and envisioned herself something other than Lucy, the youngest, the clumsiest, the least listened to and the most overlooked. She was Mary, her life a constant struggle to look out for those around her, to avoid unleashing the deadly power that would, unless contained, turn the whole world to silver.

"All right," she said. It was Mary's voice, not a quaver, not a quiver.

"You'll do it?"

"Yes," Mary said.

The young pirate poked his head in twice more before she was bundled back into the Captain's cabin. Another black candle guttered in the corner. She couldn't tell much difference between the air outside and the candle smoke, but she was so weary by now that everything seemed unreal and brighter than life to her, like a hallucinatory fever-dream.

"Well?" the Captain demanded.

"What did you want with me?"

"Are you the Pot King's son?"

"Maybe…" she stammered.

He leaned forward to stare into her eyes.

"Yes or no!" She flinched back from his shout. Her mouth worked noiselessly, terror taking her tongue.

"Bring the other in and cut his throat to show this one we mean business," he said to the pirate holding her.

"Aye, sir."

Mary, she thought, I'm Mary. If I reached out to touch this man, he would be dead in an instant. "No!" she managed to squeak. Her voice was barely audible.

He slouched back in his chair, looking pleased, but did not speak.

She gasped, fighting to shape the words. "Please, you mustn't!"

The door opened again and the pirate stood there, holding Devon against his chest, a wicked silver line against the boy's throat.

"I am, I'll do it, please don't!" she shrieked. The Captain held up a forefinger to the pirate holding Devon. The knife stayed where it was.

"I'm his son, I am, I'll help you however you like," she babbled.

"Clearly the canary is of more use here than stowed away elsewhere," the Captain said. He stroked his beard, eying them. "Do you intend to take your true form, Prince Nikolai?"

She pulled herself up out of her panic, clinging to the thought of Mary. What was the story Devon had provided? "I can't. The magic went awry. I need another mage to lift it. A Master Mage."

His eyes narrowed. "I see. Pity we didn't keep the sorcerer around longer. I congratulate you on your ingenuity. Who would think such a trifling form would mask a budding mage?"

"Trifling?"

"We have no use for you until we reach the Coral Tower. But I'm presuming you would rather see the sky and sun than spend the entire journey in the hold?"

Lucy frowned at him.

"All that I require," he said. "is your word on your name. The vow that no wizard can break without losing his or her magic."

The frown stayed on her face, knitting her translucent brows together.

"And you," he said to Devon, who still dangled, his chin stretched upward to avoid the blade. "You'll swear to make no attempts at escape either."

"How could I escape?" Devon said. "Jump overboard and walk away on the water?"

"Just do it!"

They repeated the words after the Captain.

"When do we set sail?" Lucy asked. Perhaps there might be way to get word to her family if she was allowed on deck.

The Captain laughed.

"When?" he said. "Two hours ago, that's when. We're far out to sea by now."

"Where are we headed?" Devon asked.

The Captain pointed at Lucy. "Her...I mean his father's spawning grounds, the Lesser Southern Isles."

He looked to the other pirates. "Take them away for now."

They were fed, although it was a dried fish, some hard biscuit and a half mug of sour watery beer apiece.

"The Lesser Southern Isles will take us two weeks to reach," Devon said.

"How do you know? Are you from there?"

"They teach us geography—that's maps and how to read them—in the College." He stared forward, thinking. "Magic is unpredictable in the Lesser Southern Isles. There are artifacts there from other ages, like the Coral Tower and the Speaking Skull. They say anything can happen in the Lesser Southern Isles, that gods are born and remade there. I guess we'll see."

Lucy sighed. "Two weeks."

"Will your family miss you?" Devon asked. Back in the echoing hold, Lucy wondered how she had not understood the departure sounds, the heavy timbers' creak and sway and the distant shouts and clatter of footsteps.

"Two weeks," she repeated. "No, they won't. Well, yes, they'll miss me, perhaps, but they'll have no idea where to look."

"I am sure that the College will set seeking spells after me," he said. "It's just a matter of holding out until this ship stops and the spells have a chance to catch up."

"You're a wizard—can you send word back about where we're headed?"

"Not without violating my oath and jeopardizing my magic's source."

"What would happen if you broke your word?"

He looked away.

In the morning, they were allowed to stroll the deck. Lucy would have liked to lean on Devon's arm but as the supposed Pot-King's son she felt it necessary to exhibit a masculine swagger. She hoped it was more convincing than it felt.

They exchanged histories. Devon had grown up in the Old Islands, magic-wracked lands populated by scattered tribes. The Pot-King, he said, struggled to recruit as many as he could.

"Everyone says they know the secret of his power and everyone says something different," he said. "But he's a match for any three sorcerers on the Old Continent."

"Then why isn't his son a powerful wizard?" Lucy said.

"Mages don't manifest power until they start to come of age," he said. "You know, when they start getting beards." He blushed and left the rest unsaid: his squeaky voice and downy cheek showed no trace of manhood.

Lucy told him about being the youngest, an unexpected and unwanted child trailing after her louder, bolder, braver siblings.

"Mouse," she said. "And Meepling, and Slink, and Little Miss Silent, that's what they call me."

"I have no brothers and sisters to call me anything," Devon said. "I envy you."

As they approached the Lesser Southern Isles, the days and nights grew balmier. The cook taught them how to fish and how to throw a weighted hand-net to catch the schools of small fish or shrimp swimming in the wave tops. Whatever they caught showed up in their evening bread and fish stew.

After dinner they were allowed to listen to the stories of the sailors, who sat passing tobacco pipes, telling tales of kraken and merfolk and great living islands that dove when unwary sailors went ashore and built fires to cook their meals.

Captain Miryam did not take part in the storytelling. Lucy saw him rarely—a glimpse now and again as he paced the front deck, green eyes gleaming in the evening shadows.

Two days later, the Captain sent for Lucy again. He unrolled a map and gestured at her to look.

What she presumed were the Lesser Southern Isles spread across the parchment in coin-shaped irregularities. One blob that aspired to hand-sized sat towards the map's upper edge. The Captain tapped the space beside it.

"This," he said, "is where we are now."

He pointed to a circle halfway down the map. "And here is the Coral Tower."

"Which is?" Lucy asked.

He snorted. "Your daddy keeps it all close, eh, son?" He stroked his moustache, eying Lucy. "Or are you playing it coy so I'll underestimate you?" He smiled. "I presume you know the perils of a young girl caught on a pirate ship. They may be all charm and fishing lore while you're under my wing, but should that…protection be withdrawn, you would find your form more disadvantageous."

"I told you, I can't lift the spell," Lucy said.

He studied her. "Very well. The Coral Tower is an ancient artifact, discovered when these Isles were first settled. It sits in the water, surrounded by coral reefs. Inside, a staircase leads down. Some say to the Earth's center, others to chambers filled with treasure."

He shrugged. "What I know is that your father went down there and returned with immense power, and that he had to use his own blood to pay for that bargain. Now the tower is sealed to all but those of that blood—you'll lead the way and take me down to where I can make my own deal."

"Oh," Lucy said blankly. "All right."

He smiled tightly at her. This close in the cabin, she could smell him, sweat and the sweet amber fragrance that came from the clothes chest at the foot of the uncomfortably close and lavish bed. She felt hyper-aware of his presence, the smell of the anise seeds he chewed, the way his moustache curled, the fine wrinkles at the corners of his electric green eyes.

"All right," he said. He sighed, staying where he was. "What use are you, little mage?" His hand took her shoulder; it was warm through her shirt's worn linen. She shivered. Something coiled and uncoiled in her core.

"What are you like under this disguise?" Captain Miryam's voice was husky and soft. "Is this the form you yearn for, the form of your soul itself? Are you a demure little maiden, eyelashes so blonde and fine I can barely see them in the lamplight?" His breath stirred the hairs on her neck. She gasped for breath, a sudden shocked sound that made him withdraw.

Her face burned as she was taken back to the hold.

The days and nights grew warmer yet. On a sky blue afternoon, gulls wheeling above like lookouts, they glimpsed the Coral Tower.

It was much larger than Lucy had imagined. In her head it had been the size of her home, three rooms, grown up and downward into a long thin stalk. In reality, it seemed as wide around as a small city and she understood now the awed undertone with which both Devon and the Captain had named it. It was round and windows spanned its circumference, each large enough for their ship to pass through. The lines of windows continued upward, upward, towards a top that was far above in the blueness. Its color was a rosy, warm shade, but bird droppings encrusted the lower levels, thick mottled gray and white layers.

"It's at its best right after a storm," Devon said. "Then everything is washed clean, and you can see all the details." He stared forward at the tower, eyes wide.

The Captain came up behind them. "We'll be pulling in tonight," he said. "You'll do your part, lad, or else your young friend here will die."

Not for the first time, Lucy regretted her disguise's complications.

The pirates dissented when it came time to brave the Coral Tower. Most stayed on board. They tied the ship to a railing near a set of steps a dozen horses wide, stretching upward into the tower. Two sailors shimmied down to anchor the rope ladder that most used, but Lucy and Devon were both lowered, arms tied to their sides.

"According to the sorcerer, it'll take a while for the Tower to know you," the Captain said to Lucy. "We'll stay here tonight."

They climbed the stairs, which were slippery, overgrown with wet yellow weed ribbed with shadowy purple. At the entrance they paused, gazing inward. There was no interior to the Tower, just a vast upward stretch. A narrow, unrailed staircase spiraled along the inside, leading upwards. They headed into the middle, where a black pit marked where a similar staircase led down into the earth.

The sailors built a fire of scavenged driftwood beside the pit. A small pot set amid the flames boiled with merry abandon, smelling of boiled double-fin and onions.

A sailor came from the ship, bringing a narrow wooden chest to the Captain. Opening it, he took out silken bands, each mounted with a slippery gray soapstone disk. He passed them out to everyone except Devon and Lucy, but tied one on her. Like the rest, he wore his fastened around his head, the stone disk resting flat against his forehead.

"I have been exploring and researching this Tower for over a decade," he said. "While many chambers will not open except to the Pot King's blood, since he was the last person to bind energies here, there are others that can be explored. Many hold sorcerous energies that play upon one's spirit—these disks absorb the effulgences but can hold only so much. So to find these pools of invisible, noxious influences, we use captives, just as miners use canaries in coal mines to signal deadly gas. He nodded towards Devon. "Should you fall prey to the energies and seek to destroy yourself, we will know we are in the presence of such, and hurry on."

"That is the usual sign?" Devon asked.

"A few have managed to hurl themselves into the pit that lies at the center and fall for we do not know how long."

Lucy shivered.

"There is no need to expose her to all this," Devon said.

"Who?"

He pointed at Lucy with his chin. "I'm the Pot-King's son. She's an innocent who got swept up in your plot unawares."

The Captain frowned, looking between them. "We'll take both and see who falls prey to the energies first," he said, removing Lucy's disk. "A sorcerer will have enough training to overcome the worst effects."

They slept there that night, although Lucy did not feel that she slept at all. The inside of the tower roared with the waves' murmur, magnifying it into a steady throbbing at the back of her head. She strained her ears, listening for noises from the depths of the hole. Devon was restless too. In the early hours she was roused by clamor. His restless thrashings had knocked a supply pack over the side. The Captain swore at him, but kept his voice down.

I can't do this anymore, Lucy thought, filled with despair at the anger in his words. I can't get up in the morning and go down into that pit. Tears leaked from her eyes, and a shudder passed through her as the waves cried out again.

There's no choice, she realized. They won't listen to my refusals. It's not like escaping a school day by claiming stomach ache. Mary Silverhands had no choice, she simply endured and did the best she could.

In the morning, they started down: Lucy, Devon, the Captain, and two sailors, the two who had originally caught them, Ned and Pete. Ned was the bluff-faced, stocky older man, and Pete the younger. They were all roped together as they proceeded down the stairway: a sailor, then Devon, then Lucy, then the other sailor, then the Captain. The walls were unadorned and slick with salty moisture.

The nightmarish, narrow part seemed to continue for hours but eventually they came to a place where tunnels led off in every direction, allowing them to make camp and sleep. The Captain told Devon that he might explore. The boy took a torch and headed into the darkness. His pace was quick and eager, untired where the rest ached with weariness.

A rope trailed after the Captain and back up towards the top. It led to a small windlass that had been set up beside the hole with sailors to watch over it.

"We may be a while down here," he explained to Lucy. She sat a few feet away from the pit's edge, watching the darkness while the sailors built a fire and set water boiling for tea. "And it will be easier to have them lower supplies than have someone go fetching and carrying along the staircase."

"We might be down here for days?" Lucy asked, dismayed. The oppressive darkness dampened her spirits.

"In two more circles of the rim, we will have come as deep as I ever have. There is a closed doorway that I think will open to the Pot King's blood. But who knows what lies beyond it, or how long it will take to wrestle the magic free?" He laughed. "Perhaps when all is said and done, we'll come flying up out of the pit, hovering on great wings like falcons before we burst out across the Isles in glory and splendor."

Lucy continued to watch the darkness.

"So you are not the Pot King's son?" he asked.

She shook her head. "Just a girl," she said.

"Ah," he said. "Just a girl."

The silence stretched out between them.

"Do you know why going into the earth's heart is so perilous?" he asked.

"Why?"

"Down there, we are closer to the bones of sorcery. Emotions go awry and thoughts can damage you. So it is best to be calm down here, to avoid emotional extremes." His voice was strained. "Satisfying lust, for one."

"Oh," she said. And then, "Oh!"

He stooped to whisper, "But when we are back on the surface, just a girl, we will speak of this again." He turned and went to oversee the sailors as they prepared the meal.

I am not invisible to him, she thought. Back home she was used to her sisters drawing men's stares, used to their gaze passing over her absently. But Jusef Miryam's green eyes saw her, every inch of her. She smiled to herself.

Half a day later, they stood before the portal. The rope had been fastened beside their camp at the pit's edge and they had paused to eat and drink before entering the tunnels and coming to the small, boxy room, two doors set along its northern wall.

"See?" Captain Miryam said, looking pleased. "That door and that both were closed before. We'll try the right hand side first."

They wove through roseate stone tunnels, lighting their way with fish-oil lanterns that sent out a black, stink-laden smoke. By now, she thought, they were miles below the ocean's surface. Sometimes there were signs of earlier visitors—writing scratched or painted or in one case seared into the stone, nothing that Lucy could read.

The tunnel ended in a door made of a different material, a pearly slab that reflected the lanterns' sullen glow. The Captain gestured to Devon, who jittered in place, impatient. "After you, lad."

Drawn in their wake and trailed by the sailors, Lucy entered the room. It had a sea-shell's inner glow and was far wider within than it had seemed from without. An immense ribbed ceiling stretched overhead, and white crystal veins laced like ivy across the pink surface.

"Captain Miryam," Devon said. "If you allow me to step forward and seize the same power as my father, I will take you to safety. Otherwise I will watch as you, a novice untutored in these arts, are consumed by its energies and then step forward and take the same power as my father."

His voice was altered, taking on an older, bitterer cadence but still high and excited. Lucy stared at him.

"Who are you?" she said.

"It's his son still," Captain Miryam said. He sounded amused. "So the rumors are true—he keeps you barred from adolescence and has for decades, to prevent you from challenging him."

Devon's face worked angrily. "Yes!" he spat. "Decades I've been a boy, decades I've been in this form, puny child not fit for adult company. But now I can have the power, and mature my body after all."

Lucy paid them no attention. She stepped forward, seeking the glow's source. Here in this oddly shaped chamber, the acoustics were erratic. She heard whispers in her ears, half-perceived tugs at her attention.

The Captain turned to the sailors. "Hold him," he said.

The sailors stepped forward to vanish in showers of bloody sparks. Devon's thin lips crept up from his teeth to assume an eerie rictus.

You have to hurry, Mary's voice said to Lucy. She turned back—surely she was close, so close to the source of the light. She managed somehow to turn a corner while standing still, and the light was all around her, seeping into her bones.

I'm Mary Silverhands now, she thought, distracted by the power washing through her. Someone was shouting, Devon was shouting, shouting at her, and she put out a hand and recoiled in horror as her energy and his met and marred each other.

She watched as Devon fell away into pieces, as he was unmade by the collision of the light. Sorrowfully, she kept her own edges from raveling, rewove them. The energy roiled through her, wore her like a wave, but she closed her eyes and focused, drew her awareness down into a single point, and relaxed and opened them. She stood in the chamber, alone except for Jusef, who stood staring at her. Charred smudges on the wall marked the sailors' passing. There was no sign of Devon.

She led the way back to the camp. He followed her in silence. She walked feeling the energy leak from her, feeling it collide with the world. It was a constant struggle to keep from changing it, to keep from doing things like letting wildflowers spring up in her wake, or the air in her lungs be breathed out as lastflower perfume.

At the camp and the pit's edge, she paused.

He took her hand, level-eyed. She leaned to touch her lips to his and this time she did give into the urge. With her kiss, he breathed in sweetness: the air in a pear orchard just as the first sunshine touches the blossoms open. He rocked back on his heels with the magic's passionate force, his green eyes wild and entreating.

She unfolded great falcon wings and leaped into the pit, flying upwards towards the dot of light so far above. He fell to his knees and watched, watched as a new goddess ascended towards the skies of the Lesser Southern Isles.

Up the Chimney

"Up the Chimney" was written for a flash fiction contest held by EscapePod. It did not win by popular vote, but editor Stephen Eley did purchase it for a podcast and it later appeared online in the Postcards from *series.*

I've always been fascinated by the folk story in which a man recounts having seen an odd funeral the night before. At the end of it, whatever cat is nearby raises its head, says, "Then I'm the King of Cats!" and vanishes away. Here I allowed the cat to take someone with him, a scullery lad who is, by this point in the story, heartily tired of a cat's vision of Paradise.

I should have known better. There we were dozing by the fireside, old Tom and me, and there's a stranger telling some story of funerals and cats. Old Tom, he leaps up, whiskers abristle. Shouting "Then I'm the King of Cats" and disappearing up the chimney!

I've always been a skinny lad, and quickwitted to boot, so I leaps over the embers, which were dying then anyhow, and scramble after Tom. It's my chance to get to Fairyland, I figure, and old dad, he'd always said, grab opportunities as they presents themselves.

If I'd known then what I know now, I'd have kept sitting there and waved Tom on his journey. It's Fairyland, sure enough, but it's a cat's notion of Fairyland. Maybe there's one for all the creatures, horses and rats and huntin' dogs. But their notion here of entertainment is chasing mice, the whole kit and court does it for hours on a time, and then they drink cream and eat sardines. I'd give my soul for an honest pint of beer.

The women, aye, they're pretty enough, but they'll claw you to death sure as eagles fly, and they stink, more to the point. They reek of musk and blood, and in the evenings they all sit around grooming each other and purring, an unsettling sound that unmans me whenever I hear it.

King of Cats, be-damned. I'd search for some other Fairyland, but where might I end up? A fish's land, where it's never warm nor dry, or a beetle's, perhaps. At least I have my fireside here, with old Tom cleaning my ears while I wait for some new story to set me free.

The Silent Familiar

The Silent Familiar was originally written for a Halloween contest held by the Codex Writers' group. The prompt, provided by Jenny Rae Rappaport, involved someone in love with someone they shouldn't be and a haunted zucchini. The story of a mute familiar had been floating around in my head for a couple of years...

The Wizard Niccolo was not happy. At the age of 183—youthful for a wizard, but improbable for an ordinary human—he had thought certain things well out of his life. Sudden changes in his daily routine were one. And romance was another, even if it was his familiar's romance, and not his own.

"Could make an omelet with it, I suppose," he grumbled to that familiar, the tiny dragon Olivia. She sat on the cluttered mantle, wrapped around her egg, still marveling at its production and entirely too pleased with herself. A pair of alabaster candelabra sheltered her in a thicket of gilt spirals, and a stuffed salmon, labeled "First Prize—Thornstone Village Centennial Celebration," regarded her with a sour gaze.

"Master," she said, blinking luminous eyes. "Have I not served you well?"

"For the most part," he admitted.

She stayed silent. After a pause, he said, "Yes, invariably, Olivia. But who will hold your loyalty, that egg or I?"

"Both," she said and stoked her scaled cheek along the egg's smooth surface. "But I will never value it higher than my service to you."

Wizards' familiars are unnatural creatures. Some are much like any other animal: a cat, perhaps, with black fur, a droop-winged crow, or a snake with emerald scales. Others look less innocuous and more fantastical—homunculi and tiny, perfect dragons like Olivia, or shaggy-warted mandrake plants. Given this, it is surprising that two of them had managed to have compatible body parts, let alone produce an offspring. And yet, three months after a purely platonic sojourn of Niccolo with a sorceress whose library was vast enough to entice all sorts of other mages to her door, this had happened. Niccolo had been researching how the gods manifested themselves, and the library tomes had been unfamiliar enough to hold all his attention. Enrapt in ancient texts, he had overlooked Olivia's activities.

Niccolo scowled at her. "Do you intend to make a habit of this?" he demanded.

"Oh, I don't know," Olivia said absently. "I didn't like the last part, the laying. The getting ready to lay, though…"

Niccolo put up his hand. "I do *not* want to know." He turned away. "How long till it hatches?"

"I don't know," Olivia said. "I've never done this." She crooned deep in her throat, an unsettling noise Niccolo had never heard her make before.

Grumbling, he stalked out. It's probably not even viable, he thought. How long would Olivia fool herself into believing it would hatch? When he had created her, coaxing her winged form from a malachite shard, a bit of bone, and a lizard's scale, he had endowed her with a sardonic wit and a capability for banter—requisites for any wizard's familiar. But he had always prided himself that Olivia was smarter than most. Smarter than this deluded maternal ambition would seem to indicate.

Had he erred when making her? Familiars were repositories for wizards' emotions, one of the means by which they stripped away their humanity and became immortal. Perhaps he'd put too *much* in her, though. He considered thoughts of a new familiar, but reluctantly. At times, when Olivia rested on his shoulder or curled in his lap, he felt the struggle of his emotions, the desire to pet her like a cat warring with a shrinking away, a don't-touch-me shudder. He was still young for a wizard, still trying to learn what magic meant. Still trying to become more than human.

He sighed. After a few months, he'd try to get Olivia to see reason and abandon her effort.

Three months later, Olivia still spent most waking hours curled around her egg, drowsy contentment evident in the set of her wings. Niccolo had resigned himself to her absent-mindedness. He had been experiment with *aqua vitæ* and a supposed phoenix feather, coaxing bits of down away from the shaft. He hoped to evoke fiery gold, but so far all he had was soggy fluff.

He looked up from the alembic on his worktable as Olivia chirped.

"I've told you before, don't make noises while I'm..." he began, but she ignored him.

"It's hatching! It's hatching!" She unwrapped herself, backed away from the egg, eying it. "What do I do?"

"It's your egg!"

"I've never done this before!"

They both gazed in fascination as the egg wobbled.

"Should I get some hot water?" Niccolo said.

"What are you planning on doing, cooking it?"

"They always seem to fetch hot water for babies."

The egg rocked back and forth as its occupant shifted.

"Maybe it can't get out," Olivia worried. "Should I help it?"

"Give it time," Niccolo said.

They stared as though mesmerized. The egg tipped, tottered... toppled from the mantelpiece. Olivia shrieked even as Niccolo dove for it, his heart almost stopping.

The egg shattered in his hands and what he held there almost made him drop it. For an instant he thought it dead. Then the tiny lizard mewled and Olivia's wings were fluttering in his face even as he tried to set the infant down. Chaos reigned for a moment before Olivia was curled around her offspring while Niccolo crouched on his knees, ignoring the arthritic twinges.

The baby was, despite all of Niccolo's thoughts about mutants and monstrosities, perfect. Like Olivia, it was a miniature dragon's form, with frilled, lacey wings that stretched out now, trembling, to dry. Glistening amniotic fluid hung in thick strands from them.

Niccolo took a damp cloth and tenderly cleaned the wings as Olivia fussed and twined around his hands.

"You did well, Olivia," he admitted, looking down at her child. "You did well."

Almost all wizards have hobbies, and they refuse to taint these grand obsessions with magic. Niccolo's was fishing. He knew every trout stream in the forest surrounding his retreat, and his favorite was an unnamed brook that made its way through beech groves and sandy sloughs, past a stand of willows whose roots had gnawed away at the bank, creating holes and riddles where trout might lurk in the hot afternoons, waiting for evening. A fallen tree formed a bench where Niccolo could sit, his creel beside him lined with fresh moss and ready to hold his catch.

He threaded his rod and attached a caddis fly lure Olivia had helped him create. He wasn't sure that using her to assist didn't count as magic, but his fingers shook, and she was still as deft and nimble-clawed as when he had first created her almost a century ago. The lure's underbelly was yellow as daffodils and its wings were bits of brown feather. Deep in its guts was the hook, barbed to catch hold of a trout's tender mouth and let Niccolo coax it ashore.

Hours passed as he cast and drowsed, waiting with the patience only a fisherman knows. A few times he felt a tentative twitch on the line and paused but the trout were wary and skittish that day. With the coming of dusk, he knew, they would grow hungry and strike hard at the insects lighting on the water, his lure whirling among them.

His purpose was not to catch fish though, but to think. He contemplated Olivia. Every wizard needs a familiar, like a second voice speaking the things that she or he has left behind, the barbs and commonplace facts of life that a wizard tries to divest themselves of in the quest for immortality.

Familiars were like second souls, advice you could trust. You could make a familiar, as Niccolo had, and place bits of yourself in it, but it was hard. Few had accomplished it, and most wizards relied on familiars already fit to speak. Ravens were popular, and a line of talking cats in Loudontown had furnished familiars for the wizards' school there for decades.

Talking. That was what distinguished familiars from most animals, aside from various prophetic creatures. It worried Niccolo that the offspring, which Olivia had named Hrist, had yet to speak. Was it possible that—unlike its parents—it lacked intelligence? As the months passed, he had watched it, trying to determine what was passing through its mind. It seemed to respond to words, to "no" and "dinner" and such, but after all—a well-trained hound might do as much. Had Hrist lapsed to an animal's natural state, lacking the spark that his parents had possessed?

Olivia rejected this notion when Niccolo proposed it to her that night over a dinner of fresh-caught trout and bread from the nearby village.

"Hrist is as smart as you or I," she said indignantly. "Perhaps even more so, in your case." She looked over at Hrist.

By now, the winged lizard extended six inches from snout to tail, half his mother's size. He lay on the windowsill in the sun, regarding his reflection in the dust-flecked glass with a placid gaze.

"Indeed," Niccolo said dubiously.

Hrist swiveled his head, looked Niccolo in the eye, and nodded once.

Niccolo blinked, astonished.

"If he can understand us, why can't he reply, Olivia?" he said.

Olivia's tail swished. "He can't talk," she said.

"You and his father both have fully formed—perhaps even more so, in *your* case—vocal apparati. There's no reason why he shouldn't."

Of course, there was no reason why Hrist should exist in the first place, Niccolo thought, but Olivia would become even more furious if he said that.

And Hrist was, Niccolo admitted, a charming little creature. He loved to hunt and would spend hours in the vegetable garden, haunting the zucchini and pepper plants in order to eat squash vine borers and yellow striped cucumber beetles.

As the little dragon grew, Niccolo worked at teaching Hrist how to write instead. The dragonling learned to use his long tail much like a ink pen, dipping it with a sinuous twist in the inkwell and employing the pointed tip to scrawl on parchment. He shared his mother's quick and sometimes sardonic wit, but his observations were written out in a meticulous, careful hand.

He took to reading like a duck to water, and Niccolo would find him draped over a volume, carefully scanning the words and turning the pages with his flexible, almost prehensile tail.

"I don't know why I can't talk," he wrote when Niccolo questioned him. "I try to speak and nothing comes out but air."

He could make noises, the hisses and chirps and rumbles that Olivia regularly engaged in, which comforted Niccolo somewhat. But try as he might, he could not give his familiar's child a voice.

"What will he do?" Olivia worried. "No wizard will take him on as a familiar if he can't talk."

"You don't know that for sure," Niccolo argued, but in his heart he knew that Olivia was right. Wizards were proud. No one would want a defective familiar. Familiars were reflections of one's heart and soul.

Still, he would try.

Niccolo consulted one of the few non-human wizards he knew. Most of the magic users he was acquainted with shunned Slith, a wyvern's child whose scales, slit eyes, and sinuous, boneless grace unnerved them. His tower, perched halfway up a volcano, was rarely visited and as Niccolo ascended the mountainside, he wondered whether Slith blamed his race or his location for his isolation.

Slith listened, his golden eyes considering, as Niccolo described Hrist's condition, concluding, "How will any wizard take him as a familiar? He's defective!"

"Have you ever thought," Slith said, "that your problem may be your solution?"

Niccolo looked, puzzled, at the other wizard, and Slith's eyes took on a self-congratulatory gleam. Wizards love riddle games, and confounding another wizard was a rare prize in that competition.

"A familiar's powers develop in response to their wizard," Slith said. He nodded towards his own familiar, a lop-eared, brindled tomcat named Slasher.

Slasher yawned and said, "It's true. Before I became a familiar, I couldn't talk."

"Truly?" Niccolo said. He was not well-versed in familiar lore. Most wizards weren't, but rather took their familiar for granted, a tool like an athame or a well-crafted amulet.

"Truly," Slith said. "Find the right wizard and the problem will no longer be a problem."

"Get the house ready," Niccolo told Olivia. "We're going to take on an apprentice."

She gaped. "But, Master, you don't like apprentices! You've always said they were more trouble than they were worth!"

Hrist was outside, chasing bumblebees, so Niccolo spoke freely. "Yes, but what do apprentices grow up to become?"

"Wizards! You think that one of them will…"

"Perhaps," Niccolo said. "Don't get your hopes up too much, Olivia."

"How will you get them here?"

Niccolo tapped the thick envelope on his desk, which had arrived that morning. "I've offered to instruct them in hydromancy," he said. "I knew the College had no one specializing in it. It's obscure enough that the Dean couldn't justify the expense, but I've agreed to allow myself to be hired, for a small fee, to instruct them. Each will arrive, spend one month learning its basics, and then depart. Sooner or later the right one will arrive for Hrist."

Olivia's eyes held admiration. Niccolo allowed himself to run a fingertip along the smooth skin of her sides in an almost-caress. Surely, Niccolo thought, there was no harm in the trace of affection he felt. Wasn't that the basis of sympathetic magic, after all, a fondness of one thing for another?

The first apprentice was Albert. He had red hair that stuck out like a ransacked haystack and bright, merry blue eyes. Hrist hated him on sight, and Albert bore out the little familiar's judgement in full measure.

Niccolo, unfortunately, liked him. The apprentice reminded him of Olivia in the quickness of his quips, the slight barb to his wit. Much like Niccolo had been at his age, before he put away that side of him to focus on magic. Albert's pranks amused Niccolo more than he wanted to admit, despite Olivia's exasperation with household upsets, with salt in the sugar bowl and spiders in the tea.

Albert sensed Niccolo's mood, and his pranks expanded exponentially, knowing that punishment would not fall on him. Albert went so far as to involve the elderly wizard as a conspirator at times, much to Olivia's fury, since she or Hrist were the target.

And then one day as Niccolo and Albert were working out the Seven Aquatic Principles, Albert said, "I have a fine idea for a prank on the Dean of Loudontown."

"What's that?" Niccolo asked, intrigued. The Dean was a stiff and formal woman, and Niccolo found the thought of her discomfited in some way an appealing one.

"We'll ship Hrist to her and say that he's under a curse, that's why he doesn't talk. Either the Dean will try to lift it herself or she'll set it to someone as a test." Albert laughed. "Imagine how much time they'll spend on the runt, thinking they can fix him!"

"Hrist...is not broken," Niccolo said slowly.

Albert didn't catch the warning undertone in his teacher's voice. He continued, "Might as well use him for something, he's useless for much else besides catching spiders." He laughed again.

"Pack your things," Niccolo said. "You're going back to Loudontown. And if you want to be a wizard, Albert, you'll put away this sense of humor. When you have a familiar that you can store it in, you'll understand."

And so, bewildered, Albert departed to play his tricks elsewhere.

The second apprentice was Chloe. Niccolo had to admit, he was pulling for her as well. She was clear-eyed and grave, and wore her pale hair tightly knotted atop her head. She played chess well, and she and Hrist would sit for hours over the chessboard, the dragonling studying the pieces from a higher vantage point before fluttering down to move a pawn or bishop with his tail.

And yet once Chloe had finished her studies with Niccolo, she came to him and said, "I do not want Hrist as a familiar."

Niccolo found himself awash in denials. "I didn't...I mean, we weren't intending..."

Chloe's eyes were remote. "You want to find him a wizard. I picked up that much. After that it was simply a matter of thinking why a wizard who had never shown any previous interest in teaching would have suddenly acquired it. It's very kind of you."

He was not sure whether or not the words were a compliment.

But Chloe was young enough that they were the praise they seemed—though she might not think the same in another century or two. She smiled at him.

"Have you ever thought," she asked, "that Hrist might find some path other than familiar?"

"I had," Niccolo said. "More than once. But Olivia has her heart set on it—she doesn't want him to become 'some ordinary pet,' she said."

"A chess-playing dragonling whose penmanship is as good as any monk's?" Chloe said. "I do not think anyone will ever consider Hrist ordinary." She smiled again and Niccolo decided it was a good thing that she was moving on, perhaps. Chloe made him think of altogether too many human things, and that would be good for neither of them.

The third apprentice was Ibbi, who had a rounded face and the merest intimation of fuzz on his cheeks.

He was a disaster. He arrived with the bottle of brandy the Dean had sent to Niccolo shattered and dripping through his luggage, which retained the smell of expensive alcohol for weeks. He broke three plates, a mug, and Olivia's favorite candlestick washing up the first night. Things went downhill from there. He could not master the simplest cantrip that Niccolo set him, his pronunciation of Latin was atrocious, and his fingers seemed all disjointed thumbs.

Hrist adored him. And so, despite misgivings, Niccolo let him stay and be taught. And at the end of a month, when Ibbi had failed to learn even the simplest water-based charm, Niccolo lied to the Dean and said that Ibbi was doing so well that he intended to keep him an extra month, continuing through till Samhain.

Privately, he thought perhaps a clumsy wizard and a defective familiar might fit well together. Perhaps Hrist could give Ibbi the assurance he needed. And Ibbi… well, Hrist needed a voice.

But the days went by, and Ibbi showed no signs of improving, or of bonding with Hrist.

Samhain was celebrated in the nearby village, and when Niccolo went there a few days before, he saw the preparations underway: festoons of ivy disguising the doorways, plump jack-o-lanterns set to illuminate the square, wood piled for the holiday's bonfire. When he mentioned it at home, Olivia clamored to attend, while Ibbi's eyes sparked with enthusiasm. Even Hrist seemed intrigued, asking question after question on a parchment scroll as Ibbi tried to answer.

"Why is this celebrated?" Hrist wrote.

Ibbi stammered, "It's when the veil between worlds is torn. Barriers drop on Samhain."

"Barriers?" Hrist wrote the word in a single twist and flick of his tail.

"Barriers," Niccolo said. "They're thinner on Samhain. Things disguise themselves as each other, and alliances that might not be made on other nights are enabled."

"The God of the Darkest Night, Cerunnos, appears," Olivia said. "He will grant one boon. But no one ever asks."

"Why?" Ibbi said.

"Have you learned nothing? Because gods twist wishes," Niccolo said. "It takes a well-trained mind to construct a wish that a god can't weasel out of. They split hairs finer than any lawyer. So the god appears and blesses the participants, and then we are done."

Ibbi gave him an uncertain look. Increasingly he was nervous in the older wizard's presence, as though he sensed Niccolo's growing disappointment with his performance. Niccolo felt a surge of compassion and for once did not try to battle it back.

"We'll all go for the bonfire," he said. "You will need a costume, Ibbi. Samhain is a day for pretending to be something other than you are."

"Will you wear one as well, Master?" Olivia asked.

Niccolo snorted, but Olivia was not to be deterred.

"You'll make the villagers uneasy unless you do," she said. "I'll find something."

Early on Samhain eve, Olivia presented Niccolo with his costume. He snorted once again, but put on the dress and wig. She had chosen to clothe him as a tavern maid, and he thought irritably that if he could still feel the emotion of embarrassment, he would have objected. But Samhain was a day for fools and opposites, and he would play along, for her sake and that of Hrist and Ibbi. Olivia had clearly taken care with his costume. The dress was snug, but he could fit in it, along with a false bosom. He drew the line at the cosmetics she had somehow procured and laid out. He made an ugly woman, he thought, looking in the mirror, but that was mostly the beard.

Olivia had outdone herself, though, with Hrist and Ibbi. A green mask and scaly cloak enveloped Ibbi, while Hrist wore a tiny wizard's hat and clutched a matchstick wand.

"You've disguised them as each other!" Niccolo realized, and Olivia nodded, looking smug. She had chosen to drape herself with beads and jewelry till she was simply a glittering heap.

"What are you?" Niccolo asked.

Olivia peered out from between the links of a tarnished golden chain. "A dragon's treasure horde!" she announced. "Can't you tell?"

Despite himself, Niccolo laughed.

Cheerfulness continued to buoy him, despite his best efforts to dampen it, as they made their way to the village. Niccolo was not the only person to have chosen a costume that depended on gender. Several other men minced about in dresses even more gaudily decorated than his, and the owners of the local tavern, the Greasy Eel, wore gentlemen's dress coats and buckled breeches.

Usually the villagers were standoffish (except when making their way to his cottage to ask for luck charms or philters to ward off disease) and Niccolo was pleased to note that his costume dissolved some of the usual social ice. Olivia rode his shoulder, jingling and jangling like a paste and brilliants brooch, and Hrist stayed curled around Ibbi's neck, occasionally jabbing his ear with the point of his cap.

As the darkness grew and the bonfire blazed, as the mugs of cider were passed around with potatoes roasted in the embers, Niccolo fought to keep from enjoying himself. Instead, he watched Hrist, whose presence fascinated the village children. One held Hrist in his hands, holding him up to admire him in the firelight and the little lizard permitted it, his mother looking fondly on from Niccolo's shoulder.

"Master?" she whispered in his ear. "Master, you can construct wishes. You are a well-learned man. Could you not ask Cerunnos that my child be given a voice?"

"Don't be ridiculous, Olivia!" Niccolo snapped. "I thought you claimed you would not put the egg before me, and now you're asking that I meddle with a god on its behalf? Have you no concern for my well-being? I am a poor enough wizard as it is, letting emotions sway me as I have!"

"But…" She subsided into silence as he scowled at her.

"We will hear no more of this," he said.

In the fire's dancing light, her eyes glittered like the jewels of her costume, but he could not read the emotion there.

At midnight the crowd gathered around the fire, and masks were doffed. Niccolo took off his wig, sticking it under his arm. Ibbi stood beside him, having reclaimed Hrist from the reluctant children.

The faces across the fire were horns and feathers, slips of skin and eager eyes that stared, like Niccolo and his tiny group, into the heart of the fire, waiting for the God.

He grew so slowly from the flames that no one knew when he arrived. Great curling ram's horns, dripping with ash and fire, sat his head. His cloak was night, and its lining gleamed with subdued stars.

He did not speak, but looked about the circle, waiting. There was resignation in his shoulders. Niccolo wondered how long it had been since anyone ignored the thousand cautionary tales and asked the god for a boon.

And then, from his shoulder, impossibly, Olivia spoke.

"Cerunnos, hear my plea!"

"No," Niccolo said, and grabbed at her with panicked fingers, but all he caught was a netting of gilt and rhinestone, and she was hovering in the air before that patrician figure. "Olivia, no!"

The god gestured, and Niccolo could no longer speak. The massive face, still as a statue, listened.

"My child…and my master," Olivia said. "Let them be what they want, what they aspire to! Grant me this, Cerunnos!"

Fire coursed through Niccolo, chasing away the panic.

The god considered, spoke. "No matter the price?"

"No matter the price," Olivia said, and Niccolo knew she was doomed. He was being pulled into the fire, with Hrist, and somehow Ibbi, the three of them among the flames but not burning. He glimpsed Hrist, the doll-sized wizard's hat askew, clinging to Ibbi, and hope surged in him before he was pulled inside the shadow of Cerunnos' cloak, and darkness overtook him.

After the god had gone away, after the villagers had scattered, as the dawn began to glimmer over the forest like an uncertain plea, Niccolo raised his head and spoke to Ibbi and Hrist beside the smoldering ashes of the fire.

"Well?" he said. His voice was rough. In his hands was Olivia's body, broken by the magic that had surged through her in answer to her prayer.

Ibbi and Hrist stared at each other. Then Hrist spoke. "I can speak. But I am still not a familiar," the little lizard said.

"No." Ibbi stretched out his hand and suddenly laughed. "But I am no longer a wizard."

"What?" Niccolo said, trying to understand.

They turned to look at him in eerie unison. Olivia was heavy in his hands.

"I am a familiar," Ibbi said, and looked at Hrist.

"And I the wizard," Hrist said. "You will bear the sorrow for me, Ibbi."

So Ibbi wept obediently as Niccolo and Hrist buried Olivia's tiny form in the garden, between the rows where Hrist had hunted flies and pill bugs in the summer sun. They placed her finery beneath her, as though she were in truth what she resembled, a dragon curled on a horde of gems and coins and precious metal and a caddis fly lure. She lay with her snout laid atop her paws, eyes closed and tail curled about her as they took handfuls of dirt and closed her into the earth's darkness.

Ibbi wept.

But Hrist and Niccolo were true wizards now, and they felt nothing at all.

Events at Fort Plentitude

One of the things that draws me is the idea of the frontier, of humans trying to carve out an empire from a land that doesn't share their sense of superiority. "Events at Fort Plentitude" draws from the history of American frontier forts and superimposes a supernatural menace.

I particularly like the line about the frogs.

This story originally appeared in Weird Tales *in 2008.*

DECEMBER 27TH, DUKE THEO'S REIGN, 11TH YEAR, FORT PLENTITUDE

In the coldest nights of the winter, when the new moon rides the sky's breast like an arrow, the fox women come out of the pine woods. Their flashes of hair are scarlet cardinals against the blue snow shadows. They sing, an odd, whining song like puppies who have lost the teat.

Those are the nights that the sentries are changed every half hour, and they come back with cold-chapped lips and frost crystals along their jacket fronts. Every night in the dark of the moon, we can see three or four of the animal women out among the snow banks. Ensign Caruso keeps track of the sightings in the fort's log book. Starting December 17th, there were five, immediately followed by two nights of solo visitations.

We post female soldiers more often on those cold nights, or married men with wives here in the fort. During last year in the trade village that preceded this fort, two men threw off their clothes and ran out into the snow chasing fox women. They found them frozen solid among the reeds of the river bank, the slender blades of ice fixing them like swords. When they tried to disentangle them, the men shattered like crystal and were strewn across the ice. One-eyed Bill sent two of his wives down with whisk brooms to sweep the ice for fragments, but even so, the next summer, no one would eat frogs or turtles caught from that bank.

DECEMBER 31ST, DUKE THEO'S REIGN, 11TH YEAR, FORT PLENTITUDE

The food situation continues dismal. If the Captain were a wiser man, he would seek to keep his troops busier. Instead they sit around the fort and vie to see who can complain the longest and hardest about the meals. It is impossible to spice them up, but we each carry a little skin of salt and pepper mixed according to our taste. The cook, it is rumored, has been using yellow salt to cook with, chipped from a deer lick near the fort, and saving the finer salt to sell to the soldiers.

Jan 2ND, Duke Theo's reign, 12th Year, Fort Plentitude

Captain Mercer and the cook have been arguing again. It is clear that the man has been skimming off profits and that the paucity of our meals is due to his graft. Nonetheless, he makes meals for Captain Mercer and our officer's mess that are better than the average run, and so his corruption is tolerated. But as his supply of seasonings has dwindled, the Captain's temper has grown harsher.

I went so far yesterday as to break one of my three demon gems and send the beast to the Southern Isles for an armload of fruit. If the Sorcerer Corps knew, they would court-martial me for wasting such a valuable thing, but I couldn't help it. The hunger ate at me.

I told the demon to bring as much as it could carry, but it purposely made its arms as small as possible and brought me only three apples and a shriveled fig. I had meant to share my bounty with the soldiers. But when I saw the portion's scantiness I took it all for my own and ate it in one sitting, greedily, licking my fingers, devouring even the stems and seeds, and refusing to think about what I had done.

The demon stood staring at me all the time that I ate. It was a leathery-winged *Demonica falciformus*, with silky-tendriled hair and small black eyes that seemed intelligent.

Plinot argues that demons possess the equivalent intelligence of great Barbary apes or chimera, but this one seemed possessed of a peculiar, innocent malignity. It would have torn the flesh from my bones and rejoiced in it with the happy savagery of a form Mankind has not known since we first learned to worry.

I am morose and weepy these days. At night I turn in my bed and send sparks among my bedclothes to seek out the fleas and lice nesting there. The linens smell of smoke but this is better by far than bedbugs. All the while tears stream down my face and trail among my whiskers, dampening them. My moustache curls with sorrow and I am oppressed by the sins of the world.

January 28TH, Duke Theo's reign, 12th Year, Fort Plentitude

The days and nights are tedious. I tried to organize a party to go dig along the banks for cattail roots, which according to a manuscript I read last week are edible, indeed a delicacy among some tribes. But the water had frozen so solid that there was no cracking it. We tried building fires atop the ice, but they sank, icy mud extinguishing them. We returned with nothing for our efforts—not even a brace of squirrels, because the soldiers were too loud and frightened every animal away.

The Captain has eighty troopers altogether: two Lieutenants, four sergeants, a cook, and myself, the only sorcerer in the group. All of us are miserable. Many of the men have come here in search of land grants for diligent labor, only to find a Captain ready to swindle them out of their holdings in exchange for counterfeit artifacts or stakes in dubious gold mines. Others like myself are one form of exile or another, trying to escape memories or pursuers. We are not in search of anything. We know there is only cold and misery here for us in civilization's hinterlands.

FEBRUARY 2ND, DUKE THEO'S REIGN, 12TH YEAR, FORT PLENTITUDE

I lay awake last night belaboring myself with guilt for not saving the fruit for the nursing women here. I was greedy and foolish. Still, I cannot help but think that divided among the six of them, it would have been only enough of a taste to torment. My ministry to their health is surely worth this small price, to keep me lively and able to tend to their needs while they are caring for their babies.

I have talked the Captain into having Ensign Caruso cut up the old boiler and stove that we had sitting out near the dock. He uses the forge and cuts the metal into inch wide squares that the natives prize for making spearheads or hide scrapers. They trade us five gallons of dried corn for each square. The cook soaks it and makes it into porridge that the women eat. We must keep the babies healthy and strong.

In the spring a boat will pass by and take the latest crop of babies back to the more settled lands, where people are cutting down trees and plowing fields and doing things that require healthy young workers, a new generation of settlers that can produce more in turn to man the forts and breed more babies. All part of the Duke's plan for expansion.

By the time the boat reaches Tabat, there will be half a dozen wet nurses aboard it, and the infants they supply, plus a small goat herd, sails full of just washed linens, and a few guards.

It has been a long and tedious winter. Their ranks will grow before spring comes, I am sure, since two additional women are pregnant. I see them fed better than most as well. The fort is too small to rate a doctor, so my small dabbling in medicine suffices for the ailments here: dysentery, syphilis, boils, chilblains and pregnancies.

I have been thinking about the spring, and the fish markets of Tabat, and what my mother would cook: baked black bass, spiced eels, fried smelts, boiled mackerel, fried skate wing, codfish balls, baked trout, flounder cooked with bitter greens.

FEBRUARY 28TH, DUKE THEO'S REIGN, 12TH YEAR, FORT PLENTITUDE

Today Ensign Caruso brought me up to the gun tower. The wind whistled and screamed in my ears. We looked out across the river's white sweep, nearly a mile wide, and saw a dark mass moving across it, hesitantly at first, then with mounting confidence and speed. It came closer and we realized it was a herd of buffalo.

The ice was frozen thick enough all the way across that the animals, hundreds of them, could make their way to our eastern shore in fruitless search of fodder. The Captain dispatched several men to shoot stragglers in order to relieve the tedium of our meals. They killed several dozen and dragged them into the main yard of the fort.

I took my spyglass and watched from atop the outer wall. One-eyed Bill Lafitte and his wives moved back and forth on the scarlet ice, engaged in the same task of butchery. I imagined the ice under them, thick as layers of rock, shadows swimming underneath, deep down in the dark water.

Two wives stripped the hides off the carcasses and piled them on a rickety sled that the four other wives pulled. One of them had an infant tied to her back. I imagined the last wife was at home, tending the brood of children.

The human women were flat-faced and expressionless as they moved back and forth, taking the best of the meat to pile on the sled. The two Snake women were equally expressionless, but their tongues flickered in their reptilian faces, bright as flames against the winter white of their scales.

The cook roasted buffalo steaks and the fort smelled wonderful for an evening. Everyone went around smiling. But at table the meat proved stringy and tough. This far into winter, the animals are themselves half-dead of hunger and have little flesh to spare.

MARCH 1, DUKE THEO'S REIGN, 12TH YEAR, FORT PLENTITUDE

Big White, the Shoshal shaman, came to see me. It was his third visit to my cabin, but the careful attention he gave every detail was the same as the first two times. I drew the structure of the universe and its concentric circles of realms, like a vast onion, on the wall and we debated its shape, for he insists that it is different, and that spikes from other realms protrude upon our own.

At least that is what I believe he tried to sketch out for me. His English is bad, and my Shoshal non-existent. Rumor back at the College of Mages in Tabat held that the native mages, as well as the Snake people, are sophisticated in their understanding of magic, but this seemed like rank gibberish to me.

He made tea for both of us, a pleasant brew of flower petals and leaf fragments that made the inside of my cabin smell like summer. Tension dropped away as though I had shrugged it off with my buffalo-hide robe and hung it on the peg just inside the door.

Cold winter, he said and touched the demon gems on my desk, shaking his head sorrowfully. They do not believe in trafficking with spirits, and if he knew I had traveled here in one's arms, he might not speak with me again.

Demon travel is unpleasant at best. The beast has one duty and one duty only to discharge, to convey their burden from one point to another. They will not pause to rest, no matter how long the flight, and they are not at any pains to make their passenger comfortable. I came in the summer, when the weather was warm, but at one point we flew through a great lightning storm, and the demon would not change its course no matter how I shouted at it.

I asked Big White about the fox women, but he pretended not to know what I meant. I will have one of Lafitte's wives teach me more Shoshal, so I have words for the magical concepts I want to convey. If there is an easy way to drive them off, I would like to know.

MARCH 2, DUKE THEO'S REIGN, 12TH YEAR, FORT PLENTITUDE

Slept exceedingly well last night.

MARCH 5, DUKE THEO'S REIGN, 12TH YEAR, FORT PLENTITUDE

My sister Sarah's birthday. I sent her a pile of pelts last fall, martin and beaver, to make herself a coat, and warned her that, come winter, communications would be at a standstill due to the frozen river. I imagine her sitting in her comfortable, well-appointed house, eating sandwiches spread with a layer of butter and cress, the thin leaves from the greenhouse sharp and bitter against the bland bread.

She did not want me to leave Tabat, but after the failed experiment that killed Melissa and our unborn, I could not stay. Could not endure the eyes of the other mages knowing what I had done, how badly I had predicted events. Even this privation is better than that shame and sorrow.

I caught a handful of snow sprites in the afternoon, near the outer wall of the fort. They look like crane flies—insects as big around as a Spanish doubloon, but all wing and legs, and little else. They have tiny faces made of ice, but they do not speak. Why has God made these creatures that resemble us in all but intelligence?

Deep in the woods, Lafitte claims to have seen winter sprites as big as wolves or buffalo, enormous flying things that move along the edges of snowstorms, riding the winds in a flurry of icy chitin. I put the ones I caught in a glass jar. They fluttered for twenty-two minutes before succumbing to the heat of the room and dying, melting away into a noisome, clotted liquid that smelled of vinegar.

MARCH 6, DUKE THEO'S REIGN, 12TH YEAR, FORT PLENTITUDE

When Big White came today, he shook his head and said over and over, bad, very bad. He led me outside the fortress walls and showed me ice runes on the outer walls, twelve feet high, two-thirds the height of the walls.

I asked him who had put them there, for I did not recognize the language or the writing, but it was clearly set there by sorcery. I had sensed none the night before, but I am so exhausted and hungry in the evenings that I do little but imagine meals at my mother's house back in Tabat.

He said winter and then a word I did not know, and indicated this entity had put them there. He threw handfuls of snow at the markings until they were partly obscured, but his face was troubled.

Inside the fort, I showed him a sketch Caruso had made of one of the fox women the night before. Did this woman draw the marks, I asked.

He shook his head and said dead, very bad, tapping the paper. That was all I could get out of him.

I asked him about trade for food, although I hated to throw myself on his mercy like that. But the pieces of iron were all gone and we have very few other goods. I indicated my belongings, trying to keep the whine out of my tone—surely there must be some equipment there he would like, I said. It would be easy enough to replace next year when spring came and the river thawed. Perhaps I'd even make the trip myself, and go to see Sarah in her fine new coat.

He took three small prisms, the most valuable objects there, and that evening dropped off two bushels of smoked trout. He must have said something to Lafitte as well, for one of the wives brought a sack of flour and another of dried meat. I distributed it among the pregnant women, despite the grumbling of the others, but saved a handful of each for myself.

MARCH 7, DUKE THEO'S REIGN, 12TH YEAR, FORT PLENTITUDE

Last night I stayed awake, resolved to see the fox women. I sat in the tower with the sentry, watching the wood's edge. When I saw a blur of silver and blue fog, I looked with my spyglass.

She had Melissa's face and she looked straight at me.

It was only the bowl in her hand, steaming beef stew with dumplings, I knew, that kept me from running to her. The smiling lure was too broadly painted and I realized it must be reading my thoughts somehow. No wonder men have run out to them.

In the morning, I told the Captain what I had discovered, that the fox women were trying to lure us out, but he would not listen. He had maps spread out across his desk. Come spring, he would take a patrol gold-panning, he said cheerfully to me. Wouldn't that be an adventure? His fingers trembled as he traced a line across the mountain, translucent blue as frost.

The cold has driven him mad. I broke my second demon gem and sent a letter to Tabat, to the Army Corps Headquarters. I explained our circumstances and the dangers. I explained that the Captain was unresponsive. I said 'Send food and more demon gems, and word of hope, or we will perish.' The demon took the scroll away. This one was feathered like a peacock, and had an odd snout that lolled loosely when it sniffed at me. I wait for the reply.

MARCH 8, DUKE THEO'S REIGN, 12TH YEAR, FORT PLENTITUDE

I have been advised that the winter has affected all frontier forts adversely and that food has been dispatched overland. Due to the frozen river, it will not reach here for at least six weeks. They sent no gems or other devices of aid. I have been officially demoted for using the gem, and reminded of their cost and scarcity.

In six weeks we will be licking the bones of the three horses left to us.

I sent to Big White to ask for more food, but he did not come. At length I donned snowshoes and walked over to the Shoshal camp.

Winter has not hit them as hard as it has us. There are fewer of them, and they spent the summer gathering food while we were building the fort walls. He gave me handfuls of smoked meat and a kind of thick biscuit baked with dried berries. I ate greedily until my stomach hurt and washed it down with gulps of hot bark-scented tea.

He said danger to the fort, babies, babies.

There is danger to the children, I asked.

He shook his head and drew a figure in the snow, a woman amid pine trees. You say fox women, he said, because hair red like fox. But not fox, not women. Babies that die go into the winter and make more. They want.

I was not sure what he was saying. That babies died and became fox women?

He tapped the figure with a gnarled finger. Baby want, he said. Just want want want. No more.

Was there no way to ward them off?

He shook his head. No.

MARCH 9, DUKE THEO'S REIGN, 12TH YEAR, FORT PLENTITUDE
Yielding to my entreaties, the Captain sent several soldiers out hunting again, but they came back with only a bony elk, barely a mouthful or two of meat apiece. The cook stewed the heart for the officer's mess, but there was nothing but meat and water. The vegetables had gone long ago.

I found tracks all along the walls. Light tracks. Barefoot tracks, each foot tiny and arched, like that of a child. Snow sprites clustered motionless along the runes like a fuzz of white velvet.

I brought the Captain out to look at them, but he only smiled and patted my arm. This is a land of plenty, he said. In the summer, the bees will sing in the sour gum trees and drip honey into our mouths.

Another seven soldiers have died of dysentery so far this week, bringing our numbers to forty-two. We cannot make it till spring.

I lie awake trying to figure out a plan. Should I use my last demon gem and summon a final messenger to plead our case? Did they not understand that we will die without immediate surcease?

There are eight babies here now, aged between two and six months. They are thin and sickly, and they cry from the cold. I imagine the fox women taking them away, making them into new monsters. I imagine them walking across the snow slopes, clothed in glittering snow sprites, legs lengthening with each stride, faces elongating, hair falling into blazes of crimson longing.

Why do they only prey on the men? Are we weaker in our hearts?

MARCH 10TH, DUKE THEO'S REIGN, 12TH YEAR, FORT PLENTITUDE
For dinner we had watery gruel, a scant cupful per person, measured most strictly. More hunting parties dispatched.

MARCH 12TH, DUKE THEO'S REIGN, 12TH YEAR, FORT PLENTITUDE
Lafitte and his wives are dead. They found them frozen in their building. The children were all taken. We brought the last of their food to the fort, but it is sufficient for only a few more days.

Hunting parties still unsuccessful. We ate the last horse today.

MARCH 13TH, DUKE THEO'S REIGN, 12TH YEAR, FORT PLENTITUDE
There are definitely more of them now.

MARCH 18TH, DUKE THEO'S REIGN, 12TH YEAR, FORT PLENTITUDE
Finally I take up the last demon gem. I walk across the fort, pass by the dead and dying. The cook is dead now, died of bloody flux, and the Captain has holed himself up in his office, crouched over his maps.

Faithful Caruso helps me. We sew an immense bag of buffalo hide, lined with the softest, warmest furs we can find among Lafitte's bales. We make it open at the top. We put the babies in it, one by one. The mothers that are still alive help us. I shatter my last gem and give the directions to the demon.

We can only hope a few will survive. The ones towards the outside of the bag will succumb to the cold first. They say freezing is not an unpleasant death. And when the demon arrives, perhaps it will only be delivering a package of frozen or drowned corpses. Demons are unreliable, to say the least.

But perhaps one or two will survive.

We watch the bag float up towards the sky. The demon is a kind I've never seen before, with rounded ivory horns and glittering silvery skin, immense wings that claw upward at the chilly air. It is quite splendid in its own way.

When night comes, I can hear the runes working on the outside of the walls, cracking them with icy pressures. Caruso and I wait in the watch tower, near the swivel mounted cannon, snow sprites swirling around its barrel.

I can hear them coming, whimpering with want as they walk forward through the snow. Perhaps one will look like Melissa again.

Dew Drop Coffee Lounge

"Dew Drop Coffee Lounge" was sparked by an incident where someone approached me in a donut shop, thinking I was her blind date. She was so pleased that I had a hard time saying I wasn't the woman she was looking for. The title came from a restaurant in my home town, the Dew Drop Restaurant, a name that has always amused me.

This story originally appeared in Clockwork Phoenix, *edited by Mike Allen, in 2008.*

The minute the woman walked in, Sasha sensed it. Her head went up, that characteristic Sasha motion, like a blind bear sniffing the breeze. The well-dressed suburbanite glanced over the surroundings as she entered the coffee shop. Her hair glimmered with red dye and was cut in a Veronica Lake bang that obscured one eye. I couldn't see more from where I sat.

Sliding her notebook back into her bag, Sasha leaned forward, her gaze intent on the arrival, who looked back, first sidelong, then openly. As though pulled by that stare, she moved through a clutter of tables towards Sasha.

Her interrogatory murmur was inaudible except for its tone. Sasha nodded, gesturing to the seat across from her.

First there was coffee to be ordered, and the obligatory would-you-like-something, no-nothing-thank-you while Sasha cleared an old mug and several napkins away from the shared surface.

Then just as the redhead was pulling her chair back, Sasha's voice sounded, pitched loud and clear. "I only agreed to meet with you to say I can't do this anymore. My husband is in Iraq, stationed in Basra."

The other woman stopped, looking as though she had been socked in the gut, halfway between heart torn out and tight-lipped anger. Sasha studied the table, tracing a finger across the constellations of blue stars. She looked as though she were worrying over a grocery list rather than declaring an end to a romance.

In the other woman's blank face, her eyes were a shuttered, washed-out blue. The Universe watched as the painful moment played itself out, watched with a grim and inexorable regard that I was glad was fixed on Sasha and the stranger rather than on me.

When the redhead had vanished onto the street without a backwards glance and the door had jangled shut behind her, Sasha claimed the untouched latte and croissant.

"Pig," I said from my seat.

"Don't you have some gathering of finger-snapping beatniks to get to?"

"I'm writing a poem about you right now. I'm calling it 'Sweet Goddess of the Dew Drop Coffee Lounge'."

The name of the shop was originally the Dew Drop Inn, back when it was a bar. As it had passed through the successive hands of owners who had not understood the original name's charm, it had become The Dew Drop Restaurant, The Dew Drop Donut Shop, The Dew Drop Take and Bake Pizza and most recently, the Dew Drop Coffee Lounge.

In this incarnation, the owner, Mike, had decorated the walls in neo-mystic. Posters showed translucent, anatomically-correct figures with chakra points set like jewels along their forms, backed by Tibetan mandalas. Sunlight slanted in through the crystals dangling from monofilament line in front of the French doors, and sent wavering rainbows across the glass cases by the counter, trembling on the scones and dry-edged doughnuts. Painted stars and moons covered the Frisbee-sized tables.

At first I hadn't liked the hearts of space music Mike insisted on, but after hours, days, weeks, now months of it, the aural paint of synthesizers and whale song had crept into my thoughts until mall Muzak now seemed strange and outré to me.

Sasha went back to her reading. I got up and started opening the doors to take advantage of the spring weather. The breeze ruffled the foam heart atop Sasha's latte and tugged at her newspaper. A skinny man in a red baseball cap came in, looking around, and she caught his eye, gestured him over, preparing her next brush-off.

"Everything's alchemical," Mike had told me the week before. We were cleaning out the coffee machines with boiling vinegar and hot water. Wraiths of steam rose up around his form, listening as he spoke.

Whenever we were working together at night, he would deliver soliloquies that explained the secret inner workings of the world. While much of it was dubious and involved the magnetic poles, UFOs, and a mysterious underground post office, it was a world that I found more appealing than my own. More interesting, at any rate.

It was a decent job, all in all, and it paid fair money in an economy that was so tanked that my already useless English degree was worth even less. So I tidied up the coffee shop, carryied ten gallon bottles of water in, swept, and refoldednewspapers after customers had scattered them like ink-smeared autumn leaves. It did mean the occasional late night labor, but Mike was a good sort and helped with the scutwork.

"Yes," I said noncommittally. I had learned that the best thing to do with Mike was not to stand in the way of the current rant.

"The thing is this. You know Tarot cards?"

"Like fortune tellers use?"

"Yeah, sorta kinda. See, Tarot cards have pentacles and swords and cups and rods, and that's diamonds and spades and hearts and clubs. With me so far, yeah?"

"Yeah."

"There's twenty-two cards beyond that. The Major Arcana, they call them."

"Aren't there Minor Arcana too?"

"Yeah, those are the pentacles and stuff. Anyhow, each Major Arcana shows a step in our life journeys."

"Which is how you use them for fortunetelling," I said.

"No, well, kinda sorta. But they're steps that everyone goes through, the stages of life."

"All right," I said. I tipped the jug into a tank and drained it, frothing with heat. I sniffed the steam. Was that a last trace of vinegar?

"You should write about it," Mike said. "A lot of great literature is based on alchemy."

"Yeah, that's certainly a thought," I said. "Is that one done?"

He sniffed at the tap. "Another pass, maybe. Then let's mop the floor, as long as we have the hot water. Call it a night after that."

"The thing is this," he said after a long and reflective silence in which I'd forgotten what we were discussing. "There's these Avatars that walk around. They're foci for the Universe's attention, moments that get repeated over and over again, like in the Tarot cards. Sasha's one, for example."

"Sasha?"

"That skinny blonde who comes in around ten, reads and drinks coffee for a couple of hours, turns up in the late afternoons sometimes."

"She's a what?"

"An Avatar. It's the shop. It's a Locus."

"I thought you said it was a *foci*."

"No, people are the foci. The Avatars. The shop now, it's a *Locus*, a place where foci converge. Like Stonehenge, where all the ley lines meet."

"The Dew Drop is like Stonehenge?"

He laughed. "Yeah, crazy, isn't it? I don't understand why, either." He pulled a bottle of whiskey out from behind a blocky pyramid of stacked coffee bags. "But we'll drink to it all the same."

The next day, I watched Sasha.

It was a little before ten, a slack hour with only a couple of customers. I appreciated the lull, since I was hung-over and queasy from last night's drinking.

A kid came in, maybe fourteen or fifteen. He had long brown hair tied back with a red bandana, bell bottoms, the kind of teenage body that looks like one long stick. He slouched in the doorway until she gestured him over and said something.

His jaw dropped.

I'd always thought that was a figure of speech until I saw him go literally slack-jawed with surprise at her words. And I would have said something, done something, but I felt it. The weight of the Universe's attention, just for a moment, not on me, but so close that you'd think space and time had collapsed at the point where Sasha sat, looking up at the kid.

He turned and pushed past me to the door. The back of his jacket had a picture of a chimpanzee with the legend "Got Monkey?" under it.

I gave her a little *wtf?* look and she shrugged at me and went back to the paperback she was reading, *The Biggest Secret*. But fifteen minutes later, another person came in, an elderly woman carrying a yellow flower in her hand.

She was taken aback by Sasha's wave, and made her way over to the table like someone advancing to feed a stray dog that they don't trust. Sasha stood and held the chair out for her, but the woman shook her head, laying her daffodil down.

"He's not coming," Sasha said. "He's happily married, and he asked me to break it to you. He gave me a little money to buy you a coffee, a pastry perhaps." She fumbled with her wallet.

"No," the woman said. She wore a lavender pants suit and was carefully made up, her colorless hair freshly combed and set. "No, that will be all right."

With chilly dignity, she left.

"That was awful!" I let Mike take the register and sat down across from Sasha, indignation pulling at my vocal cords. "What the hell was that all about?"

"It's my role in life, sunshine," she said.

"You pretended to be someone else! You're interfering in those people's lives!"

"It's not as evil as all that, Clay." She pointed at the front entrance. "It's something about this place. Maybe it's the dumping ground of the Universe but I noticed it when I first started coming here to get coffee and read. People come here to meet blind dates that never show up all the time. I've never seen anyone actually meet here, but I've seen plenty lingering in the doorway, looking around, trying to catch your eye to see if you, you're the one."

She leaned forward. "So I started leaping into the breach. I give them a reason to run, to have a story they can tell at dinner parties for the next few years, the Blind Date from Hell, who seemed so nice in e-mail, then turned out to be…" She twisted her hand. "…a little cuckoo."

"You're not just a little cuckoo, you're insane," I said. "There ought to be a law about people pulling crap like that. How many dates have you thwarted?"

"You're not listening. I don't thwart them. They only show up here if the other person isn't arriving."

"Bullshit."

"Watch." She pointed at a small ginger-haired man as he stepped in. "I can spot them a mile off. I can hear it in the cadence of their steps coming along the sidewalk and read it in their faces when they open the door. But I won't catch this one, and you'll see what I mean. He'll linger and wait."

I rose and took his order, a double espresso. He wore horn-rimmed glasses and a robin's egg blue cashmere sweater. He looked around as I prepared the coffee, glance falling on Sasha. She didn't look up, just kept on reading.

He took the drink with a thanks and sat down by the door, checking his watch. Each time someone came in, he looked them over. After forty minutes and a dozen people, he drained the coffee and exited, shoulders a tight line of anger.

I went back over to Sasha, not sure what to think.

"See?" she said.

"How can you field all of them?"

She gestured at herself. "Online I could be anyone."

"So you stand in for the men too?"

"Sure." She licked crumbs from her fingertips.

"How do you make them think you're the same person they've been talking to?"

"They come pre-fooled," she said. "Ready to drop into the seat and talk to the one heart in all of the universe that knows them."

"You disillusion them."

"I teach them what the world is all about. What doesn't kill you makes you stronger, and what you can laugh at, you can live with."

"Is this tied in with that crap Mike was spouting last night? You're an Avatar?"

"A whatty-tar?"

"An Avatar. Mike said something about Avatars and Tarot cards and focuses."

"Mike says all sorts of things and only ten percent of them actually makes sense. You should know better than pay attention."

"Like any of this makes sense? Sasha, it's just weird and awful that you do this."

"Fuck you, emo-boy," she said.

I guess I wouldn't have minded so much if I hadn't been having shitty luck with blind dates myself. I'd set up match.com and yahoo.com and OKCupid and FriendFinder and all the rest.

I got replies from women who wanted me to send them money so they could come visit, one hard-core rock chick in Alaska who said flat-out that she didn't do in person but was fine with "long distance commitments," and a Chicago woman who said she'd seen me at a poetry slam when visiting Seattle. She wouldn't post a picture of herself, leaving me to believe that she was actually a fourteen year old boy.

But at least I was getting a trace of hope every night. I'd log on to the computer and check my messages, send a couple of Woo!'s or raves or whatever the flavor of the flirt was. And here was Sasha, skinny unappealing Sasha, dirtying the taste of it. Making it meaningless.

"You're a sadist," I said. "A goddamn sadist."

"Do you think I really like it?" she said.

"Yeah, I think you do. You get off on it, the power of crushing people's dreams," I spat out.

"So I can sit here and watch them die, or I can give them a little closure."

"Seriously, it's screwed up," I said. I stood and went in back to rinse filters.

Mike caught me there later.

"Hey, did you and Sasha have some kind of fight?" he said worriedly.

"I told her she's a twisted fruitcake," I said. "I know you're a friend of hers, but the blind date crap...Jesus, it's wrong!"

He held up a hand, forestalling me. "Yeah, well. It's a long story." He looked unhappy in his long-nosed, spaniel-eyed way. "Look, you know how she started coming here?"

I guessed. "Did she work here at some point?"

"No. See, I'd answered this ad in *The Stranger* personals, couple years ago, you see?"

"I don't know what you're trying to say."

"I stood her up," he said. "I told her to meet me here at 10:30 on a Thursday morning, and I was so ready, but then there she was and I chickened out and just served her coffee and watched her wait. She waited half an hour, ate a warmed butter croissant and drank a hot chocolate and left. The next day she showed up at the same time and brought a book with her, something by Camus. Ever since then, she shows up three, four times a week, sometimes more."

"Why didn't you ever say anything?"

"She's an Avatar," he said, his voice dropping in awed intensity. "You felt it too, didn't you? Larger than life. It's what's so frightening, so appealing about her." He stopped, looking at me as though the thought had just occurred to him. "You're attracted to her, too, aren't you? Is that why you're so pissed at her?"

"I'm pissed at her because she's acting out some sort of outrageous psycho-drama that you're enabling and messing with people's lives in the process," I said. "Does she know you're the one she was supposed to meet?"

"Don't you get it?" he said. "It's a genuine supernatural occurrence that happened. I brought her here and she became an Avatar. I don't know how."

My head throbbed. "I need to go home," I said. "I'm going to throw up."

"Go, go." He flapped a hand at me. "But come back when you feel better and don't fight with Sasha anymore."

I didn't show up for work for four days. I went out with old college friends every night to a hip bar in a former barbershop. Vintage hair dryers had been lined up like studded alien helmets along the wall and baggies stuffed with peroxide curls were thumb-tacked to the ceiling. Band after band sang each night's anagrammatic lyrics in smoke-hoarsened voices. When I came back, I was still tipsy. Mike didn't say anything, just eyed me and served up a jumbo mug of the coffee of the day, a Tanzanian roast, before I swept the floors and used clothespins to clip the day's newspapers to the rope racks on the north wall.

Sasha came in a little before noon, pausing when she saw me. She laid her book —some Charles Williams title—down on the table in front of her while sorting through her pockets for bills.

"Clay," she said, carefully unfolding the crumpled ones. "Clay, man, I wanted to say, with the blind dates, I don't mean they can't work. I'm sure they can, I'm sure they do."

The words tumbled through her lips like pebbles, like diamonds, like some fairy tale princess speaking truths.

"The ones that end up here, those are the only doomed ones, you know what I mean? I'm not dissing the love thing. You're a nice guy, and I don't mean to be saying anything about that at all."

The sun gleamed through the window and fell on her straw-like hair, as yellow as the daffodil. I said something reassuring and offered to buy her next coffee, and realized somewhere in the middle of that transaction that one thing Mike had said was true. I was attracted to her, an attraction as mysterious and unexpected as though I'd found an impossible door, opened a closet to find Narnia waiting instead of coats.

What could I do? I lapsed into silence. From then on, Mike and I exchanged glances whenever she came in, both of us acknowledging that lodestone pull, so elemental and so deep within our bodies that we couldn't imagine wanting anyone else.

And I wondered about the Avatars. Was Sasha right, did she fill some cosmic gap? Were there others? Did I know them, had I seen them walking down the street or taking a double hot chocolate, no whip, from my hand?

When he appeared, when the magnet that governed our movements jolted in galvanic response to his presence, Mike and I both knew it instantly. It was something in the way Sasha's breath caught, something in the way her shoulders shifted, the way she set down her cup and lifted her head.

He was clean-jawed as some young Galahad, and there was an aquiline elegance to the planes of his nose, to the curls that clustered on his scalp in Greco-Roman order.

His stare went to Sasha and for once she didn't smile or beckon. She just sat there staring wordlessly at him, her eyes as wide as windows. He came over to her table in three graceful strides and stooped to say something.

"Yes," she said, giving him her hand. "That's me." He drew her hand to his lips and kissed the palm, a gesture as startlingly intimate as though he'd taken off his shirt.

Was he an Avatar as well? Was his job to console selfless women? To pick up people in coffee shops? To piss off unrequited lovers? What role did *he* fill?

Mike and I stood side by side, watching, ignoring the customer trying to get a refill on her mocha. We stared while Sasha gathered up her things and the young man helped her into her jacket, tucking his arm around her hand.

For a moment she looked back, and it would have been the time to say something then, but Mike's heel ground into my foot. I yelped and she half-laughed, and waved at Mike, and left.

"Give the poor girl a little happiness," Mike said. "Breathing room."

"Will she be back tomorrow?"

He shrugged, finally looking to the counter and the empty mocha cup sitting there. "Maybe. I don't know. Maybe she won't be an Avatar any more."

The customer gathered her drink after he refilled it and looked around, meeting my eyes. She took a step towards me.

It felt as though someone were watching me from just past her shoulder—I slid into focus. She opened her mouth to speak and each word was the click of an immense non-existent cog.

"Excuse me," she said. "I'm supposed to meet someone here at two fifteen…"

I squared my shoulders, meeting her eyes. The bell over the door jingled as another customer entered: plaid jacket, crew-cut, elderly, his gaze scanning the shop.

"First off," I said, leaning forward to touch her sleeve. "Everything I told you in my e-mail was a lie."

Narrative of a Beast's Life

This story ends in Tabat, the fantasy seaport in which I have based numerous pieces, including others in this collection. Tabat exists in a slightly steampunk magical world where intelligent beasts such as unicorns and dragons exist but have no legal rights. Their status is in part a reaction to the depredations of the sorcerers who created many of them in the Shadow Wars, which destroyed an entire continent.

Tabat started as a proposal for an area for an online game my friend James was creating in the mid-nineties. I wanted to do a seaport, and I was inspired by the building system that James had created, which allowed one to add conditional descriptions to a room.

The game never came to pass, but several years later I returned to Tabat. At the time Armageddon was closed to players every Saturday in order to allow the staff to coordinate and conduct maintenance. I suggested that a MUD set in a very small area would allow the players to socialize and roleplay, and set about recreating the city. That project also never was completed, but finally in 2004 I began writing stories set in Tabat, because I knew it so well.

PART I
An account of my family and village—our circumstances—childhood pastimes—Bozni's fate—Adrato's lesson

Like many of my fellow Beasts, I was born to freedom, in a small village named Dekalion, the confluence of five centaur herds. The youngest of seven, I was a favorite of my family, not just of my parents and siblings, but of my aunts, uncles, and cousins as well. They named me Fino, which means "Quickwitted" in my milk tongue, and I grew up in an atmosphere of love and encouragement that any Human child might envy.

Since many have asked me of that initial society, I will set down what I remember of life there. Our village resided in the shade of sandstone cliffs, which overlooked plains of acacia trees and brambles. My people hunted, and the men had farms of cassava and gourds, corn and plantains.

The village was located three or four days inland from the sea, and only a scant number of our women went to trade on the coast or with other neighboring settlements. Only bold women, past their first childbearing and used to fighting, because slavers were common. The traders traveled in groups of five or six, armed with bows and spears, and took goods: bark cloth, carved water gourds, reed baskets. They brought back bright cottons and bits of metal, and sometimes dried fish, tasting of salt and smoke and unfamiliar spices.

When I was a child, my favorite playmate was Bozni, a clever boy perhaps a year younger than myself. We played together, along with our fellows, under the watchful eye of an elderly centaur, Adrato. In the hot afternoons, he was prone to falling asleep in the shade, and we would play where we liked while he drowsed.

The town was a series of huts, woven of thorn and branches, thatched with grass. In the morning, pairs of centaurs would take clay jugs to fill them in the mud-colored river that ran near the village.

This river was not a safe place, and we children were forbidden to go near its shores, which naturally rendered them the most desirable of playgrounds in our eyes. We learned that dangling a branch over the deeper pools might bring a grim-jawed crocodile boiling out of the water.

While leaning out over a pool with a branch one day, Bozni was snatched by such a monster. The rest of the children screamed and ran for help, but I leaped forward, trying in vain to pull him from the reptile's maw. I took up the fallen branch and beat the creature about the head, Bozni shouting and screaming all the while.

Alas! Try as I might, the crocodile withdrew further into the water, where it spun itself sideways several times as quickly as a child's top. Bozni thrashed past in the foaming water—I believe he perished early in those moments, but the crocodile continued to shake the corpse.

I stood horrified, staring into the reddening river, and caught a last glimpse of his ensanguined face, barely visible against the water's rusty color. By the time Adrato came galloping up, summoned by the others, Bozni was gone.

Adrato demanded an account of what had transpired, and forbore his anger at my inability to express the horrific scene I had just witnessed. Bit by bit, he coaxed the tale from me.

At its conclusion, we stared at each other for a long moment. He took me by the shoulder and pointed a doleful finger at the river. By now, the current had washed away any stain from the glistening banks, although the dents and troughs dug in the mud by the frantic action of Bozni's legs bore testament to the struggle.

"That is the price of disobedience," Adrato said sternly, and shook me once or twice. His demeanor impressed me so gravely that it would not be until I was an adult that I fully realized that in some cases, the price of obedience might prove still more costly. I was free then, as I said, and a child. I did not understand many things, and so I swore I would always obey, lest I meet Bozni's fate.

Part II

My early education—anticipation of a hunt—a raid in the night by Shifters—my capture—our journey

We children were taught mathematics, which I took to with great delight and facility of mind. We learned nothing of the written word, but we were taught to calculate with cabi, which means "counting beads," carved of ivory and strung on cords.

The arts of hunting and self-defense were also taught to us. When a centaur youth came of age, he or she would kill a lion in order to receive the tattoos of adulthood along their arms and chest. As the day for my hunt came nearer, dreams of what was to happen filled all my nights. I made two spears for the purpose and Adrato promised me an iron knife for the occasion.

But a week before the ritual was to take place, a slaving clan of Shifters—who sometimes walked in two-legged form, and other times ran as hyenas—attacked us. Our traders had left that morning, and our attackers must have been watching for that signal. In the darkest hours of the night, they set fire to several huts and shouted angrily beside the windows, thrusting spears inward at the sleepers, before withdrawing.

In the confusion, amid the noise and flames, I ran in the wrong direction, fetching up against a fence and knocking myself sharply on the head. I reeled away into the darkness outside the village walls and was seized by rough hands, which pulled sacking down over my head, obscuring my vision and binding my arms. I kicked out, but my captors quickly secured me and I found myself trussed and thrown on a cart with several others. We tried to ascertain each others' identities, but savage blows rained down on us with imprecations and commands for silence. The cart trundled into motion and we rumbled away.

The next few days we traveled in this manner. My companions in captivity were revealed as three other youths, ranging in age from myself, my age-mates Tsura and Kali, and an older boy named Flik. We tested our bonds, but our captors were evidently well-experienced at their brutal profession. They watered us and fed us with grain porridge, but so little that we were weakened by hunger and tormented by thirst, along with biting flies that crawled over us as we jostled along in the miserably hot sun.

Sometimes I tried to convince myself that my family would come for me, but at least a week would pass before our traders returned from their mission. They were the only ones brave enough to dare searching for us, but by the time they were set on our trail, it would be cold.

PART III

We are taken to market—I am sold to a new master—our journey and its hardships—a garden feast—the sphinx's name—we come to Samophar and are taken aboard ship

We were taken to a market in a city. None of us had ever seen such a place before and there were sights and sounds and smells such as I had never witnessed. The buildings were made of clay brick, laid together so snugly that no mortar or cement was necessary. Some buildings were built on top of each other, and stairs meant for no centaur led up and down the outside.

Here we were sold, each to separate masters. Mine fastened me in a coffle with other beings: a sphinx of that city that had committed murder, two djinni, and a snake-headed woman. Oxen drew the cart to which we were shackled, and chained on it was a dragon, not a large one, but some eight feet in length. A small herd of goats marched behind us in turn, intended for the dragon's sustenance.

We traveled northward for three days, during which I picked up a scattering of my comrades' languages, and they of mine. The dragon, as it chanced, spoke the sphinx's tongue. As they talked back and forth, I listened and tried to make sense of what they said. I could not assemble the dragon's words into meaning, but they drove the sphinx to silent tears. She wept all day and well into the night, and did not speak again for days.

I had never seen a sphinx before and when at last she could be coaxed into speech, I gave her my name and tried to learn her own. But my companions informed me that no sphinx speaks their name outside their own kind. I was much amazed at this strange practice, for it was the first time I realized that it was not simply places that differed from those I had known, but customs as well.

The djinni were kindly disposed towards me, saying that I reminded them of their own child, who had been sold away from them. They tried to give me a portion of their food, but I refused it, even though it tempted me sorely. They were as hungry as I, and I had no right to deprive them. Even then I thought it unfair that one creature should eat while another starved, before I had seen how bitter injustice might be.

On the second day, we came across a village that lay in ashes. Its living inhabitants were all gone, but here and there in the blackened ruins were corpses: long-armed apes and centaurs like myself. Our master allowed us to forage in the gardens, although we were kept chained together, rendering walking laborious. While much was trampled, I found some yams there and put them in a sack I found to one side, along with stalks of sugar cane, two lemons, and a handful of orange fruit that I had never seen before, sized to match my thumb tip, thin-skinned, and full of a sour savor. We roasted our pickings in the guards' fire that night, and considered ourselves to be dining as well as royalty.

The next day we came to a seaport, which a passerby told us, in answer to our entreaties was Samophar. Here the larger buildings were made of white stone and the streets underfoot were paved with yellow brick. Fatbellied ships rode at anchor in the harbor and we realized that our owner intended to sell us away from our homeland.

I had never seen so much water. I stared at it, imagining crocodiles beneath the glittering surface. At the docks, we were passed over to a ship's master. I witnessed other slaves being loaded onto the ship, and saw the weeping of several families being parted.

Here a sad incident came to pass. The two djinni were chained together and contrived to jump into the waves. The woman drowned before they could be drawn up out of the water and the husband was savagely beaten by the sailors, angry at the trouble he had afforded. Try as I might, despite the blows aimed my way, I could not force my way up the gangplank at first, but the djinni's blood, his cries, forced me, lest I push them to such lengths, for I knew they would have no mercy.

Below decks I found myself amidst a throng of other captives, including dog-men from the east, ghouls, several griffins, a family of harpies, ogres, unicorns, and a rakshasa. Above decks, I could hear the roaring of the dragon as it was chained into place and we set underway.

PART IV

The voyage—we are rebuked by the sphinx—I am given a new name—the fate of a cyclops

Brutality was a common practice of the Human crew towards the cargo. They affected to despise the Beasts they conveyed, and yet they used us venially as they desired, particularly the ogre women. Few of the crew did not undertake such practices, either with each other or with the miserable captives in their care.

We were given a measure of gruel and water each day, which our keepers were not careful to hand out. Some bullies among us made it their practice to take the provisions of those who were sick or otherwise unable to defend what was rightfully their own. After a few such incidents, though, the sphinx spoke to us. Those who could understand her words rendered them into other tongues and others translated them in turn so a constant subdued whisper spread outward from her throughout the cramped hold.

She discoursed most remarkably in her deep, grave voice. She said as thinking beings we owed each other civil treatment and that it was the duty of the strong to protect the weak from the worst of our common oppression. She looked at each face in turn with her great brown eyes and some faltered under that stare.

After that, the bullies seemed abashed. From then on we kept better order among ourselves, despite the taunts and jeers of the sailors, who were angered by such behavior. It was as though it were a reproach that their captives might act more civilized than they. But we knew that without such acts, we had nothing.

Not even our names were our own. During the journey we were given new names, chosen by the Captain from a book which he carried as he walked the levels below decks, trailed by two sailors, pointing and giving each the appellation by which they were to be known from then forward.

The sound he gave me seemed strange and unrepeatable. Phil-lip. But the sailor behind him paused and said the name aloud to me and made me repeat it back until he was satisfied and moved on to the next beast. Phil-lip. Resentment blazed in my chest, for it was not my name, not the name by which my parents and beloved siblings had known me. Was that not part of who I was—my very innermost nature? My name. Phil-lip.

But I did not give voice to my objections, for I had seen the example made of a resistor. A monstrous cyclops, who was incongruously soft-spoken to the point where one must strain their ears to hear him, proved quite adamant on the subject of his name, refusing the one given him—Jeremy—and was beaten till he "should acknowledge it," which rather proved to be the point where he fainted and pails of sea water thrown on his face failed to revive him. He died two days later.

As the days passed, the realization struck me that I was moving away from my home, and that even should I escape my servitude, I would find myself in a strange land, where I knew no one to help me. Despondent at the thought, I refused to eat and gradually sank into a deep melancholy. It was evident that the sailors cared not whether I lived or died, but the Captain, who had a financial investment in his piteous cargo, forced them to shift me up onto deck in the sunshine and wind. I was placed towards the aft of the ship, in a somewhat sheltered spot, with several other invalids also deemed to be in danger of being carried away by their maladies.

One of these we knew doomed. A tree spirit named Malva faded with each mile stretching between herself and her tree. The Captain swore greatly upon discovering the nature of her malady, for the seller had deliberately not warned him. She was the sweetest of souls and it was painful to watch her skin grow dull where once it had been luminous. The strands of her hair fell prey to the sea winds, which snatched them away day by day and bore them who knows where.

After a week and a half of this existence, Malva finally breathed her last. The captain lost no time disposing of the corpse overboard and I forbore to watch, lest I see the gray sharks that followed us quarreling and tearing over the body.

The ghouls pleaded to be allowed to dispose of the corpse, as they did each time some unfortunate passed away. The Captain said he did not like to encourage their habits, and for the most part they were denied fresh meat except for such occasions as they were able to hide someone's death below decks.

In doing so, they did not have to hide their activities so much from the sailors, who paid us as little attention as they could, as from their fellows, most of whom objected to the thought of being disposed of in such a gruesome wise, although those entirely resigned to their fate said they did not mind being eaten by the ghouls.

Once again, Providence stepped in. Prompted by a chance fondness for my form and face, another being intervened and saved me from following Malva's dreadful fate. The cook, Petro, was a fat man who had once worked in a racing stable. He confided in me that his great desire had been to be a jockey, and that when at the age of twelve, he had realized that his frame would outstrip a rider's dimensions, he had run away to sea in despair.

Only Petro's nursing me with what fresh fruit he had stored away kept me alive. He took me as his pet, and delighted in asking for stories about my village and the Beasts I had encountered in the course of my travels. He was fascinated with the equine part of my body and would groom and caress it, while avoiding that part which seemed Human to him.

I went so far as to offer him my real name, but he shook his head and insisted that I must think of myself as Phillip from now on, else I might expect to gather unnecessary punishment on myself.

He explained to me that the world was divided into Humans and Beasts, and that the Gods had given Humans dominion over Beasts, which meant that such creatures could not own themselves, and only be the possession of Humans. He would have offered to buy me, he assured me, except that I was far outside his meager savings. He spoke of the highness of my price as a good thing, because it ensured that someone wealthy, who would be able to maintain me well, would be my purchaser.

The dragon was kept at the very back of the ship, which was reckoned less imperiled by its flames. Most of the time its jaws were kept prisoned, but at dawn and dusk, they would release its mouth to feed it a goat from the dwindling herd and let it drink its fill of water. The diet did not suit its bowels, and by the end of the trip, the back of the ship was covered with its gelid feces, despite the sailors' best efforts to keep it scrubbed free of the substance, which burned bare skin exposed to it.

As we went north, the weather became more and more winter-like. We all found the cold and damp excruciating. Clothing and blankets were at a premium, and many traded favors or begged bits of clothing from the sailors. Petro gave me his second-best jacket, which he said he had grown too paunchy for. It hung loose on me, but I was glad of the overabundance of the fabric.

We did not sit out on the deck any more, and so I did not witness our approach to the port of Tabat. Waiting in the darkness, I strained my ears to make out what I could: the cries of gulls, echoed by the shouts of Humans, the creak of the ship's timbers and the swish of water, the slap of waves.

When I left the ship, Petro had tears in his eyes as he waved to me, but I did not think much of him. All my worries were engaged by what was to come. Under the watchful eye of the Captain, we made our way down the gangplank that led from the ship to the dock, shivering in the bitter sea wind, uncertain of our fate.

Part V
We arrive in Tabat—the fate of the dragon—I am sold—my new mistress—I am taken to Piper Hill

We were driven to a vast marketplace, a single roof stretched across hundreds of feet, and six raised platforms where the Beasts and each platform's Human auctioneer stood. Inside the walls, among the press of the crowd, it was much warmer, so warm that I felt in danger of fainting. The crowd pressed on every side, and the smells were oppressive.

I saw the sphinx and others of my fellow captives sold. Then came the dragon, which they hauled up onto the block in chains. The great iron muzzle was clamped around its jaws so it still could not speak, but it rolled its eyes in fury and tried to flap its wings.

Alas! It had been denuded of those members and only stumps remained, treated with cautery and tar bandages. At the time I wondered at the savagery of such a gesture and later learned it is customary with Beasts that possess the power of flight, lest they come loose, since in such cases they invariably fly away as quickly as they can.

The bidding for the dragon came fast and furious. At length it was sold and dragged away. The bidding was shorter in my case, and after a quick interchange, I was shoved in line behind my purchaser.

She was a lean woman with dark hair worn in an ornate braid wrapped around her head. Her skin was darker than my own and she was significantly shorter. She gestured at me to follow her, flanked by her guard, a shaggy-headed minotaur who eyed me wordlessly. His arms were as big around as my chest, or so it seemed to me.

She bought another Beast, a dog-man. He and I walked in new sets of chains behind a cart heaped with produce and other goods. I did not speak his language, nor he mine, and so we did not communicate much as we progressed along. At noon, we stopped to rest, and the woman and minotaur ate lunch, although only drinks from a water skin were given to the dog-man and me.

We arrived at our destination by early evening. A series of white-washed buildings sat atop a cliffside overlooking a small river. The houses seemed quite grand to me at the time, but after I had lived there for some time, I came to see that it was older, and had not been well tended. The bushes in the once lavish garden were overgrown, and in places the faster-growing ones had choked back the shyer, less-assuming plants. The garden grew all manner of medicinal herbs—some outright, others hidden between tree roots or in the shadows of the crumbling rock wall. The outer walls were shaggy with peeling paint, and the gutters drooped as though unable to bear the slightest thought of rain. This was Piper Hill, my new home, which it has remained until now.

Part VI

Jolietta begins my training—I am broken to harness—Brutus and Caesar—the dwarf dragons—I am sent out to work—I fall ill—I speak my feelings and am punished

I soon settled into life at Piper Hill. I set about learning the language as quickly as I could, stung by both Jolietta's scorn and her lash when she did not think I was applying myself as hard as I could. Jolietta showed me how to work in tandem with another centaur that she had in her stables, named Michael.

You would think that an intelligent creature would have little trouble with the concept of the harness, but the truth is that it required strength and dexterity that had not been developed in me by all my confined days aboard the slave ship.

My physical dexterity was also hampered by my injuries. The day after we arrived at the estate, Jolietta had me tied and whipped until the blood flowed. She told me that we should begin as we meant to go on and that to disobey her would be to get whipped again.

She demanded to know if I understood her. By now I could make out what she said, for it was the same language many of the sailors had spoken. She went on to tell me my name would continue to be Phillip, as that was the name written on my papers of ownership, but that if I dissatisfied her, she was quite capable of changing my name to something much more degrading.

By way of example, she was in the process of training an oracular pig, and she called that unfortunate being "Thing" and insisted that we all do the same, although the information quickly passed among us that the pig's birth name was Tirza.

I watched Tirza's training in tandem with my own, and found her sullen example a warning sign of my fate should I rebel too overtly. Like most of her kind, Tirza could speak aloud, as though she were Human, a clear soprano which I had the pleasure of hearing sing on several occasions. She was a good enough soul when one spoke to her outside of Jolietta's training, but few of us dared hold such conversations, for fear of the beatings that we would be given if we were caught offering the miserable creature solace, either spoken or material.

I respected the two minotaur guards that Jolietta had with her almost constantly as she went about the estate on her daily business: Brutus and Cassius. It had been Cassius who had gone with her on her buying trip. Neither of them deigned to speak to the other household Beasts, other than to pass along their mistress's orders or reprimand us if we mis-served them in some way. They had been with Jolietta, I was told, since they were calves.

Other members of the household were an orangutan, two dryads belonging to nearby trees, a satyr, two dog-men who worked in the stable, an old troll who served as cook, and Bebe, a fat old centaur mare who oversaw the household and was greatly trusted by Jolietta. She was a sly creature, and I quickly learned to confide nothing in her, for she was fond of earning treats and favors from Jolietta by paying with small betrayals—or sometimes much larger—of the other servants.

The satyr, Hedonus, professed himself content in his role. He said when he had first been captured and sold, he had worked in the Southern Isles in a salt-making establishment. The Isles were not conducive to health. Hedonus said each year one out of every ten slaves died, and that this death rate, which was better than most, was reckoned to be due to a mixture of lime juice and sulfur that the overseer forced his workers to drink each morning. By contrast to the salt pond, Jolietta's establishment was luxury indeed, he implied in conversation more than once, and Bebe seemed to feel the same.

There were others who might not have agreed. Workers served on the estate and a larger group was hired out as needed. These groups were somewhat fluid—servants out of favor might find themselves hired out and conversely a hired worker who did well might find themselves purchased as part of the household or estate workers. While the household servants lived within the house itself and ate in its kitchen, the others lived in small cabins erected at the back of the estate.

Although the household accommodations were severe, they were luxurious by contrast with these cabins, which were caulked ineffectually with mud and cloth against the severities of the wind. I have stood in one during a storm and heard the whole cabin singing, as though it were nothing but a musical instrument for the wind to sound as it would.

Mistress Jolietta also raised what are called dwarf dragons, though they are not properly dragons. The wealthy in that area used them for sport hunting. A single one could kill a creature ten times its size, and a pack of them could bring down anything. These she set me to feeding each day, which meant that I must butcher two goats and several dozen chickens every morning. Tender-hearted, I wept whenever I killed the goats until Jolietta caught me at it and beat me for my tears. After that, I steeled my heart and killed each animal as though it were nothing more than wood made animate and bleating.

The dragons, of which there were a half dozen or so, were kept in a great pen set against the cliff face that also functioned as the rubbish heaps for the estate, for the dragons preferred to nest in such, and let the baking heat combined with the sun brood their eggs. The trees had been cut back so the sunlight could fully enter the pen, and it was a malodorous and noisome place where few cared to go. I took advantage of this to seek solitude in which to heal my injured spirit. I would sit thinking and listening to the rasp of the lizards' lovemaking—a sandpaper rasp that never seemed to cease, even when eggs were being laid in the pits scraped atop each heap of trash and nightsoil.

The dragons were worth a deal of money, I gathered. There were two clutches ready to hatch, and Jolietta set me to watching over them at night, sitting up with a torch, waiting to see any motion on a mother dragon's part that would betoken a hatching taking place.

The second day of the watch, I was so tired that I fell asleep and woke only when I heard the croaking from a female dragon that announced her progeny.

The tiny animals crawled out under their mother's watchful eye and headed for the shelter of the bale of straw Jolietta had directed me to put within a few paces of the heap.

One crawled beneath me, and I raised my foot, thinking to crush it and thus deprive my owner of a fine sum of money. But it was such a pretty little thing, only a foot long, with fine mottled patterns distinct and new along its scaly sides, and so I stayed my hoof and let it crawl into the straw. Dwarf dragons are as unthinking as animals, so I did not speak to it, now or later.

Those eggs hatched fine, but the other batch did not, and when this became evident due to the length of time that had passed, Jolietta held me accountable and beat me. While she had me beneath the lash, I cried out, saying that she had no right to do such a thing to me, and that I would run away, as soon as I was able. She merely laughed at me. We both knew every hand would be against a runaway Beast.

It would not be the last time she beat me, or that I saw another servant beaten. A small hut crouched towards the back of the estate, a great hook set dangling from its blackened roof beams. She would suspend the unfortunate victim by the wrists from this hook and the rest of the household would be assembled in order to watch and learn from their unfortunate fellow's example.

Under Jolietta's tutelage, I learned the difference between the various methods of punishment: the searing flay of cat-tails, the bitter blow of a cow-hide whip, the thud of a rod against scarred flesh. Like other Humans I had met, she felt that the sooner examples were made, and the sooner a captive resigned to its life of servitude and toil, the better for all parties concerned.

Food was a constant worry among the Beasts of the household, although we did not live half so badly as the Beasts who were hired out to work on surrounding farms. They were given two pecks of corn and a pound of dried fish each week, and counted themselves better off than most. Nonetheless, they tried their best to be hired by the masters known for feeding their workers well, and the household Beasts smuggled out what they could of food. Most of the time, though, we ate the same mash and boiled vegetables that the Humans in the household, mainly Jolietta and her apprentices, consumed.

On the western edge of the estate there was a stand of apple trees. Jolietta allowed us to pick these as we would, for she disliked the taste of the fruit, and would watch one of us gobble a piece down, amazement evident on her face as she made loud remarks regarding how she did not understand how we might stomach such noisome provender. Despite this talk, we ate the apples with relish, for they were sweet and full of savor, and what was not eaten was dried and put aside against the winter.

We were severely punished if transgressions were discovered. At one point, directed to throw out some burned soup, I tried to scrape it into some sacking for transport to a work slave who was ailing. Jolietta found me at it and forced me to eat the cold, burned mass there and then before stringing me up for the lash. The food was the entirety of what I was given for the next three days.

I learned that in Tabat there were individuals known as Beast farmers—Humans who held the titles to Beasts by law but left the Beasts alone, to make their own way in the world or sometimes pay the farmer a weekly portion of their income.

Some did this out of the goodness of their hearts, while others chose to make their daily living in such a partnership, being too lazy or otherwise disinclined to keep the strict grasp that a slavekeeping arrangement would entail.

But for a Beast to belong to such a farmer, they must manage to save up a sum to give the farmer, with which to buy them—and this sum was inordinate indeed. Nonetheless, I began to put aside such small coins as fell my way.

PART VIII
Visitors to the estate—my friendship with the sphinx—I learn to read—I am trained as a physician—I escape and am caught—I father a number of children—I begin writing this account

Other creatures constantly passed in and out of Jolietta's kingdom, either in the process of being trained or nursed. I nursed litters of dog-men and groomed gryphons being trained for the Tabatian cavalry. Many institutions sent their ailing Beasts to Jolietta for doctoring. The sphinx had been purchased by the College of Mages, and when she fell prey to cough, the College sent her to Jolietta's farm to be nursed back to health with boxes of heated sand and horehound and pinetop tea. Jolietta allowed me to care for the sphinx and over the month she spent there at Piper Hill, we became fast friends. Even after her departure, we passed messages back and forth as we could.

Jolietta thought me intelligent enough to absorb some knowledge of healing. I learned to identify and pull bad teeth, to apply leeches, and to administer medicine to Beasts. She taught me the names and methods of the different preparations, and had me smell and taste each of them so I would know them in the future.

She said that if I learned quickly, she would be able to trust me with errands to outlying farms, to tend creatures too ill to be fetched to her.

As a result of learning such things, I taught myself to read and write, although my hand was poor and unpracticed. Still, I worked at improving my understanding of the art where I could, stealing pamphlets and magazines to read, hiding them away in a shed near the dragon pens.

I made it my practice not to speak much, but my mistress caught something suspicious in my demeanor and watched my actions jealously. Aware of the scrutiny, I took care to make no move that would confirm her fears. Indeed, I was a model slave, unobtrusive as a piece of furniture, quick to anticipate her wants and desires. I had feared that I might be put in a brothel, for the sailors on the ship said that most Beasts of my kind ended up under such circumstances. And to do her credit, Jolietta never spoke word or made gesture that led me to think she desired sexual congress with me.

Time wore on and I grew from my spindly youth to a broad-shouldered male. While Bebe had no interest in me, the same was not true for many of the centaur mares in the area, along with a few of the Human women. The dryads liked for me to kiss them, and stroke them with my hands, and we spent many hours in this wise, but the mares were what I ached for.

Jolietta forbade me congress, saying that the owners should have to pay well for my seed, but I managed to defy her more than once, and blame the outcome on my nature. Jolietta thought, as most Humans did, that Beasts were inevitable prey to their natures, and that I could not help taking an opportunity at congress with a mare in heat any more than I could help eating when I was hungry and food presented itself.

At first I tried to ensure that my loves produced no progeny, but when a mare is fertile, Nature takes its course and soon enough a child results. When I realized this, I attempted to deny myself such pleasures, but I was young and easily swayed by my body's yearnings. And so, within a few years, I had a number of colts, both purchased and gratis, in the surrounding area, and I experienced the first pangs of seeing a child sold away from me when a neighbor parted with mare and colt to a trader who took them northward to Verranzo's City.

Those who advocate slavery would deny such familial bonds. Surely they have never seen a mother, wailing and lashed by despair more harshly than any cat-o-nine-tails, trying in vain to reach to her infant! The child stands, uncertain and blinking, sensing the sorrow to come, and then is driven ever more frantic by his dam's remonstrations! More than once such a sight has torn with an eagle's claws at my heart.

After several years of study as a physician, Jolietta began to take me with her when she paid visits to check on Beasts, and I would administer medicine or treatments under her watchful eye. Several of the freeholders asked her if she meant to geld me, and she spoke forthrightly, saying that centaurs of good frame sold well, and that she reckoned she would have good fat breeding fees of me.

"Ain't you afraid that will leave him too feisty?" one demanded, and she shrugged.

"It would be a poor advertisement for my training skills if I did not trust in them," she said.

By the time she began to put me out to stud on a regular basis, my lost children ate at me. I saw their sad faces in my dreams at night, and whenever I encountered one of their mothers on a visit, I glimpsed only reproach in her eyes. What would it be like, I thought, to live in a place where I might be part of a herd. Where I might sire children and teach them as I had been taught, how to sing, how to wield a spear, how to count on cabi.

Driven by such fantasies, I entertained thoughts of escape. While passing through a farmhouse kitchen, I had the opportunity to steal a knife that sat waiting to cut pieces of a ham. While I found out later that my theft caused a great hubbub, suspicion did not land on me. I kept my weapon out in the garden, tucked beneath a little-used bench, and waited a few weeks to make sure that no late suspicions would lead to Jolietta searching my chamber, as happened from time to time.

I put food aside, mainly oat rusks that I stole from the kitchen and dried apples given me by the work Beasts. I stitched a pack out of burlap stolen from the stable, and read through Jolietta's almanac to discover the next night when moonlight would be sufficient to see at night. I kept my eyes open for other items that would not be missed, hoping for a torch or lantern, but fate did not provide such.

I knew from reading the newspaper that if I made my way north to Verranzo's City, I might find souls willing to shelter me, and eventually send me west, where the Humans were few. I did not know much of the territory that lay in my way, but I figured I might head for the coast and then work my way up along it towards that haven.

Accordingly, I left late at night, creeping out from my quarters in the stable. Under the cover of darkness, I made my way along the deserted road to the place where its cliffs overlooked the sea, and then made my way north and east from there. In the hour when dawn fingered the sky, I found a patch of woodland between fields and sheltered in its depths—the lush grass testified that only deer and smaller wildlife came there. I found a bed beneath a fallen pine and slept, dreaming of freedom, among the smell of the rotting brown needles.

My hope was that in the morning, I would not be missed since Jolietta would think I had gone to slaughter game and feed the dragons. The day was bright and sunny, and would render the dragons torpid and unlikely to complain much—I had fed them early and more than their usual the day before, and they customarily gorged themselves and then did not eat for several days. And in those hours while I was not missed, traffic would pass back and forth along the road, muddling and—hopefully—destroying my scent so hounds would not be able to trace me to my hiding place.

I was far enough away from the road that I could not hear the traffic or conversation there, and while once or twice I thought I heard the baying of hounds, carried on the wind, I was never certain. When evening came and I could move in the shadows, hiding whenever I came across another traveler, I continued to move up along the coast.

I travelled in this way for three days, living off the rusks in my pouch and food stolen from gardens where I could. On the fourth night, I heard pursuit behind me and the cries of hounds, which grew louder and louder. Jolietta had anticipated my path and had been waiting for it to coincide with her patrols. She tracked me into a ravine, where I slipped and slid in the clay and mud, unable to find traction. Cassius climbed down and tied me with ropes before he and Brutus drew me up out of the rocky cleft by means of pulleys.

The beating I had earned was a savage one indeed. Afterwards Jolietta let me hang by the wrists throughout the night. I lay insensible for two days afterward, and then resumed my duties.

From that point forward, I kept any thoughts of escape to myself. I was resolved that in the end, I would, but that next time I would be far better prepared.

My life in general improved as a result of my quiet demeanor, for I was determined to betray no sign of my intended, inevitable rebellion to my mistress. Jolietta allowed me better food, and the cook instructed me in culinary techniques that I might find useful in tempting the appetite of a patient or the mistress at some point. I learned how to create trifles and frumenties, soufflés and omelets, and a variety of nogs and creams and soups of medicinal nature.

Where for many, years of interaction would engender trust, Jolietta grew more and more suspicious of my motives as time passed. She stopped sending me out on errands by myself, saying that I had fathered as many free colts as she cared me to, and she would no longer allow me in the still-room, where she kept her herbs and medicines, by myself.

Word came to me through other slaves that in Tabat one of the Human presses had devoted itself to the cause of abolition, and wished to receive accounts of the lives of Beasts, in order to speak on their behalf to those who insisted that they should remain subject, incapable of governing themselves. And so I sat down to write, and penned the first part of this tale and sent it by secret means to the newspaper.

A month later, by the same means in reverse, a newspaper arrived in my room. I unfolded its stiff pages and looked throughout its sections. On the fifth page, I found these words, beginning the dense blocks of print beneath an advertisement for decorative tiles: *Like many of my fellow Beasts I was born to freedom, in a small village named Dekalion, the confluence of five centaur herds.*

I continued writing my pages, but it was difficult to get candles in order to compose at night. I limited myself to one chapter each purple month, and used any extra luminescence to correct and edit my prose. I composed paragraphs while working for Jolietta making pills or feeding the dwarf dragons, and polished them as I sat eating or doing handiwork in the evenings.

I did not grow up believing in Gods, such as the Humans follow. And even now, when the Humans insist that everything is theirs, a gift from those Gods, I find myself dubious, though I know I might find myself slain for such words. The Humans do as they will, and firstly say that we are like infants who must be looked over and then say we are monsters who must be controlled, creatures incapable of rising above their natures, who will do wrong to them if we are allowed to be our own agents. And so I questioned these things, and asked my fellow Beasts if they did not question them as well.

Part IX

The aftermath

It is unknown how Fino's mistress discovered his activities, but on the day he was due to pass his next manuscript to his correspondent, it failed to arrive. The messenger stopped at Piper Hill to secretly ask after him, and was told that he was ill.

Subsequent queries learned that she had performed some surgery on him that robbed him of the majority of his intelligence, rendering him able to feed and tend himself, but little else, and that shortly thereafter he had been sold to a passing trader, and taken to the Old Continent.

His fate is unknown as of this writing. The last piece of his narrative was smuggled out, but the hand is illegible and hurried, and only the first sentence can be read.

It says only this: "I am determined to disobey."

Eagle-haunted Lake Sammamish

"Eagle-haunted Lake Sammamish" is a self-indulgent story in that it draws on the relationship between my spouse and I, who do live beside an eagle-haunted lake. I also did buy land in Utah, but unfortunately there were no dryads on it, nor has a large corporation tried to purchase it as of this date.

This story originally appeared in a lovely small magazine, Shimmer Magazine, *in 2007.*

"You're nuts," my husband told me.

"Land is always a good investment," I said. "Here, I'll send you the link."

I messaged it to him and there was silence while Jonah clicked through the pages on his laptop.

"This is in Utah," he finally said. "It'll be swarming with Mormons. Or there'll be some sort of religious cult living just down the road."

"By purchasing this land for a mere 350 dollars," I said, "I have doubled our property in the world. We are landed gentry now. I think that means we can be knighted."

"A quarter acre."

"No, I got a better deal by buying two lots, so it's a half acre."

Our legal holdings now consisted of one decrepit, Key-west colored condo beside Lake Sammamish, a boat slip, and a half acre of property in Box Elder County, Utah. The deed, when it arrived a week after Paypal payment, read "The West third of the North three fifths of the Southwest Quarter of Section 13, Township 6N, Range 16W, S.L.B. & M."

I pinned it up on the bulletin board over my computer.

"Who pays the taxes on that?" Jonah said, glancing up at it.

"We do, but this year's are included in the purchase price," I said.

"Huh."

I paid him no attention and kept on working through the Ebay auction list. I couldn't see what was on his screen, but I could hear the game music shift as he stepped off the zeppelin and into the base camp in the jungle.

"Are we planning on going to see it?" he said.

"Sure, we can go camp on it."

"And get shot."

"You're just jealous of my real estate genius."

He snorted.

"Mark my words, that land will make us money someday," I said. "Land isn't a renewable resource."

"That's what you said about the condo," he said.

"And I was right, too," I said. "It's gone up 50k in two, what, three years?"

"Yeah, yeah. You said that when you bought all those Thai sapphires a couple of years ago too."

"Poophead."

"You too."

I didn't think much more about the property at the time. The summer went on and we continued about our business: I made a living selling Ebay items for people, and Jonah went off to work at untangling web issues for his company on a daily basis. We barbecued and watched the eagles fish in the evenings beside Lake Sammamish.

In September, a letter arrived about the Box Elder property. The Morton-Thiokol Corporation was offering me $3,000 for it.

"Whoot," Jonah said. "Not a bad return on your money."

"I wonder why they want the land," I said. "I mean, not to look a gift horse in the mouth or anything."

"That's exactly what you're doing, though, looking a gift horse in the mouth," Jonah pointed out.

"Yeah, well, it just seems a little too good to be true. It's a corporation. They're not offering me money out of the goodness of their heart."

Jonah Googled around that evening. "Sounds like they're building a research facility," he said. "Lots of funding, special names, a fancy opening ceremony with that singer Ivory and that guy from that one show."

"What show?" I looked over his shoulder. "Oh, that one. Huh, fancy model."

"Three thousand dollars is a lot of money," Jonah pointed out. "It's your investment and all, but maybe you want to cash it in and get us a trip to Paris or something."

"Paris?"

"I've always wanted to go to Paris."

"Well, we'll see," I said.

"You could sell the condo. Write up a fancy description of it that sells for the same kind of return. Do it."

"Live beside eagle-haunted Lake Sammamish in Washington State, beneath the shadow of Douglas firs and cypress," I said. "This quirky condo features good feng shui and its own boat launch."

"No wonder we like living here."

"No wonder."

Since there was no immediate deadline on the check and since I am a procrastinator by nature, I put it aside. Six weeks later, another letter arrived from Morton-Thiokol, this time with an offer of $30k.

"Holy crap," Jonah said. "That's so rad."

"We have to go check it out."

"Gift horse. Mouth."

"Oh, come on. You're curious too. What could be there that's worth $30,000?"

We packed the car with Trader Joe's goodies, sleeping bags, and my old camping gear.

I never minded traveling anywhere with Jonah. We'd burn a few CDs worth of music or bring the iPod. Sometimes I'd read something aloud and we'd work our way through a book of short stories or a horror novel. This trip we got all the way through the first half of a book of Hans Christian Andersen fairytales.

"They're all so dark," Jonah said. "People with their feet stuck to loaves of bread, stuck down in a bog of toads and snakes. Look at the poor little match girl—she just freezes to death."

I closed the book and put it in my lap. "Grimm's the same way. Everything is dark and people get bits chopped off them. Very un-Disney."

"I wouldn't read them to my kids," he said. Realizing what he'd said, he gave me a quick, worried glance. I pretended not to see it, just stared out the windows.

We were on I-90 on our way across the pass. On my right, pines ringed a black pool. The ghostly stumps of trees protruded up through the water, glimmering like streaks of coal pencil on the silvery surface. It was polluted. Barren.

Descending into eastern Washington, I glimpsed black and white magpies along the fence rails and watched the landscape shift from pines and firs besieged by blackberry vines to scrub trees, leggy beeches, and red-capped sumac, before we dipped further south into Utah and the landscape grew dryer yet.

Past Willard Bay, we saw hundreds of high voltage power transmission lines, metal lace against the snow-covered Raft River mountains. Shadows cracked the ground at the foot of each metal construction.

I shivered as we passed under them.

"What's up?" Jonah asked.

"Long time ago I read a book about power lines distorting magnetic energies in our bodies. They said ghosts hung out around them and people ended up with shorter life spans because of the energy changes."

"Poppycock," Jonah said. "You read too much crackpot stuff."

"Yes, but we do have magnetic fields in our bodies."

"Hippie."

"I know you are, but what am I?"

The bickering went on till the northern tip of the state, near the mountains. The car's GPS unit led us along a dirt and rut road to the precise location, bordering a hill crested with short, stubby trees.

Scrambling out of the Vehicross and stretching, I looked around.

"These must be box elders," Jonah said, nodding at the trees that surrounded us. "Hence the name."

"I always thought these were maples," I said, stooping to pick up a stout purplish green twig. It held a drooping cluster of parallel wings, each a thumb width long, rustling hollowly as I shook it.

"You're the biologist in the family," Jonah said. "You do realize that camping means no toilet or hot water in the morning, don't you?"

I shouldered a pack and the tent's bundle and did not deign to reply.

We made our camp near a stand of older trees ridged with grayish-brown bark.

"What the hell is on this?" Jonah said, unrolling the tent.

"I haven't used it in years," I said. Hand-painted ivy leaves and blue flowers stretched across the dark green surface. "I painted those on before I took it up to the Michigan Womyn's Music Festival. People liked the way it looked."

"This is a hippie tent," Jonah grumbled as he stretched the fabric over the tent poles. He tossed our sleeping bags inside.

"I'm going to go get the rest of the stuff," he said. "You might gather some wood for a fire."

I nodded, but instead I sat down on a log and watched the light gleaming on the upper sides on the mountain near us while gray clouds shaded the stands of pine further down. A trickle of sunshine danced on the tent flap.

Something rustled among the trees but I looked up too late to catch anything but a dark limb sliding in among the foliage. I blinked and looked again, but could see nothing.

Jonah returned with an armload of sleeping bags and the cooler. "Where's the wood?"

"I saw an animal."

"A big animal? What was it?"

"Pretty big."

"A bear?" he asked, eyebrows raised.

"Are bears pale brownish? I thought they were black. It didn't look very hairy."

"Bigfoot."

"Piss off, unbeliever."

"It was a dog. I bet it was a dog."

"Maybe," I said.

We built a fire and roasted hotdogs and marshmallows while watching milky moonlit clouds scud overhead, touched with the red sparks of our fire.

In the middle of the night, I roused to pee. Outside in the starry night, I groped my way to a safe spot. A scuffling came from the side of the car, and I clicked on my flashlight's beam and sent it there.

She crouched near a tire, her head barely topping the square of the gas cap, a bag of marshmallows in her dirty hands. Twigs and leaves filled her hair. Her face was narrow as a fox's, inhuman as she blinked at me.

"It's okay," I said, directing the beam to the ground between us.

She stuffed another marshmallow into her mouth and watched me, chewing. Her feet were bare and black.

"You can have those," I said. "There's some hotdogs in the car, too."

She swallowed. "Really?" Her voice was higher-pitched than I expected.

I nodded. She crouched beside the remnants of the fire. "Make it hot again?" she said.

I dragged more wood onto the fire and sparked it alight before threading a hotdog onto a skewer.

Once she was holding her meal out over the flames, the marshmallows a lump inside the coarse hide of her vest, I felt more comfortable asking questions.

"I'm Stacie," I offered. "What's your name?"

"Deirdre." Her gaze stirred past my shoulder. "I like your tent." Her voice had a lilting burr to it, a slowness that marked each statement, as though she searched for words.

"Yeah, I do too," I said. "So do you live around here?

"Right here," she said. She nodded at the thicket of trees.

"Out here in the country?"

"Yah," she said.

"Seems like that would be lonesome."

"There's been people that have lived here," she said. "There was a house over there, a man and two little girls." She pointed with her chin at a nearby ridge.

"Doesn't look like much there."

"Before that, a while before, there was a Shoshone camp," she said. "They all moved along."

I studied her. Sunlight was creeping up over the ridge, slowly moving the leaves from haze to clear definition. I tugged more wood into the fire and began to make coffee. She watched me, placid and accepting.

"Who was the man with the two little girls?" I asked.

"Reverend Kingsley, Algernon Kingsley. Algie. And his girls, Amalfa and Lulu." She sounded wistful.

"What happened to them?"

"The Shoshone came through here, hunting for a pair of horses they'd lost," she said. "They killed them all. Cut their throats in the middle of the night."

I stared into the heart of the fire. "Seems like it would have been lonely since then," I said.

"It has."

I heard Jonah stirring inside the tent and looked towards it. When I looked back, she was gone already. He came crawling out of the tent, ready for coffee.

"You're up early," he said.

We watched the sunrise come up over the hills in sleepy companionable silence, drinking the coffee laced with the small carton of milk that had been in the car.

"What are you grinning at?" Jonah asked me.

"It's been a weird morning," I said. "And it's still pretty early."

We drove into Brigham City so I could check the courthouse records. I told Jonah about Deirdre along the way.

"It's not April Fool's," he said, "*so* why are you messing with me?"

"I swear this is true. Honest."

"Are you serious?"

"Seriously serious."

"No shit, cross your heart and die?"

"Anything you want to name."

"Holy shit." He lapsed into silence, staring at the road. "That's so rad. You're pulling my leg, right?"

In Brigham City, in a basement underneath the courthouse that smelled like pine cleaner and tinny fluorescent lights, I looked up Reverend Kingsley and his children. Lulu's actual name turned out to be Lucille. They'd died in 1890. There were no pictures, just the Reverend's spidery brown signature on the deed to his land, the Northernmost three fifths of the Southwest Quarter of Section Thirteen.

"So?" Jonah said.

"So they existed at least, and she's probably not a mental patient." We stopped at the QFC and I picked up several bags of marshmallows. "I want real coffee," I said. We went into a Denny's where a surly waitress named served us gritty lattes that tasted of burned grounds. At a nearby table, two men in blue coveralls and another in a business suit, were making their way through identical portions of Moons Over My Hammy.

The badges on their coveralls read Morton-Thiokol in poisonous green cursive.

"Well," the one in the business suit said, coming up for air from his hash browns. "I want the soil tests started today."

"Don't have all the tracts signed off on," a coverall man said.

"Just start testing the soil. No one will chase you off if you happen to get a little too far over. There's only that one tract left, I think, anyhow."

I caught Jonah's eye and tried to make a "Listen to the people at the other table" face but he only stared at me blankly.

"What?" he said.

I mouthed "listen" at him and rolled my eyes to the right but he just stared.

"I'd like my biscuits boxed," he told Jolene. And to me, "Did you want coffee to go?"

At our campsite, I set a bag of marshmallows out and gestured Jonah to a seat on a toppled log.

"Deirdre," I called. "Got more marshmallows for you."

"Holy shit," Jonah said as she seemed to materialize, walking out of the heart of the thicket. She ignored him, moving over to tear open the bag of marshmallows and pop three down in quick succession before looking at the two of us.

"Hi Deirdre," I said. "This is my husband, Jonah."

She nodded at him as he managed a feeble wave.

"We want to talk," I said. "Do you know why someone would want to buy this land?"

"They come and look at the plants all the time," Deirdre said.

I couldn't tell much difference between the trees here or further off. Perhaps a little healthier, a little greener? I wasn't really sure.

"They want to cut it all down and grow new trees," she said. "I heard them talking about clearing it all and setting out new lines of trees."

"What will happen to you if they do that?"

She shrugged fatalistically. "I won't be able to live here any longer."

"Can you move to a new tree?" Jonah said.

She looked at him for the first time, and I felt a flare of jealousy at the warmth in her face. "If I move quickly, within a day or two." She patted the bole closest to her, a little larger than its fellows. "I have lived here for many years."

He looked at me. "Plenty of places within a day's drive. Eagle-haunted Lake Sammamish, for that matter. Marymoor Park is pretty close."

"How long have you been here, Deirdre?" I asked.

She shrugged again. "Many years."

"How did you come here?"

"I grew here."

"With no parents? Who gave you your name?"

"I awoke to sunlight and rain; I don't know how long ago that was. I have never seen another like me. Algernon said I was a dryad, a tree spirit. He named me for one."

A pair of voices came from the road. It was the two men in blue coveralls.

"Hey," one shouted, and waved as they came over to us.

"Camping, huh?" he said, looking at the marshmallows.

"Yeah," Jonah said. "What are you guys up to?"

"Testing the soil all along here."

"Oh, yeah? Some kind of government project?"

They exchanged glances. "Yeah, our company's testing all the soil, building a research facility along here," he said. "You folks own this land?"

"Yeah, just figured we'd come up and say goodbye to it before selling it," Jonah said easily. "You guys want some marshmallows?"

They shook their heads and moved along.

"We need to get her out of here," I said to Jonah. "They'll find her and dissect her or something."

"You always assume the worst," he said.

"It's a corporation. Remember?"

His eyes dropped. "You'll never forgive them, will you?"

"Thirty years ago a corporation—a big corporation, just like Morton-Thikol—decided burying chemical waste was fine, and then didn't say anything when someone decided to build a playground on the site, managing to twist the genes of every child that played there. I can live with that, Jonah. But I won't let them take someone else's future away."

"I don't want to get out of here," Deirdre said. "I've lived here all my life."

"It's that or be dead," I said. "I don't know what you believe as far as life over death goes, but I find the former preferable."

"I know it's unfair," he said to her. "Sometimes the world is unfair. But you don't need to be one of the tragedies. You don't need to be one of the fairytales with an unhappy ending."

She wavered, looking between us.

"It's your land," she said. "That's what those men were saying, weren't they?"

I gestured around myself. "Even if we don't sell the land, the machinery will come and be all around you. And it's a corporation—you never know when they're going to do something like come chop everything down and then go 'Whoops, our bad'. Or get the government to use eminent domain to grab something for a project that will bring a lot of money to this area?

"We can offer you someplace to think about what you want to do next," I said. "A respite."

She stared at me, searching my face, before she sighed and nodded. Sunlight slanted across the clearing, and the trees whispered in the breeze. She went across to the clump of trees and laid her hands on the bark, bowing her head to it. Jonah watched her. His eyes were sad. I hadn't seen that look in his eyes before, even on the day we found out we'd never have a child, and it made my chest hurt, a hopeless, hard ache.

I filled a paper grocery bag with dust and dirt and tree branches and laid it on the floor on the passenger sidee.

Deirdre insisted on sitting on my lap, saying that she did not want to touch the seat. She was surprisingly light, like holding a sack of leaves. Her long toes coiled down to the sack of dust, nestling into it.

She lay in my arms and I cradled her. I laid my cheek atop her head for a moment, and the fierce wild green scent of her filled my lungs, pushing them outward. Jonah touched the radio into a dim and drowsy music. We talked quietly, but her answers grew drowsier and drowsier as the afternoon's warmth filled the car. I let her sleep, figuring it was the state in which she'd most easily take to transportation.

The day was flat and sunny hot.

"Do you think she'll do okay by the lake?" Jonah said.

"I think so. Plenty of trees around there. Enough people to keep her entertained watching them. And with the park, she won't have to worry about her tree getting cut down."

"What do you think she is?"

"I dunno. A dyrad maybe. Or something entirely different. Maybe an alien."

"What do you think she would have done if no one had come along?"

"Lived there for centuries more, maybe. Her and her memories of the Reverend Algernon."

The road dipped and we came into the flatlands. Up ahead lay the desert of wind sculptures and power lines, gleaming in the late afternoon sunlight like knives of incandescence lacing the sky.

As we approached the host of power lines, Deirdre stirred in my arms.

"She's waking up," I said. Her eyes opened, then rolled up in her head. Her mouth opened and closed like a fish's kissing the air, gasping for life.

"Deirdre, what?" I said. Then, urgently as we passed under the first interlacing of power lines, their intersection a mathematical bird's nest above us, "Jonah!"

She spasmed helplessly in my arms.

"Turn around!"

"I'm trying!" He spun the wheel, despite the honking of the truck behind us and we bumped across the median still under the web of tangled lines, there at its edge, waiting for an opportunity to get back into traffic.

"Hang on," I said to Deirdre, holding her tightly as Jonah gunned us into motion and the wheels ground at the road with a desperate roar. "Hang on. Hang on."

"It's...all right," she said, smiling as her body twisted. She kept smiling. "Algernon." Her back arched and the car was full of the smell of wet wood and rot as she fell apart into tangled branches, damp roots, and skeletal leaves in my arms. I held the dead weight as we lurched out from under the power lines' shadow and swerved over to the side of the road.

"God, Jonah," I said. "God, she's gone." I couldn't stop crying, crying as I never had in my life. Bits of root and twig covered my lap, a hopeless scattering that could never be reassembled.

We buried her beside Lake Sammamish, over in Marymoor Park, near the communal gardens and the off-leash area, taking the thin armful of twigs and spindly roots in the dead of night to lay it to rest it where I figured she would see people daily. Last time I was there, a thin, weedy tree had sprouted there among the blackberry tangles in the shadow of the white-railed fence.

Jonah was more shaken than I. I've held onto the Box Elder land to spite Morton-Thiokol, but we're still going next month to Paris, to see if I can coax the shadow from his eyes. Morton-Thiokol Corporation may not have come through for us or for Deirdre, but the Thai sapphires did last week.

Sugar

"Sugar" was another of my pirate anthology inspired stories. Ironically, Sean Wallace picked up "Sugar" for his Fantasy *sampler before I had a chance to send it to any of the pirate anthologies and it appeared there in 2007.*

They line up before Laurana, forty baked-clay heads atop forty bodies built of metal cylinders. Every year she casts and fires new heads to replace those lost to weather, the wild, or simple erosion. She rarely replaces the metal bodies. They are scuffed and battered, over a century old.

Every morning, the island sun beating down on her pale scalp, she stands on the maison's porch with the golems before her. Motionless. Expressionless.

She chants. The music and the words fly into the clay heads and keep them thinking. The golems are faster just after they have been charged. They move more lightly, with more precision. With more joy. Without the daily chant they could go perhaps three days at most, depending on the heaviness of their labors.

This month is cane-planting season. She delegates the squads of laborers and sets some to carrying buckets from the spring to water the new cane shoots while others dig furrows. The roof needs reshingling, but it can wait until planting season is past. As the golems shuffle off, she pauses to water the flowering bushes along the front of the house. Placing her fingertips together, she conjures a tiny rain cloud, wringing moisture from the air. Warm drops collect on the leaves, rolling down to darken pink and gray bark to red and black.

Inside the house is quiet. The three servants are in the kitchen, cooking breakfast and gossiping. She comes up to the doorway like a ghost, half fearing what she will hear. Nothing but small, inconsequential things. Jeanette says when she takes her freedom payment, she will ask for a barrel of rum, and go sell it in the street, three silver pieces a cup, over at Sant Tigris, the pirate city. She has a year to go in the sorceress's service.

Daniel has been here a year and has four more to go. He is still getting used to the golems, still eyes them warily when he thinks no one can see him. He is thin and wiry, and his face is pockmarked and scarred by the Flame Plague. He was lucky to escape the Old Continent with his life. Lucky to live here now, and he knows it.

Tante Isabelle has been with her since the woman was thirteen. Now she's eighty-five, frail as one of the butterflies that move through the bougainvillea. A black beak's snap, and the butterfly will be gone. She sits peeling cubes of ginger, which she will boil with sugar and lime juice to make sweet syrup that can flavor tea or conjured ice.

"If you sell rum, everyone will think you are selling what lies between your thighs as well!" she says, eying Jeanette.

Jeanette shrugs and tosses her head. "Maybe I'd make even more that way!" she says, ignoring Daniel's blush.

Tante Isabelle looks up to see Laurana standing there. The old woman's smile is sweet as sunshine, sweet as sugar. The sorceress stands in the doorway, and the three servants smile at her, as they always do, at their beautiful mistress. No thought ever crosses their minds of betraying or displeasing her. It never occurs to them to wonder why.

Christina is a pirate. She wears bright calicos stolen from Indian traders and works on a ship that travels in lazy shark-like loops around the Lesser and Greater Southern Isles, looking for strays from the treasure fleet and Duchy merchants. The merchants, based in the southernmost New Continent port of Tabat, prey on the more impoverished colonies, taking the majority of their crops in return for food and tools. The treasure fleet is part of a vast corrupt network, fed by springs of gold. This is what Christina tells Laurana, how she justifies her profession of blood and watery death.

When Christina comes to Sant Tigres, she goes to the inn and sends one of the pigeons the innkeeper keeps on the roof. It flies to Laurana's window. She leaves her maison and sails to the port in a small skiff, standing all the way from one island to the other, sea winds whipping around her. She focuses her will and asks the air sylphs, who she normally does not converse with, to bear her to her lover's scarlet and orange clad arms.

Tiny golden hoops, each set with a charm created by Laurana, jingle in Christina's right ear. One is a tiny glass fish, protection against drowning, and the other is a silver lightning bolt to ward off storms.

Christina likes to order large meals when she comes ashore. Her crew hunts the unsettled islands and catches the wild cattle and hogs so abundant there to eke out their income. They sell the excess fat and hides to the smugglers that fill these islands. So she is not meat-starved now, but wants sugary treats, confections of butter and sweet, washed down with raw swallows of rum, here in harbor, where she can be safely drunk.

"Pretty farmer," she says now. She touches the sorceress's hair, which was black as Christina's once, but which has gone silver with age, despite her unlined skin and her clear, brilliant blue eyes.

"Pretty pirate," Laurana replies. She spends the evening buying drinks for Christina and her crew. The pirates count on her deep pockets, rich with gold from selling sugar. Sometimes they try to sell her things plundered on their travels, ritual components, scrolls, or trinkets laden with spells. The only present Christina ever brought her was a waxed and knotted cord strung with knobby, pearly shells. It hangs on her bedchamber wall where the full moon's light can polish it each month.

Laurana brings Christina presents: fresh strawberries and fuzzy nectarines from her greenhouse. In Sant Tigres, she trades sugar for bushels of chocolate beans and packets of spices. Someday, when circumstances have changed, she would like Christina to spend a day or two at the plantation. Jeannette would outdo herself with the meals, flaky pastries and flowers of spun sugar.

It is time to send for a new cook, she thinks. It will take a few months to post the message and then for the new arrival to appear, and even more time for Jeannette to train her in the ways of the kitchen and how to tell the golems to fetch and carry.

Someone leans forward to ask her a question. It is a new member of Christina's crew, curious about the rumors of her plantation.

"Human slaves are doomed to failure," she says. "Look what happened on Banbur—discontented servants burned the fields and overtook the town there, turning their masters and mistresses out into the underbrush or setting them to labor.

"And," she added, "Whites do badly in this climate. I can take care of myself and my household, but it is easier to not worry about my automatons growing ill or dying."

Although they did die, after a fashion. They wore away, their features blurred with erosion. They cracked and crumbled—first the noses, then the lips and brows, their eyes becoming pitted shadows, their molded hair a mottling of cracks.

Time to redecorate soon, she thought. She did it every few decades. She would send a letter and eventually a company representative would show up, consult with her, and then vanish back to Tabat, soon replaced by rolls of new wallpaper and carpets, crates of china, and porcelain wash basins. She looks at Christina and pictures her against blue silk sheets, olive skin gleaming in candle glow.

Later they fall into bed together and she stays there for two hours before she rises, despite her lover's muffled, sleepy protests, and takes her skiff back to her own island. Overhead the sky is a black bowl set with glittering layers of stars, grainy as sandstone and striated with light. Moonlight dapples the waves, so dark and impenetrable that they look like polished jet.

At home, she goes upstairs. A passage cuts across the house, running north to south to take advantage of the trade wind, and open squares at the top of each room partition let the wind through. Britomart's is the northernmost room.

The air smells of dawn and sugar. Sugar, sweet and translucent as Britomart's skin, the color of snow drifts, laid on cool white linen. The other woman's ivory hair, which matches Laurana's, is spread out across the pillow.

Tonight her face is unmasked. Laurana does not flinch away from the pitted eyes, the face more eroded than any golem's. Outside in the courtyard, the black and white deathbirds hop up and down in the branches, making the crimson flowers shake in the early morning light.

"Pleasant trip?" Britomart says.

Laurana's answer is noncommittal. Sometimes her old lover is kind, but she is prone to lashing out in sudden anger. Laurana does not blame her for that. Her death is proving neither painless nor particularly short, but it is coming, nonetheless. A month? A year? Longer? Laurana isn't sure. How long have they been locked in this conversation? It has been less than six months so far, she knows, but it seems like forever.

She goes to her room. The bed is turned down and a hot brick has been slipped between the sheets to warm them. A bouquet of ginger sits on the table near the lamp, sending out its bold perfume.

She lies in bed and fails to sleep. Britomart's face floats before her in the darkness. She is unsure if she is dreaming or really seeing it. She wonders if she remembers it as worse than it really is. But she doesn't.

Two weeks later, the pigeon at her window.

Christina has a bandage around her upper arm, nothing much, she says, carelessness in a battle. She pushes Laurana away, though apologetically. Rather than sleep together, they stay awake and talk. It is their first conversation of any length. Two hours after their first meeting, in the Sant Tigres market, they had fallen into bed together, four months ago.

"So she's sick, your friend?" Christina says.

"You were raised here in the islands," Laurana answers. "You don't know what it was like in the Old Country. In the space of three years, sorcerers destroyed two continents. Everyone decided to make their power play at once. They called dragons up out of the earth and set them killing. The Flame Plague moved from town to town. Entire villages went up like candles. Millions died, and the earth itself was charred and burned, magic stripped from it. Some fought with elementals, and others with summoned winds and fogs, but others with poisoned magic."

She pours herself more wine. Christina's skin is paler than usual, but the lantern light in the room gleams on it as though it were flower petals.

"And you were here…" Christina prompts.

"I was here in the islands, preparing to go. I heard that Britomart had blundered into someone else's trap and was dying of it. I brought her down. The magic is clean here, and there are serendipities and artifacts. I hoped to heal her."

"But that hasn't happened."

The wine is mulled with cinnamon and clove and sugar that has not completely dissolved, a gritty sweet residue at the cup's bottom.

"No," she says. "That hasn't happened."

Christina smuggles Laurana onto her ship while it's at harbor. She and three other sailors are supposed to be watching it. Laurana sits with them drinking shots of rum until the yellow moon swings itself up over the prow, its face broad and grinning as a baby's. It reminds her of Britomart and her tears well up. She savors the moment, for magic removes almost all capacity to weep.

She nudges Christina and points to the distant reef. Out on the rocks, mermaids cluster, fishy eyes shining in the moonlight, fleshy gills pulsing like tidepool creatures shuttered close by the light. She kisses Christina as they watch.

Eventually, the two climb into Christina's bunk for frantic, slippery, drunken lovemaking, careful of the still healing arm.

She leaves in the small hours, past the stares of the mermaids. It is still planting season and the golems work day and night.

When she first came to the island she tried yellow-flowered sea-island cotton. Then indigo and ginger. With the arrival from the Mage's College of Tabat of schematics for three-roller mills and copper furnace pots, sugar cane has become the crop of choice. Her workers perform the labor that must be undertaken day and night when the cane is ready to harvested and transmuted into sugar and molasses. She makes rum too, and ships barrels of it along with the molasses casks and thick cones of molded muscovado sugar to Sant Tigres, which consumes or trades all she can supply.

Most sorcerers are not strong enough to animate so many golems. She has the largest plantation in this area. Others, though, have followed her lead, although on a smaller scale. It took decades for them to realize how steadily she was making money, despite the depredations of the Duchy merchants or the pirates they paid to disrupt the western shipping trade.

She had been to the Old Continent before all the trouble, two years learning science at a school, where she had met Britomart, who was an actual princess as well as a sorceress. She had been centuries old when she met Britomart but she had dared to hope that here was her soul mate, the person who would stay by her side over all the centuries to come.

But in the end, she wanted to return to her island, full of new techniques and machineries that she thought would improve the yield. Rotating fields and planting those lying fallow with clover, to be plowed into the soil to enrich it for planting. Plans for a windmill to be built to the south-east, facing into the wind channeled through the mountains, with sails made of wooden frames tied with canvas. Lenses placed together that allowed one to observe the phases of heaven and the moons that surrounded other planets, and the accompanying elegant Copernican theories to explain their movements.

She swore to Britomart that she would return by the next rainy season and she kept her promise.

But by then, the trap had been sprung and Britomart had begun to rot away, victim of a magic left by a man who had died two weeks previously.

"You're ready to be rid of me," Britomart says.

"Of course not."

"It's true, you are!"

She goes about the room, conjuring breezes and positioning them to blow across the bed's expanse.

"You are," Britomart whispers. "I would be."

Two breezes collide at the center of the bed. Britomart wants it cold, ever colder. It slows the decay, perhaps. Laurana isn't sure of that either.

Outside she sees that the golems are nearly done with the south-east field. One more to go after that. She glances over the building, tallying up the things to be done. Roof. Trimming back the bushes. Exercising the horse she had thought Britomart would ride.

Half a mile away is the beach shore. Her skiff is pulled up there, tied to a rock. Standing beside it, she can see the smudge of Sant Tigres on the horizon.

She is so tired that she aches to her bones. Somewhere deep inside her, she is aware, there is an endless well of sorrow, but she is simply too weary to pay it any mind. It is one of the peculiarities of mages that they can compartmentalize themselves, and put away emotions to never be touched again.

She does this now, rousing herself, and prepares to go on. She has a pact with the universe, which told her long ago when she became a sorceress: *nothing will be asked that cannot be endured.* So she soldiers on like her workers, marching through the days.

She is still tired a week later.

"Go to her," Britomart says. "I don't care. You don't have much time with her."

"I have even less with you," Laurana says, but Britomart still turns away.

It is harvesting season's end. Outside in the evening, some of the golems are in the boiling house, where three boilers sit over the furnace, cooking the sugar cane sap. The syrup passes from boiler to boiler until in the last it begins to crystallize into muscovado. Two golems pack it into clay sugar molds and set the molds in the distillery so the molasses will drain away.

In the distillery, more golems walk across the mortar and cobble floor in which copper cauldrons are set for molasses collection, undulating channels feeding them the liquid.

They mix cane juice into the brew before casking it. In a few months, it will be distilled into fiery, raw rum and sold to the taverns in the pirate city.

She goes and fetches her notebook and sits in the room with Britomart, her pen scratching away to record the day's labors, the number of rows harvested, and making out a list of necessities for her next trip to Sant Tigres. She estimates two thousand pounds of sugar this year, three hundred casks of molasses, and another two hundred of rum. Recently she received word that the sorcerer Carnuba, whose plantation is three days south, renovated his sugar mill to process lime juice. Lime juice is an excellent scurvy preventative, and much in demand—she wonders how long it would take a newly planted grove to fruit. Her pen dances across the page, calculating raw material costs and the best forms of transportation.

"Is she pretty?" Britomart asks. Her face is still turned away.

Laurana considers. "Yes," she says.

"As pretty as I was?"

The anguish in the whisper forces Laurana put down her pen. She takes Britomart's hands in hers. They are untouched by the disease, the nails sleek and shiny and well-groomed. Hands like the necks of swans, or white doves arcing over the gleam of water.

"Never that pretty," she says.

The next morning Laurana goes through the room, touching each charm to stillness until the lace curtains no longer flutter. Until there is no sound in the room except her own breathing and the warbling calls of the deathbirds clustering among the blossoms of the bougainvillea tree outside.

She hears a fluttering from her room, a pigeon that has joined the dozen others on the windowsill, but she ignores it, as she ignored the earlier arrivals. She sits beside the bed, listening, listening. But the figure on the bed does not take another breath, no matter how long she listens.

All through that day, the golems labor boiling sugar. Jeanette brings her lemonade and the new girl, Madeleine, has made biscuits. She drinks the sweet liquid and looks at the dusty wallpaper. The thought of changing it stuns her with the energy it would require. She will sit here, she thinks, until she dies, and dust will collect on her and the wallpaper alike.

Still, when dinner-time comes she goes downstairs and under Tante Isabelle's watchful eye, she pushes some food around on her plate.

Daniel cannot help but be a little thankful that Britomart is dead, she thinks. He was the one who emptied her chamber pot and endured her abuse when she set him to fetching and carrying. The thought makes her speak sharply to him as he serves the chowder the new girl has made. He looks bewildered by her tone and slinks away. She regrets the moment as soon as it is passed but has no reason for calling him back.

Upstairs the ranks of the pigeons have swollen by two or three more. She lies on her bed, fully clothed, and stares at the ceiling.

The next morning she takes two golems from their labors to carry Britomart's body for her. They dig the grave on a high slope of the mountain, overlooking the bay. It is a fine view, she thinks. One Britomart would have liked.

When they have finished, she stands with her palms turned upwards to the sky, calling clouds to come seething on the wind. They collect, darkening like burning sugar. When they are at the perfect, furious boil, she brings lightning down from them to smash the stone that stands over the grave. She does it over and over again, carving Britomart's name in deep and angry, blackened letters.

At home she goes to lie in bed again.

One by one, the golems grind to a stop at their labors, and the sap boils over in thick black smoke. They stand wherever their energy gave out, but all manage in their last moments to bring their limbs in towards their torsos, standing like stalks of stillness.

It may be the smoke that draws Christina. She arrives, knocks on the door, and comes inside, brushing past the servants. Without knowing the house, she manages to come upstairs and to Laurana's bedroom.

Laurana does not move, does not look over at the door.

Christina comes to the bed and lies down beside the sorceress. She looks around at the bedroom, at the string of shells hanging on the wall, but says nothing. She strokes Laurana's ivory hair with a soft hand until the tears begin.

Outside the golems grind to life again as the rain starts. They collect the burned vats and trundle them away. They cask the most recent rum and set the casks on wooden racks to ferment. They put the plantation into order, and finish the last of their labors. Then as the light of day fades, muffled by the steady rain, they arrange themselves again, closing themselves away, readying for tomorrow.

A Key Decides Its Destiny

"A Key Decides Its Destiny" was written in response to the challenge posed by Say's *"What's the Combination?" themed issue in the winter of 2005. It is set a few hundred years ago on the Old Continent, in Tabat's world. It started with the image of the magician making his key and thinking about what a key is for. Superimposed over the creation of the key and its fate is a love story of sorts, albeit one that only exists in the apprentice's mind.*

Because Solon DesCant was the greatest enchanter of his time, which spanned centuries, Lily had chosen him for a teacher despite the peril. He had produced wonders for the Duke of Tabat, performed miracles for the Emperor, and even vanished mysteriously for a decade, returning to claim he had undertaken certain unpalatable tasks for the demons of S'Keral.

Every fifty years Solon took an apprentice, whose work was to straighten the shelves of his workroom, to fetch and carry, cook and clean, tend his chickens, and run those errands beneath the magician's dignity. In return he taught the apprentice the ins and outs of enchanting and the secrets he had spent his life discovering. And sometime in the forty-ninth year, Solon would kill the apprentice before they could carry his secrets out into the world. Two had escaped this fate by fleeing before that year arrived. But the final year was the year of true knowledge and many had let their thirst for secrets keep them there until it was too late and they found death in one of the ingenious poisons of which Solon was master.

Today's creation was a minor magic. He made the key out of cats' whiskers braided together and hardened with the chill from a heart that had never known love. He couldn't resist embellishment so he carved roses from mouse bone and attached the beads on strands of lignum vitae. Handling it required care—whisker tips protruded along its length like tiny thorns and a drop of blood swelled on his finger where one pricked him. The manticores stuffed and mounted on the walls of his workroom watched him with glassy eyes as he held it up.

"Is that it?" Lily asked from the doorway. He nodded, setting the key down on the table so they both could study it. She tucked her hands behind her back as she looked at it like a child examining a fragile heirloom, afraid of breaking it.

"What will it unlock?"

He shrugged. "Enchanted keys choose what they will unlock. But I've made this for a witch, who hopes to persuade it to the destiny she prefers." He wrapped the key in a length of velvet before handing it to the apprentice. "Lily, you'll take this to her. There will be no payment; I'll ask her for a favor in due time."

She chewed her lip at the thought, looking down at the bundle.

"You'll have to learn to deal with witches at some point," he said. He reached for an alembic and pulled it in front of him, readying his next experiment. "It might as well be now."

"Is there anything I need to know beforehand?" she asked.

"Don't look in her eyes and be polite above all else. Witches take offense very easily."

Lily went down the winding stone stairs. The thought of delivering to the witch made her dizzy with nerves—witches are uncanny sorts and dangerous to cross. Girding herself with charms and amulets to fortify her courage, she slung a cloak around her shoulders, dark as night, soft as a smile, and went down the road towards the Thornwoods. She hunted up and down the paths, stepping right and left, walking deosil rather than risk the bad luck of widdershins, and trying to ignore the boggarts that hunted through the branches, watching her with sly eyes like cracks of light in a darkened room.

The key rested heavily in her pocket. A key that could open any door if it were persuaded. It burned in her mind like Magnesia Alba, which ignites hot and white when exposed to the air.

The witch lived in a cavern. Two great beasts crouched on either side of its entrance, mawed like panthers, tailed like scorpions. The apprentice did not look at them directly but she could feel their eyes like flames against her back as she walked down into the darkness.

The air was cold on her face and the plink of falling moisture echoed in the distance. Once something small and leathery-winged flapped past but she pressed on.

Up ahead an archway held the warmth of torchlight and through it was the witch's chamber, unexpectedly cheerful. Rugs woven in scarlet and purple covered the rocky floor, swallowing Lily's footsteps. The witch sat at a table, laying down cards made of stiff paper and painted in elaborate detail, colored with powdered lapis lazuli and gold leaf.

The witch did not look up until the last card had been laid down. Then finally she raised her gaze.

"You're new," she said. "Got you running errands, does he?"

"I've brought the key you wanted made."

"Have you now? Let me see it."

A touch of reluctance slowing her movements, Lily put the velvet bundle in the witch's hands. She unwrapped it like a long-awaited present, her eyes gleaming with avarice.

"I'll lift a curse with this," she gloated, fondling the haft and ignoring its tiny thorns. She frowned as it twisted in her grasp. "What's this? This key has already decided its purpose—one that is no good to me."

"I brought it straight from Solon's hands," Lily said, bewildered.

Drawing back her arm, the witch flung the key in Lily's direction. It glanced across her cheek, drawing blood as it hit and fell without a sound to the carpet. "Take it back and tell Solon I demand a new one within the next century."

Shaking with fear, Lily picked up the key and put it back in her pocket. She moved to retrieve the scrap of velvet but the witch motioned her away. "Be off and be glad I don't set the blood in your veins to boiling! It's you I blame for the key's decision."

The trip back through the corridors seemed longer than it had going down but at last she saw the light of the entrance and made her way out. A beast snapped at her, rending her cloak, but she hurried on.

Back at the tower she hesitated at the foot of the stairs. Solon's temper was slow to rise but fierce as a dragon's blaze when awakened. She wavered on the bottom step, slipping a hand into her pocket. The thorns stung her and she thought, *Why bring pain upon myself now? He won't know until he asks the witch for a favor, and that may be centuries away.* She turned and went to the workroom to grind sulfur crystals into the fine powder that summoning spells demand. Distracted by the demands of constructing a matrix for water elementals, Solon never asked about her errand.

Days passed and the key remained in her pocket. At night she puzzled over what its purpose might be—if she and Solon were the only people who had touched it before the witch then it must be shaped to the desires of one or the other of them. *If it is Solon's, it could be anything,* she thought, *but after all he took precautions and great care in shaping it. He must, after all, know the best way to prevent such things.*

Perhaps it's my desire that gave it purpose, she thought. *The witch did say she blamed me. Perhaps it is the key to Solon's heart.* She fell into daydreams of romance where Solon declared his passion and vowed to lay the world at her feet, where he slew hippogriffs and kings for her and built a castle of rose-colored crystal on the slopes of Berzul, the dwarf-infested mountain that is the tallest in the world.

Yes, he'll love me, she thought. *He will be unable to kill the woman he loves.* She began to watch him for signs of passion: sighs or glances, or uncharacteristic lapses into poetry. Sometimes she thought she glimpsed warmth in his eyes as he demonstrated how to dissect a basilisk and preserve its delicate, fan-shaped heart or as he leaned over her to show the steady back and forth of the pestle necessary to produce a diamond powder as fine as flour, glittering particles floating in the air around the mortar, falling onto the sheet of parchment Solon had placed on the table to catch them.

But there was nothing certain as the years passed and finally Lily thought, *He's waiting until I am no longer his apprentice, but his equal, before he approaches me. How just of him! For he knows that otherwise I'd be distracted from my learning.*

And learn she did.

In the twentieth year of her apprenticeship, she learned to tie time in a loop to keep herself from aging; in the twenty-fifth year, how to weave moonlight and sunlight together in a rope that neither creatures of the day nor creatures of the night could escape. In the thirtieth year, Solon showed her how to make a saddle that could sit any steed, from dragon to crocodile, and more. At night the knowledge dancing in her head kept her from sleeping and she took to midnight walks around the tower roof, walking in circles until the cloud of facts settled, sifting into layer upon layer in her mind.

In the fortieth year she became aware that Solon watched her covertly, gazing when he thought she would not notice. It confirmed her hopes and she took to wearing fripperies and furbelows, making sure her shirt fit snugly, and putting belladonna in her eyes to make them shine.

As the forty-ninth year approached, Solon taught her more and more and praised her for her quickness. "No apprentice has ever taken to things so swiftly," he told her and she glowed with happiness.

The beginning of the year came and went. Lily took simple precautions such as checking her food and drink with a unicorn's horn because she did not want Solon to think her stupid or that she knew his secret love. The moment that he announced it would be all the sweeter if he thought she did not know. She imagined it over and over again, wondering how he would choose to tell her, picturing his handsome face creased with worry that she might not reciprocate. She was pleased to see that he took over more of the work that she had previously performed, such as preparing his morning meal and doing his laundry. *Getting used for the rearrangement of the household when I become his wife,* she thought.

On a day that dawned clear and bright Solon asked her into his workroom. *Now,* she thought, *he'll tell me now.* He stood framed by the sunlight coming in the window, gazing at her. She gathered her skirts and took a chair.

"I regret to tell you," Solon said, still looking at her, "that you will be dead by tomorrow. The laundry soap has had a poison in it for the last two weeks—I calculated it to match your body weight and allow it to cumulate into a dose sufficient to end your apprenticeship at midnight. Give or take a half hour."

She looked at him, horrified. Her fingers played over the key in her pocket. "But you love me," she protested.

He looked surprised. "Dear child, where would you have gotten that idea? I am sworn to celibacy for the sake of my art."

The thorns on the key pricked and stung her but they were not the source of the blood warm tears rolling down her face. She felt the key stir beneath her touch and finally realized its purpose.

And when she plunged it into his heart, piercing it as love could not, he was as surprised as she had been, dying with a startled look fixed on his lean and timeless face.

She went downstairs and put her things in order, tidying the shelves and sweeping the floor one last time. She dusted the tall glass jars of powders and set the flock of chickens loose, shooing them away. Then she went to sit on the tower roof, listening to the owl's call, and waited for midnight to arrive.

The Towering Monarch
of His Mighty Race

I was doing some freelance writing that involved researching P.T. Barnum's acquisition of Jumbo the elephant. The actual story was too fascinating not to get used in a piece of speculative fiction.

This story originally appeared in Orson Scott Card's Intergalactic Medicine Show. *I had not thought it particularly experimental, particularly for a genre story, but some readers found the idea of writing from an elephant's POV too radical for them. Personally, I think we need* more *stories from non-human POVs.*

It was a peanut butter jar, not even a brand name but generic, the two and a half pound size, as big as a lantern. Oily dust roiled inside.

The woman dressed in gray picked the jar up and held it between her large flat hands. There was something reflexive about the gesture, as though her mind were very far away.

The boy said "Those are Jumbo's ashes."

Her eyes returned to regard him dispassionately. It was an old look, a look that had been weighing the universe for many years now and found it lacking.

"Jumbo," she said in a leaden voice.

He pushed on, fighting his way against her indifference, wanting to see her thrill and liven, if only he found the right fact.

"There was a fire in 1975, here in Barnum Hall, and Jumbo, who was the Tufts university mascot by then, burned up. They saved the ashes in that jar."

She turned it over, watching the flakes stir.

"Of course, he was stuffed then," he added. "The bones are in the Smithsonian. His keeper, Matthew Scott, donated them."

For the first time her gaze sharpened, though not to the degree he wanted. "Is Scott still alive?"

"No," he said. "He died in 1914. In an almshouse. How could he still be alive?"

She turned the jar with slow deliberation, letting the contents tumble once, twice, three times. "Stranger things have happened."

There wasn't anything Jumbo was afraid of but the big cats, even years and years later, when he was much too big for them to terrorize him. The wind would shift and bring him the tigers' musty reek and his eyes would roll while Matthew laughed and thumped him on the side, calling him a big baby.

But that wasn't true. He hadn't been afraid of any number of things that were worse than lions. Even the swaying of the netting holding him hadn't frightened him as it hoisted him aboard the ship among the gulls' harsh screams, in a dazzle of blinding light that left his eyes red and weeping and unable to see until much later in the hold's darkness, smelling like hay and saltwater.

The thing he remembered best from those first captive days was the hunger. They had lowered him into a pit too deep for him to free himself. He searched the ground over and over again, ravenous. He had been used to constant grazing, being able to snatch a trunkful of grass or leaves as he wanted. But here they did not feed him, and his bulk, even at less than a year old, demanded fuel.

A narrow ledge spiraled down along the side, too narrow for him to climb. He trumpeted his anger, his fear as a face peered down at him from one side before saying something to another face. He had been here two days now, and starvation weakened him. When the man came down the ledge, he could not rise, despite the grain smell. The man came nearer and he tried again to stand, but could not. The hands ran over him, an unthinkable touch that gradually became no more bothersome than a tick-bird picking parasites from his skin. Reluctantly at first, he let the man feed him handfuls of mash from the bucket, tasting of dust and metal, becoming more eager as the strength returned.

For a while the man lived with him, slept by his side, and he became used to him. Even acquired a fondness for him. But no matter how much food the man brought him, it was never enough, and the hunger ate at him during the nights, making him fretful and weak.

Later Matthew had found him in the Paris Zoo, huddled with Alice. *Puniest elephant I've ever seen*, Matthew said, tipping his head back to consider him, *think he can make it to London?* The Frenchman shook his head, *Mais non.*

P.T. Barnum liked things big. Say that, he told the reporters in his mind, rehearsing the spiel mentally, "P.T. Barnum likes things big. Why, right now, he's chasing after the world's largest elephant, Jumbo, seven tons and eleven and a half feet tall!"

Right now he stood in the offices of the London Zoological Society. He'd been in these sorts of places, smelling of formaldehyde and dusty feathers. He'd bought the Fiji mermaid from such a place, knowing when he saw the nappy black hair, the scaly lower half, that here he had a moneymaker.

"You want to buy him as a sideshow," Abraham Bartlett said politely. He was a wispy, fine-haired man with a heavily waxed mustache and tendrils of hair protruding from his ears, which Barnum stared at in fascination.

"A sideshow? No—for the circus, my circus!" Barnum said. "I'm willing to pay you $10,000 for him!"

The silence in the room changed to a new and waiting quality as the two Englishmen exchanged glances.

"No, I'm afraid not," Bartlett said with genuine regret in his tone. "Jumbo is one of the greatest attractions here. Hundreds of thousands of children have ridden on him over the last fifteen years."

On the way out of the Zoo, Barnum ducked through the East Tunnel and made his way to the Elephant and Rhino Pavilion. Inside, he stopped and stared at Jumbo. "There's got to be a way," he thought.

Clusters of children were lined up to ride the elephant, who stood beside his keeper. Three little girls were arranged in graduated height with their nanny, each dressed in blue with red bows riding their hips and matching bows perched like butterflies on their hats. One held up her hands to Jumbo and the elephant's trunk explored them for the peanuts she held. Her face shone with joy.

"I will have you," Barnum mused. "P.T. Barnum doesn't take no for an answer." He imagined his friend Charles, the world's smallest man, in the place of the child the keeper was lifting up. The biggest and the smallest together in one ring and himself in the background proclaiming, "General Tom Thumb and Jumbo!"

"Mr. Barnum," a voice said beside him. It spoke in English, but the accent was indefinable, a rumble beneath the words like a distant echo of thunder.

"You have the advantage of me, madam," he said, turning.

"You seem entranced by the elephant." She was a small woman, dressed all in gray, the lustrous, colorless cloth giving her a pigeon's drab appearance. "Surely you have seen one before?"

He laughed. "Hundreds!" he said. "I used one to plow my farm in Bridgeport."

"As advertisement, I know," she said.

"Every agricultural society in the States wrote to me, asking if the elephant was a profitable agricultural animal."

"And was it?"

He chuckled. "No. One eats up the value of his head, trunk, and body each year, not to mention that he can't work at all in cold weather. Tell me, why are you so interested in elephants?"

She looked at Jumbo. "In Africa, the elephant hunters leave piles of corpses, only the tusks removed," she said. "It is a savage, barbaric sight. Have you ever witnessed elephants mourning? They speak their sorrow in sounds too low for the human ear to comprehend, but you can feel it vibrating in the ground beneath your feet. They gather around the corpses, walking in circles and mourning. They throw handfuls of straw and grass upon the corpse as though trying to shield themselves from the sight."

"A pity," Barnum said.

"More than that. An atrocity. If more people knew elephants as something other than distant monsters, perhaps the public outcry would make the trade cease."

"So you are their advocate."

"After a fashion."

He sighed, following her gaze. "Jumbo here is no ordinary elephant. The largest of his kind. What a draw he would be!"

"And yet you speak as though you cannot have him, Mr. Barnum."

"I will have my way. It's only a matter of time."

"The curators will be reluctant to part with him. So vast a creature and yet so gentle."

Her voice gave the last word a lingering caress.

"Gentle, yes," Barnum said. An idea flickered in his mind.

After Lord Corcoran's death, Matthew Scott had come to the London Zoological Society along with the animal collection the Lord had left to that Institution, elands to cheetahs, Amazonian parrots, and a lone pink-headed duck.

"I'm just a jumped-up ostler," he'd say when drinking. "My fellas just look a lil' more unusual than most." At first he'd balked—the animals he cared for ate better than any member of his family, which seemed obscene. But with time, he'd become proud of the variety of animals he'd nursed through illnesses or helped birth their scaled or spotted offspring. When the directors sent him to Paris to scour the zoos there for possible additions, he'd been pleased.

He wouldn't have found the elephant without the woman, though. He'd been in the Champs Élysées when she approached him. At first he'd reckoned her for a whore, but her dress was muted, unlike that of the tarts who seemed to vie with each to see who could more closely resemble the brightly-plumaged macaw that he'd found in one zoo. Surely no decent woman would accost a man in order to speak to him.

"You might be interested in the Jardin des Plantes," she said. Her English was perfect.

"Eh, Miss?" he said.

"The Jardin des Plantes," she repeated. Her eyes were brown and fluid as a gazelle's, but he could not determine her age. She turned away but he caught at her shoulder.

"Miss, how did you know?" he began.

"I saw you at the Parc Floral and overheard your conversation with the curator about their peacocks," she said.

"What will I find at the Jardin des Plantes?" he said.

"Two elephants," she said. "Young ones. They're very ill."

He frowned. "Ill from what?"

"The climate. Lack of care. Improper diet."

"What makes you think I can save them?"

"You know elephants," she said.

The two young elephants, Jumbo and Alice, were indeed ill. Matthew looked into the long-lashed eye as big as his clenched fist and saw despair there. He laid his palm flat across the warm gray hide.

"Hang on," he said. "I'll get you out." The zoo tried to bargain with him, but he pointed out that the two might not even survive the journey and that in that light his offer of a full-grown Indian rhinoceros in trade was quite generous. He suspected the curators had miscalculated how much an elephant could consume. Going to the market, he paid for a cart of hay and brought it back to the Jardin to feed the pair. He bought a bushel of peaches as well and fed them to Alice and Jumbo in alternating handfuls, smelling the sweet pulp as the elephants plucked the fruit from his fingers.

Jumbo wouldn't have done it, but when the man offered him the handful of peanuts, he didn't realize the trick until he felt the terrible burning in his trunk. He cried out and the children ran, screaming as shrill as gulls, as he reared back on his legs, trying to find the source of the red pepper. Matthew was there between him and the tormentor and he could not find him with all the burning, as though the world of smells had gone away and he was forced to rely on his own weak eyes. He turned to the water tun, drinking with frantic need, but the burning barely ceased, and he trumpeted angrily again.

It was hard for Barnum to keep from grinning whe he signed the papers in the Zoo's office. Sunlight slanted across the page as he finished the bold loops of his signature and blotted it. He'd celebrate at the Madagascar Hotel tonight, drink champagne with the Swedish Nightingale, Jenny Lind, who'd come to see him. As he'd suspected, the directors were worried at Jumbo's temper tantrums, which Barnum had paid two sub-zookeepers to provoke by every method they knew. The pepper had been the most effective.

"You will be taking him back to America as soon as possible?" Bartlett asked.

"Oh, I reckon not," Barnum said. "Figured I'd leave him here long enough to say goodbye to you Brits." He smiled and tipped his hat to Bartlett.

Within the week the journalists he'd paid off had done their work. "England to Lose National Treasure!" one said. Another demanded, "Are We Shipping Our Largest Asset to America?" More newspapermen, who'd missed the original story, were waiting for him as he exited the Regent's Park Hotel, and he stopped despite the rain's fine drizzle to address them, standing back on his heels with his thumbs in his suspenders, surveying the crowd craning to hear him against the hubbub of passing carriages and foot traffic. The English didn't have a chance against good old American scheming.

"Is it true the Prince of Wales himself asked you to reconsider taking Jumbo?" a tall man in a porkpie hat asked, pen poised over his notebook.

"Well," he drawled. "His Majesty and I are old friends from my other tours. He did bring it up, but I said nosir, a deal's a deal."

"Visitors to the London Zoo have tripled," another said. "All saying goodbye to Jumbo. Do you have any message for the children pleading with you to leave Jumbo here in England?"

"They're welcome to come to the U.S. of A. and see their pal there. He's not a born British citizen, so maybe the fellow will like a little travel," Barnum said.

"When are you returning to America?"

"I'm setting sail tomorrow, actually."

"With Jumbo?"

"No," Barnum said. He refrained from adding "with all this publicity he's generating I'd be crazy to" but the thought had crossed his mind.

He would have stayed to talk to them longer, but he wanted to pick up presents for his wife Nancy at Harrod's. He strolled the aisles, finding Jumbo dolls, mugs, tin banks, booklets, everything he could have thought up himself and more, and it brought a constant smile to his lips, even when the salesclerk recognized him as the man taking Jumbo away and charged him twice what he should have for a stuffed elephant waving the Union Jack in its trunk.

Jumbo knew what the crate was as they rolled it into his yard. It smelled of oak and iron and the canvas padding that lined it. Big enough to hold him, the largest elephant in the world. He'd smelled that smell before on his trip to Paris, and then later to England. He remembered the water's feel underneath him, and the nausea that came as unwelcome accompaniment to the hunger, as though they were alternating, angry monkeys on either side refusing to let him rest.

He flapped his ears, warning them, but they continued to urge him towards the crate. He lay down, flopping onto his side with a grunt. Let them try to get him up. He wouldn't go.

TELEGRAM FROM GEORGE COURO, AGENT FOR PHINEAS T. BARNUM, MARCH 1ST, 1882:
JUMBO IS LYING IN THE GARDEN STOP WIL NOT GET IN CRATE STOP PLEASE ADVISE STOP

TELEGRAM FROM PHINEAS T. BARNUM TO GEORGE COURO, MARCH 1ST:
LET HIM LIE THERE A WEEK IF HE WANTS STOP BEST ADVERTISEMENT IN THE WORLD STOP

Couro crumpled the telegram in his hand and threw it to the ground. All very well for Barnum to say such things, but he didn't have Parliament and the Queen ragging on him, nor had he been threatened with imprisonment if any force was used to remove Jumbo. He went to the window to look out across Regent's Park towards the Zoo's distant blur. Overhead, clouds like mottled lead filled the gray sky.

TELEGRAM FROM PHILLIP HARBOTTLE, EDITOR OF THE LONDON DAILY TELEGRAPH, MARCH 3RD, 1882:
BRITISH PUBLIC DEMANDS JUMBO STOP WE ARE AUTHORIZED TO REQUEST YOU NAME YOUR PRICE STOP

TELEGRAM FROM PHINEAS T. BARNUM TO PHILLIP HARBOTTLE, MARCH 4TH, 1882:
HUNDRED THOUSAND POUNDS WOULD BE NO INDUCEMENT TO CANCEL PURCHASE STOP SINCERELY PHINEAS TAYLOR BARNUM.

Matthew didn't trust this Barnum fellow. Slick American, and by all accounts a flim-flam man. There was a story circulating about an earlier visit to Europe when Barnum had gone to see the antiquities at Warwick Castle. He'd had the gall to ask the curator how much he'd sell the antiquities for. When the man declined, Barnum said, "I'll have them duplicated for My Museum, so that Americans can see them without coming here, and bust up your show that way." Was this the right person for Matthew Scott, a man of good character even if he was just a jumped-up ostler, to associate with?

He went out into the Pavilion. The transportation crate loomed in the middle and off to one side was Jumbo's bulk. The elephant stirred as he approached, and the trunk caressed his face when he stooped.

"Look, old man, this won't do," he said. He sat down beside the vast head, the straw crinkling below him. Overhead through the skylight, the night stars were bright as diamonds. He leaned back against the knobbed plane of the top of Jumbo's head, and the elephant gave a low soft rumble of pleasure at the contact.

"You can't lie here forever," he said. The elephant rumbled again. Matthew sighed.

"Barnum's offering me five times my wages here to travel with you," he said. "America. It's a frightening thought, but an alluring one. I'd have to leave the other elephants here. Alice, for one."

He could hear the elephant's breathing in the darkness, a great rush of straw-scented air, regular and rhythmic.

"You're my success story, you know," he went on. "The largest elephant in the world. Who would have imagined a sickly little thing like you turning into that?"

He laid his arm along the elephant's side, exploring the deeply grooved skin. To the south, a hyena's whiny warble sounded from their enclosure.

"I'll do it," he said. And sighed.

He didn't want to, but with Matthew urging him on Jumbo entered the crate, trumpeting once to show his indignation before he went in. Sixteen matched Percheons pulled the cage through the streets towards the docks. Word of Jumbo's departure had spread, and thousands lined the streets, following the team. Matthew stared forward, ignoring the crying children.

The thirteen-ton crate was swung aboard their freighter, the *Assyrian Monarch*. Crowds filled the docks. From his vantage point, Matthew could see a blond five year old whose father had lifted her onto his shoulders to see. Tears glinted on her face but she waved a small flag in her hand, imprinted with the elephant's outline. Gulls circled overhead, watching for stray food, and two artists stood where they could see it all, trying to catch the scene on sketchpads.

Barnum, standing beside Matthew as they watched the crate's progress onto the ship, rubbed his hands together.

"Worth every penny," he said. "You know they charged me for the freight they can't ship because of Jumbo? And steerage passage for 200 emigrants. I'm in the wrong business. But it's all advertising. There's a banquet on board tonight and I expect you there."

"I want to settle him down," Matthew said.

"Sure, sure, see him settled. I sent up fruit for him. And a bushel of candies. I hear he has quite the sweet tooth. But come to the banquet. All sorts of lords and ladies there, all to say goodbye to him. I sent a tux along to your quarters."

"I won't know how to act," Matthew said in a sullen tone.

Barnum clapped him on the shoulder. "You'll do fine."

Despite his fears, Matthew was able to take to the sidelines during the banquet. At the head table with the Captain and the scowling Prince of Wales, Barnum led toast after toast, drunk in the best French champagne. "To Jumbo," he cried, ignoring the English nobility's dark looks.

Beside him, a woman said, "Is he well? Are his quarters sufficient?"

He turned and recognized her, again in her gray dress. A pearl necklace rested around her throat, surprisingly opulent against her olive skin.

"You again," he said. He was a little tipsy from the unaccustomed drinking. "Are you traveling with us?"

"Yes," she said.

"Come tomorrow and I'll show him to you."

"I'd like that."

"Tell me your name this time."

"Miss Laxmi."

There was plenty of food, and a boy who shoveled his droppings as fast as they fell. Despite the swaying deck beneath Jumbo's feet, he did not feel queasy this time. He ate the sugary candies delicately, one by one, so small he almost could not taste them.

When he smelled Matthew, he rumbled his greeting.

"Got a friend," Matthew said, producing a handful of peanuts. Jumbo began to alternate between them and candies.

The woman touched his side near his foreleg. "So big," she said. "A magnificent ambassador for his race." She smelled comforting, like grass and hay in the sun.

"Careful," Matthew said. "I'll get jealous."

"Of me or him?"

As she touched his skin, Jumbo raised his head, looking at her. His trunk touched the side of her face in return and she half-closed her eyes. An odd tension filled the hold, lingering in the air. As Matthew watched, the massive elephant slowly bent his legs, kneeling down as though bowing before her. Smiling, she whispered something.

"I'll be damned," Matthew said. "I never taught him that trick."

Her hand lingered on the wrinkled skin, each fold thick enough to swallow her slender finger. "Perhaps he is preparing for life as a performer," she said, her voice low and husky with a sorrow Matthew did not understand.

Later, Matthew and the woman sat together on the freighter's rear deck, watching the trail from the ship, moonlight gleaming on the frothy waves.

"Twenty years I've been with that elephant," Matthew said. He'd liberated a bottle of Barnum's champagne. The cork came away with a pop and spray and he offered it to her. She took a sip and laughed.

"It's like drinking fizz," she said.

He chuckled at her. "You can't tell me you've never drunk champagne before."

"I haven't," she said. "Really."

He loved the way the light played on her dark hair. "Laxmi. That's not a European name."

"You may call me Gaja, if you like," she said. "And no, it's Indian."

He studied her. As though the words had evoked it, he saw the subtle but apparent exotic cast to her face, the almost slant of her eyes. He took another drink to give himself time to think.

"That bothers you," she said.

"No," he said. "No, it doesn't."

She shrugged. "No matter," she said. "This can only happen here, between worlds."

"What do you mean?"

"The Old World and the New. Right now we're in neither."

"I don't know what you mean," he said helplessly.

She looked out across the water, watching the moonlight drifting on the waves. "Imagine there was once a goddess," she said. "The world is changing, and no one believed in her anymore. Which was a relief, actually. No one asking to win at dice or father sons or find gold hidden beneath their doorstep.

"But the goddess found herself looking at the humans in another light. She found that they had taken one of her favored creatures and made it an animal like any other, to be slaughtered for goods to sell."

Her dark eyes regarded him. "For a god and a mortal to touch is perilous in any world. Do you understand now why we have so little time?"

She was pulling his leg, he figured. Flimflamming like Barnum. He drew her close and tilted her face to his. "Then we should make the most of it," he said and kissed her.

Thousands met the ship when they arrived on Easter Sunday. April in New York didn't seem that different from London. The sun shone in a watery blue sky, and danced on the water as the ponderous crate swung ashore. Cheers went up as Barnum ceremoniously swung open the massive door and when Matthew led Jumbo out, a shout came from the crowd. Children waved pennants, each printed with Jumbo's likeness, or had stuffed elephants tucked under an arm. The air smelled like a circus—peanuts and popcorn vendors vied with men selling sausages or meat pies. Matthew looked for Gaja, but saw her nowhere. As though she had vanished.

"We're taking him to my Hippodrome Building," Barnum shouted in his ear over the crowd's clamor. "The circus opens there tonight. See the team of ponies pulling the steam calliope? Fall in behind them."

The buildings here seemed taller than London's, and there was a cold edge to the wind that blew through the scarlet coat Barnum had made him wear. Like London, the air was full of coal smoke and the smell of people living too close to one another. The parade moved along the street and the delighted faces made him feel better about the tears that had accompanied Jumbo's departure. He looked again for Gaja, but she was nowhere to be found. He didn't know that it would be years before he'd see her again.

Barnum stood in the center ring of the Hippodrome in a dazzle of torch light. Next year, he thought, he'd bring in that new invention of Edison's and make the inside of the tent shine as though it were daylight. To his left a tiger's angry scream rent the air. It was a windy night, and the canvas tent roared like a windjammer under full sail.

"Ladies and gentleman!" he shouted as the other rings stilled. "I direct your attention to the center ring! It is Barnum and Bailey's greatest pleasure to present to you one of the wonders of the world! I give you the towering monarch of his race, whose like the world will never see again! I give you...Jumbo!"

The elephant was bedecked in spangled harness, stepping slowly, enjoying the roar of applause as Matthew led him around the ring. The other circus elephants were lined up around the ring and at a signal, they backed onto their hind legs, sitting with their front legs up, and let out a unified trumpet of acclamation. In their center, the smallest elephant, Tom Thumb, knelt to stand on its head. Jumbo glowed in the light like a fairy tale figure, so brilliant and bedazzling that he took the crowd's breath away.

"That elephant cost me $30,000 all together, and every penny well-spent," Barnum gloated in his trailer as he thumbed through the receipts. "Pulled in $3,000 a day in the first three weeks. They've even named a town in Hardin County after him."

"He's a champ, all right," the accountant said, totting up figures.

"Drinks a bottle of beer every night with his keeper. I'm thinking about having a special mug made in his shape. It'd sell, all right, but the Temperance folks would pitch a fit. I'm having a special train car made for him, with his picture painted on the sides so whenever the train pulls into the station, the people will know to come."

The best thing about the circus was getting a chance to sit around with the other elephant keepers. Some of them had been in the business longer than Matthew. He liked the easy camaraderie, the friendship of men who knew how to figure out whether or not a tiger would take to flaming hoops, the ways to keep fleas from spreading, or the best method for lancing a boil on a baboon's ass.

Every Thursday was poker night, and they sat around the table playing with dog-eared cards and drinking beer and swapping stories.

"Used to have a little elephant, dainty as could be, named Siri," Joe D'Angelo said. The cigar in his mouth puffed, sending up blue smoke around his dark face, mounted with a beaklike nose. "You know what she'd do? Give her an apple or an orange and she'd put it on the ground, tap it dainty as you please with her foot, then pick what was left and rub it all through her hay, like she was flavoring it. What a sweetie she was—real little lady. Hit me with two cards."

"I had an elephant used to cry like a baby if he made a mistake," George Arstingstall said.

"Go on, I never seen an elephant cry."

"He did," George insisted, throwing his cards on the table. "I'll pass. Yell at him and there he'd go, crying away. Tears as big as a china cup."

"They're strange critters," Joe said. "Gotta admit them Indians, the real ones, are onto something when they worship them. They got a god called Garnish, got six arms and an elephant trunk. Got a straight."

"Beats my hand," Matthew admitted.

"All sorts of elephant mysteries," Joe continued. "I had a friend who said he'd met the Queen of the Elephants in human form. Walking around like you or me. Said you always knew her because she dressed all in gray. Your deal."

Thoughts of Gaja flickered across Matthew's mind as he shuffled the cards.

"What's she doing walking around then?" he said.

Joe shrugged. "Hey, I seen elephants do all sorts of things. Who says they think like you or me?"

Jumbo didn't mind the circus, although he still didn't like the smell of the tigers. Matthew knew it, and he always took care to make sure the big cats were safely stowed away, twenty cars up the line, before they boarded Jumbo's car. It was custom-built for him, painted crimson and gold, with double doors in the middle to let him enter.

He didn't feel hungry anymore. Whenever he was hungry, food was there.

"Gotta keep up your strength, you're the star of the show," Matthew said. He brought him fruit and hay, and handfuls of peanuts.

It was a good life. The children came and petted him, and Matthew would help him lift the bravest ones to his back, clinging there like fleas. At night Matthew slept in his stall with him, and would talk into the night, the small voice washing over him as he swayed into sleep.

"You can't go to Toronto," Gaja said.

"You show up after three years and your first words are, 'Don't go to Toronto?'" Matthew said. "Where have you been?"

She looked the same as ever. He'd swear it was the same dress.

"Walking up and down the earth," she said. "Does it matter?"

"I thought we had… I mean I thought we were."

"It was nice," Gaja said. "It was very nice. But I can't get attached."

"Attached, is that what you call it? Simple human decency would have meant saying goodbye, at least!"

"I'm telling you not to go to Toronto."

"But why?"

"I can't tell you."

Matthew laughed. "And I should go to that prick Barnum and say we can't go because some woman's got her knickers in a twist?"

She looked down. "Can't you just trust me?"

"Are you the Queen of the Elephants, that I should trust you?"

"Not the Queen," she said. "Just a goddess who saw the plight of the animals she loved."

"Not even the right kind of elephant, is he? African rather than Indian. You're insane!"

"Please," she begged. "They're all my children. Please. I thought if you loved me you'd listen and we could prevent it. You can't let it happen."

He turned away. "Go away, Miss Laxmi. I have no reason to listen to you."

Barnum was there the next day with a long thin skeleton of a man. "Wanted to introduce the two of you," he said. Matthew started to hold out his hand but Barnum said, "No, no! Him and Jumbo, I mean. This is Henry Ward. He's a taxidermist from Rochester. Stuffed all sorts of things for me. He wants to be the one to stuff Jumbo."

Ward was gazing up at the elephant, enraptured.

"Anything ever happens, we telegraph him immediately so he can save the skin and skeleton," Barnum said.

"That's macabre," Matthew said, appalled. A chill ran down his spine.

"It's good business practice, that's what it is," Barnum declared.

Matthew led Jumbo and the smallest elephant in the circus, Tom Thumb, along the tracks to the waiting cars, through the darkness lit by flickering torches. Overhead the incurious stars glimmered like a dancer's spangles across the sky. The trio were the last to board. The small elephant squealed and danced along, still happy from his performance. Jumbo rested his trunk for a moment on his companion, perhaps to calm him, or perhaps only to show affection. They paced along the tracks, steep embankments on either side, the blare and glare of the Big Top behind them and the sounds of the departing crowd, the last visitors leaving with the smell of cotton candy on their hands and glamour pervading their minds to haunt their dreams that night.

When he heard the chill whistle of the express train behind him, his first thought was, "But there's none scheduled." The ground shook underneath his feet and he heard the roaring of the coal engine, the screech of the brake, applied too late, too fast. Then all was chaos. The train crashed into Tom Thumb, scooping him onto its cowcatcher—elephant catcher was Matthew's next thought—pushing him screaming along the track before he rolled down the embankment.

"Run!" Matthew shouted but Jumbo shied away from the slope, trying to flee and unable to see the gap in the fence in his panic.

Train and elephant met. Jumbo was driven to his knees, a massive blow to the earth that Matthew felt to his bones. The train shuddered, its length crumpling, falling away from the tracks.

All thoughts vanished from Matthew's mind. He knelt beside the groaning, dying elephant, sobbing. The trunk crept around his waist and the two held onto each other until Jumbo's grip slackened. Matthew clung to his friend in desperation, but the light in the massive eyes died away.

"It's taken three years," Henry Ward announced to the Powers' Hotel banquet room, filled with journalists. "But at last Jumbo's remains are preserved. All of you have received a piece of the trunk, suitably inscribed for the occasion, but I have another surprise for you. You'll note the jelly before you. It is a most unusual dish. In the course of preparing the body, I accumulated a pound and a half of powdered ivory. The cook here used it to create the dish, allowing each of you to assimilate a little of the mighty creature."

He held up his champagne glass. "To Jumbo. Mightiest of his race, *Loxodonta Africana*."

"Did you hear that?" one newspaperman said to another.

"What, the toast?"

The man frowned, shaking his head. He was a slight, dapper man, his waistcoat figured with a print of green elephants. "Maybe not hear, but feel. Like a vibration shaking the floor, some sound too deep for the human ear. Maybe a train is passing outside."

In the corner of the room at an obscure table, Gaja Laxmi sat. She took a spoonful of the pale green jelly, sprinkled with flecks of white, and ate it deliberately, her tears falling to the white tablecloth like slow warm rain.

In Order to Conserve

I originally wrote this flash piece the summer of 1991. It was a response to the gas crisis of the time, and recently became pertinent again.

1.

In order to conserve color, the governments first banned newspaper inserts, the ones where dresses and dishwashers and plastic toys and figurines of gnomes with wary smiles tumbled across glossy surfaces. Readers faced columns of type interspersed with dour black and white line drawings, no slick sheets cascading on their laps as they unfolded the newsprint to gaze at the reports of latest developments in The Color Crisis. Others turned to the Internet, monochromatic monitors scrolled by blogs denouncing the Administration, the liberals, the conservatives, the capitalists, alien spiders, and a previously obscure cult known as the Advanced Altar of the Rainbow Serpent.

The change had been almost imperceptible at first. Only artists, fashion designers and gardeners noticed the dimming of shades, the shadows of reds, blues, purples that blossomed from less verdant stems. They brought the shift to the attention of white-coated scientists, who measured the changes in angstroms, then announced that laboratory results proved it true. Somewhere, somehow, color, once thought an inexhaustible natural resource, was running out, and doing so quickly.

The National Guard quelled the initial panic, while their counterparts did the same in other countries. Marching along in their drab uniforms, they shook hands with the populace and rescued black and white cats from birch trees. Waving for the cameras, they smiled that all was well before having them shut down and bundled away by nervous newsfolk, breaking up crowds that had gathered to discuss the situation. Color TVs were piled in broken heaps on on street corners, awaiting pick-up by the shadow-hued trucks that lumbered and clanked their way through early morning beneath a colorless sky.

As the months passed, more stringent measures were introduced and more and more things were rationed out with booklets of black on black stamps. People tried to use the rarer colors, magenta, fuchsia, pale lavender, but even so, the fashion industry unwillingly made black and white houndstooths, seersuckers, plaids, and ginghams the next statement of style. Grade school students were introduced to the fine art of cross hatching. Studios set to work, uncolorizing old movies.

Color became totally contraband. The majority of police car paint jobs were unchanged. Taxi cabs, on the other hand, turned gray striped with silver, a gleaming paint that reflected a thousand shades of concrete.

You would have thought that people would have mobbed art museums, to stare at the last canvases ever touched by color, but attendance fell off. People didn't want to be reminded of what they were missing, and security guards, their eyes welling deep with tears, moved among the lonely paintings before going to collect their last paychecks.

2.

An acute scientist, whose hobby was the cello, was the first to notice the decline in sound. The blackberry finches and house sparrows that flocked to her feeder each morning to feast on thistle seed were morose, silently pecking at each other. Sighing, she picked up the telephone, then changed her mind and bicycled away to send a telegram to the White House.

Teachers were forced to come up with new classes to replace band, orchestra, and music appreciation. Playground shouts were monitored. The uniformed guards held up placards to the students: "Conservation begins with you!" and taught sign language during the lunch hours.

Flashing white lights took the place of bells and buzzers. Audiences, after watching their black and white movies, took flashlights out of the purses and pockets and flicked them on and off to demonstrate approval.

Mimes were still unpopular.

People thought, and thought again, before they said anything. Therapy sessions often consisted of fifty minutes of silence, therapist and patient staring at each other, signaling with raised eyebrows, hesitant smiles, gentle nods, and at times inexplicable tears signaling some breakthrough.

The scientists wrote furious notes to each other, denouncing various theories for the shortages. Jeanne Dixon predicted that the San Andreas Fault would open and Elvis swagger forth, flanked by Jim Morrison and John Lennon, bringing with them new supplies of color and sound that would swell forth across the world like a nuclear explosion of color, expanding outward in concentric rings in a single joyous shout while the Angel Gabriel blew back-up saxophone.

"Silence is silver," read the billboards. "Walk softly and carry a big gray stick."

3.

When imagination began to ebb, the government again took active measures. Some philosophers and scientists pointed out that in order to solve the problem, creative thinking would be necessary. Death squads were immediately dispatched to their houses.

But still, overall there was a surprisingly lack of protest, if anyone had bothered to think much about it. Polls showed no one cared enough to vote.

Sure, it sounded good to protest creativity's absence, but there were benefits to not thinking too hard. Pluses to not worrying about things too much.

The television programs were still the same, after all: a black and white flicker, with dialogue in a slow scroll along the bottom of the screen, hazy snow hovering around the edge as through to signal the arrival of some gray winter of the soul.

Rare Pears and Greengages

"Rare Pears and Greengages" takes its title from Christina Rossetti's "Goblin Market." It takes place in Victorian times, in a world where Fairy overlaps the human world, and both worlds emerge the worse for the encounter. In flavor, it is somewhat influenced by Kipling and Dickens as well.

The narrative moves between two POVs, one a transplanted African shapeshifter who has lost her child, and the other an abused household servant faced with an unwanted pregnancy.

LILY:

Violet is one of the halfies—mixed blood. Don't no one talk much about where they come from, mostly whores who took on too many Fair Folk. Means a nice purse for the lady, and then the fairies educate the baby and bring it back here. Why they don't stay in Fairyland, I don't know, but I know Violet don't call it Fairyland, and gets pissy-like if she hears me say that. It's the Old Country to her.

Violet sleeps in the same cold servants' room as me, where the wind whistles at night, like knives coming through the walls, but she don't seem to mind, not that nor eating cabbage and bone soup like me and Cook, nor not having no money of her own. Her wages goes to the King and Queen of the Old Country, she told me once.

Mr. Smith pays a lot for her because the nobs like maids and butlers with fairy blood. But he don't have to spend on her room and board, any more than mine, so she shares my room, up at the top of the stairs.

She comes to me after Mr. Smith has been up the stairs and gone again, leaving a shilling on the bed stand. It hurts, deep down inside, and I'm crying, not even worrying about saving the tears. It'd make him mad as thunder, seeing all them tears sliding down to soak into the blanket. Violet catches them, though, in the little bottle she wears around her neck. She whispers to me and hugs me and it's nice, so nice that I don't mind her taking my tears. Better her than Mr. Smith.

He don't come to her. I heard him talking to his friend, Mr. Ryan, about it. "Give me the creeps, that one," he said. "I think she doesn't bother breathing unless someone is looking at her."

Mr. Ryan laughed, nasty-like. "Doesn't matter so much between the sheets, does it?"

"Be like swivving a fish. That clammy. And worse—a dead fish, since they don't move."

He ain't always so picky. Sometimes he does a vampire girl down at the mill when he's been there inspecting it. I can tell—he comes back from those trips with a stink of old blood clinging on him. But he never comes to Violet.

When she first started a year ago, I said, "You're Violet and I'm Lily. A regular boo-kay. Like sisters." She looked at me blank as an empty window and I gave up on any visions of that right quick. But on these nights when she creeps into bed aside me and touches me with her cold fingers, it takes away all the bruises Mr. Smith left.

She whispers in my ear, "Maybe you'll have a baby, Lily," and the moist words are like ice water spilled down my spine. I'd lose my place if I did, sure as Sunday. I'd lose my place and no other respectable establishment'd have me.

"No," I whisper back. I fumble to light the candle end and find the bottle of vinegar and water. I try to wash all trace of him, all nasty slimy trace of him, off me while she watches. The wind shrieks and whistles like it was screaming *No* over and over, and it's cold, so cold.

"Maybe," she whispers again as I get back into bed. It makes me want to slap her face, ghost-white as a cellar mushroom. She never smiles, but sometimes there's a spark behind her eyes. A little spark, like when you set flame to paper, and don't know whether it'll glow and go out, or leap up in flames. Is Violet a glow or a leap? I have no idea, and so I don't say nothing, just pull the blanket around me.

I think about the lady next door, the foreign one, the one that looks so sad. What about her? Leap or glow? Violet tucks her pointed chin into my shoulder and lies against me, cold and solid as a stone. She wraps her skinny arms around me, but I don't feel her breathing.

Mela:

The Colonel Sahib came to me and said come to England with me, and I will teach you how to read, and you can return someday and teach your people.

I came, but not to learn. I came because the smell of the acacia trees, the way sunlight combed through the long grass, the grunts of the cheetahs chasing down an antelope all made me think about my son, grief like a spear in my side.

I would go to England and learn Iron and Progress and the death of the baby Jesus and how to forget. I made my goodbyes to the Elephant People and the Hyena People, but I did not tell my clan, the Lion People, what I was doing. They knew, they caught word of it, but they did not approve, and pretended that the goodbye did not exist, as is our custom when there is something we do not want to say.

I came to London, where the air smells of smoke and despair. There were people like me, who walked as animals, the Colonel Sahib said, but only in one form—wolves. And in the twenty years he'd been in Africa, in Nakuru with me, they had become the pack leaders—the upper crust, he called them.

"Demmed if I know just how they managed that, but they've made it clear enough they've no wish to associate with the likes of us, old girl." He patted my head awkwardly. "I had thought to find you more company. But since the fairies came, everything's topsy-turvy. The streets are full of Fruit addicts."

I said I didn't mind and I didn't. My own people reminded me too much of my dead son, and other animals reminded me of my people. Now I go into the courtyard in the back of the house and sit smelling the frozen earth and watching the little sparrows flutter the complicated patterns of their wings and cock their heads, one side, then another, to examine the snowy gravel.

A gate in the garden wall leads next door. Originally the houses had been owned by a pair of brothers, the Colonel said, but they had moved on and now the gate between the houses was locked and curling plants grew along the bars in the summer, blue, odorless flowers kissing the space between them. I walk through the dead, icy grass and it leaves tear trails on my gown's hem, lines of black against silvery-gray, to look into the other garden.

Another woman sits there. Her hair is piled atop her head in a messy mass like a thorn-weaver's nest, and her clothing is white and filmy. The old Mem Sahib, the Colonel's wife, died in a garment like that after three years in Nakuru. A nightgown. This woman is alive, sitting humming to herself as though the sunlight were warm here, as though there were no wind or snow.

I do not make a sound, but she turns to me nonetheless. Her eyes are dreamy, a madwoman's or an addict's, or both.

"Who are you?" she says.

"My name is Layla." I stare at her through the bars.

She is a little dik-dik of a woman, but she shows no fear of me. She stands and comes over to the gate.

"You're not human," she says, looking at me. "One of them, one of the funny people, like the wolves or the fairies or the vampires, all come out of hiding."

Her breath smells of vanilla and her eyes are all pupil. She sways where she stands, and another woman darts out from a doorway, a maid, dressed in magpie black and white, to slide her arm around the first woman, supporting her.

"Leave me be, Lily," she says, pushing her away. "I'm human," she tells me. "I'm Arabella Smith. Why are you here?"

"I remind the Colonel Sahib of my homeland."

"And who reminds you of your homeland?" she demands, swaying again. The maid says something, but Mrs. Smith ignores her still. The maid is small and plain-faced and smells of sweat and soap and watery soup. Her hands are red and rough, and when she sees me looking at them, she pulls again at Mrs. Smith's sleeve.

"No one," I say. "I do not want to be reminded." A sparrow flutters too close and I slap a hand out, leaving only a smear of feathers and blood. Arabella Smith does not notice, but the maid does, and her eyes are wide as she looks at me.

LILY:

We all run errands at the same time, or try to, the other housemaids and I. For one, it's safer. Men don't come looking so eager if they know they'll find you in a group, and anyhow the streets ain't safe. Betty knows a girl who got abducted, taken away into white slavery, and never seen again. I ask how she knows it was white slavery she was abducted to then. Tabitha says she knows for a fact witches come out at night and grab people, fly them up in the sky and drop them for the fun of it.

Betty gets cranky at that point and says maybe it was white slavers or maybe it was witches but the important thing is that she got taken and no one ever saw her again.

And that's the main point, really, of going together. Gossiping and telling each other all the little bits—whose mistress done what to who. Tabitha's not here one day and when I ask about her, no one will say nothing in front of the others. I get it out of them in whispers, crumbs at a time.

"She got in the family way."

"Missus found out and she were that angry."

"Said she'd have no doxies or children of sin in her house and threw her out."

"But Tabby had enough saved for coach fare back to Sussex. Said she'd keep house for her brother and her mum."

"Think her mum will let a disgraced woman in? I don't. I wouldn't."

At least she had that chance. What can a woman do if she has no family? Become a whore. That's the only door open to me if Violet's whispered words come true. "Maybe you'll have a little baby," she says in my head. Tears start to my eyes, but I fight them back. No sense wasting them.

Some women get hired to cry in the Weeperies. They say it's a cushy pull while it lasts, but you must cry on command, or be so soft that the Weepery can start you off by telling you sad stories or killing kittens. No one lasts long, though. They end up dry-eyed and hard-hearted as stones, while their tears get shipped off to Fairyland. The Old Country. How can it be old, when no one knew it existed until a few years ago?

I remember that day, when folks came running in to say one of the Parliament Members had said he was a fairy, and then suddenly it all came out, there was fairies an' werewolves and all sorts of creatures, all around us. They'd been around us all the time.

One of my errands today is the Fairy Market. It's down Threepenny Lane, near the river. Tents all jumbled and confused and everything glittering, glittering, shiny, the minute you come near. Glimmers of light, gone if you look straight at them. Ghosts of shapes. Goblins with their funny cat eyes, squinting against the sunlight.

I have two bottle of tears in my basket, and when I enter the market, the vendors swarm me, pulling at me to look here, look there, pinching me if I don't move quick enough to suit them.

They shout, "Rare pears and greengages, pomegranates full and fine, figs to fill your mouth, citrons from the South." I pick out two peaches, soft and juicy, warm as if they were full of fever, one for each tiny bottle.

At home, Mrs. Smith takes the peaches greedily and vanishes into her room. When she can't get fairy fruit, she drinks laudanum and vanilla, but the fruit is most to her liking. She'll be lost in dreams for days. Time enough to cry more bottles full, to buy her more fruit. I sniff my fingers, and smell the peaches, sweet and lush, and imagine their skin, soft and furry as mice.

Mela:

Some afternoons, the dreamy-eyed, rumpled woman suns herself in the courtyard. I sit near the locked gate and tell her stories, the ones I whispered to my cub, long ago with the warm mud under our bellies and the blood of a fresh kill on our lips.

I tell her stories of crocodiles and storks, and the sinuous pythons that search through the acacia branches. I tell her how the little basilisks live on the insects and dormice they can stun, and how they dig their underground nests to lay clutches of eggs that may stay there in the dark and dirt for a decade or more before the eggs crack and their moist contents crawl out, bellies dragging in the dust, to make their way back to the safety of one of the big trees, its canopy grown up far past the depredations of elephant and giraffe.

Sometimes the maid Lily sits with her. The other one, the one that is part fairy, pays me no mind and I pay her none in return. I have seen her kind before, dealers in scraps, trying to buy the affection of their full-blooded kindred. She has her own thoughts, her own mysteries to contemplate. But the other, the human one, sits listening, wide-eyed. She thinks I am a great sorceress come from Africa. When I tell the story of my son, of how I nested him in a thorn-thicket every day when I hunted, to keep him from danger, she listens. She never asks what happens next and I do not tell her.

Lily:

The first month my bleeding don't come and I tell myself it's because I don't eat much. Then it don't come again, and again.

I try to ask the other maids what they would do without letting on why. I know whores do something, something to make the baby go away, but I also know it's a sin. I don't know what to do.

Violet lies in my bed, and puts her hands on my stomach and sings. She brings me all her food, don't save so much as a scrap for herself, and so I let her touch my stomach. Her singing goes all through me, like something humming out from her hands.

"I can hide your growing belly," she whispers to me. "And when the baby is born, I can take it away where it will be happy. It'll only cost twelve pounds."

"The Missus will notice," I say. "Or Mr. Smith."

"I'll take care of them," she says, her eyes gleaming like candle flames while the wind shrieks. "And Cook won't say anything. Can you get the money?"

"Where will you take my baby?"

"To a place where they raise babies and educate them. Fine people run it, generous and wealthy. Your baby can learn to be something other than a servant."

I sell my best clothing and my mother's necklace, and that with all the shillings Mr. Smith has left beside the bed comes to a little under eleven pounds. Violet is angry—she rummages through my things, looking for something else to sell, but finds nothing. Finally I cry for her, and she catches the tears in her bottle, several spoonfuls worth, and smiles before bringing me a cup of water.

As the weeks pass, I cry more and more. Violet takes the tears away and comes back with fruit, knobby melons and glossy limes. She gives Cook something to put in Mr. Smith's soup, and he dreams his way through the days like the Missus. Cook doesn't like it much, but when Mrs. Smith is doped on fairy fruit, she gives Cook no trouble in the kitchen, and when she's not, she orders two puddings a night and changes her mind on the meat on a regular basis, right after Cook's just finished the marketing.

I grow bigger and bigger, I float my way through the house like a cloud, carried along by Violet's song. I think she gives me fruit as well—the weeks pass too quickly, too quickly, and then one nightmare of a night I dream my belly splits and I wake up in the middle of blood and soreness. Violet is wrapping up the baby in my coat.

"Give it to me," I say, but she holds it away.

"It'll just make you miserable later, trying to remember," she says. "I'm taking her to a nice lady, Mrs. Sucksby. She'll give her a good life." She gives me a glass of water, so sweet I know there must be fruit juice in it, just a spoonful or two to send me back to the coolness of the pillow and dreams of sleeping a thousand years, like Sleeping Beauty, with all them plants and thorns.

In the morning Violet and the baby are gone, but I am still sore. Downstairs everyone is cranky, but there is no fruit, and no tears in the house. I cannot cry no matter how much Mr. Smith raises his voice or hand. Finally he sends for the physician, who comes and leaves behind a blue glass bottle. More laudanum.

Mela:

I smell the birth on the wind and it makes me restless. On the night my cubs were born, the rains were just starting. The clouds were low and lightning played over them as though the storm were thinking, dreaming. Then rain fell in sheets bending the grass flat, drops as warm as blood.

All my babies were born dead except my son. I was prepared for this. My people do not live long, and we are few. But he lived, and I washed him clean, there in the torrents of rain, my tongue and the warm water sluicing away the afterbirth.

The Elephant Women and the Hyena Women came to look at him and congratulate me, for their children are few as well. Three groups rule the lands where the acacia trees grow, the Elephants and the Hyenas and the Lions, because we walk most easily between the land of humans and the Real World. There are lesser beings there—we have fairies too, but they are little, malicious things, and rarely come down from the branches.

Lily:

It's cold going to market without my coat. The other maids are stand-offish at first—Betty says they ain't seen me in months, and maybe that's true, judging by the differences in some of them. But they know what I need to find out—Miriam's heard of Mrs. Sucksby's.

"It's a baby farm."

"Whozzat?"

"They take the baby and board it for ya, or adopt it if you give 'em enough."

She gives the word "adopt" a nasty twist, so I say it. "Adopt?"

"One payment and they make sure you won't see your baby again. Got what they call a high mor-ta-li-ty rate." And she twists the words again like a knife. "That means the babies die."

Back home I go about my duties. Mr. Smith's angry, so angry.

"Where's Violet?" he snaps.

"I don't know, sir."

He scowls something fierce. "Have to replace her if she's run off." He reaches out and touches me, and the gentleness scares me more than the scowling. "Been a while, eh, Lily?"

"I'm having my woman time, sir," I say, very soft, looking at the floor. "Just started."

He ain't happy, but he goes off to examine the mill.

I slip out before dark, that gives me a head start. I know the address for Mrs. Sucksby. It's a part of town I never seen before, buildings leaning on each other for support like they was drunk, and everything dirty, so dirty.

The house hunches up between two others. A few lights on, but not many. I go round the back and almost walk into a woman sitting on the steps, but duck back afore she can spot me. She's a mangy old thing, sitting there enjoying the stars coming out, and finally she rises, gathering up her skirts, and goes off to the privy. I dart up the stairs and inside before she returns.

The pantry has a big cupboard under the sink. I hide under there and wait.

It may be been less than an hour I wait, but it seems like days. I keep hearing footsteps, and it don't seem like everyone is going to sleep like I'd hoped. Finally I crawl out and go up the back stairway to the second floor.

There's rooms and rooms full of babies up there. How will I know which is mine? But I spot her, wrapped up in my coat, on a cot with two others.

Footsteps sound, two pairs? Three? I duck under a cot just as they come in. All I can see is three pairs of feet, one set of black ladies' boots, the others men's shoes.

"Take the ones against the west wall," the woman says. Light from the lantern one of them must be holding shines on the wooden floor, showing dust mice as big as kittens, and places where diapers have leaked. "That's a half-dozen disposed of, and not so many dying at once that anyone will notice."

"Do you think anyone really pays much attention to the death rate of bastard babies?" a man says.

"I think that we carry out this charade so no one will know they have been taken, and that we will play it out as fully as we have been directed," she says. Her voice is colder than any wind. It sounds like Violet's.

Her footsteps clack away, and I peek out enough to see what the men do. My baby is on the east wall, safe enough, but they pick up the other babies, and each time take a bundle out of the burlap sack one carries and lay it in the first baby's place.

The babies cry and whimper as they are picked up, but the taller man touches a finger to each forehead, and they still, snuffling themselves asleep. Arms full of babies, the two men leave.

I go over to see what they've put in place of the babies, but there are still babies there. One yawns and looks up at me. They look like any of the other children. I don't understand.

Voices, coming back up the stairs, and shouting, somehow they know I'm here. I grab my baby and one of the others, one of the new babies, and scramble out the window, out along the slanted roof. The old window frame slides back down after me.

It's cold on the roof but calmer than I expected, once I get over the fear that they'll figure out which way I went. Shouts come from the alleyway and I hear footsteps in the room underneath, but I sit where I am, in a nook between the chimney and the roof, with the coat wrapped around the three of us, while we get acquainted.

Mine has black hair, which I don't like, because it reminds me of Mr. Smith, and blue eyes, which I do like. The other baby isn't much to look at—brown hair, brown eyes. Its skin has a funny feel to it, like old leaves. It don't make a sound, just looks at me and reaches up a hand, tiny perfect fingers curling around my rough red one.

It's like me, this other baby—it doesn't know what to do. All three of us stay there, my baby asleep, the other baby watching me. The church clock, far away to the west, is chiming three when the witches find me.

Mela:

You can hide a cub, but they will not stay hidden. You can tuck them among thorn branches, but they will not stay, and even when they do, death can come slithering down the trunk, a python to whom a cub is only a mouthful, a little mouthful, what the Mem Sahib called an appetizer when she served dinner to other English folk. When fever came, we thought the Colonel would go away after she had fallen, but he stayed, and little by little, we became friends, because we never spoke of our losses to one another.

Pythons eat cubs, and when they have, you cannot recover your baby, no matter how much you roar or moan. No matter how much you weep, even though lions never weep.

After we came here, a fairy came visiting, curious about me, about the Colonel. She told me what they could offer: fruit full of sweet hallucinations, combs and charms and little cantrips to keep a house clean or a man faithful.

And memories. They offer dreams and memories. But the price is high, too high and I have no coin with which to pay.

Lily:

Witches! When they swoop down, grabbing me, pulling me into the sky, I scream and almost drop my baby, but one of them grabs it as we whirl up in a rush of wind and stars.

"What's this then?" one demands. She looks like something out of a storybook: all long nose and beady eyes and hairy chin. I would have known her for a witch anywhere. "A baby!"

"Two of 'em, even," the other says. Her tone is regretful. "I don't want to drop er while she's carrying babies, Grizz. That's too wicked."

"Soft as pudding, you are, Sophie," Grizz scoffs. "Set her down on the clock tower, we'll find out what's going on. Mebbe we can take the babies and then drop her."

"I don't want no baby," the first says, but we are already tumbling through the sky, whirling like scraps of paper or feathers on the wind, to land on the narrow lip of the clock tower, gritty bricks nice and solid under my feet.

Grizz has my baby, and Sophie takes the other. She spits when she looks at it. "This ain't no real baby," she say. "It's a changeling, be dead before the day is through. How'd you come by a fairy husk, girl?"

I tell them my story, holding onto the edge of the tower. Below us are London streets, and the faint distant lanterns of night watchmen.

The witches debate whether or not to drop me—"Keep the populace a little worried, after all, so they respect honest English witches," Grizz argues. Sophie reaches out for my hand and looks at the palm before she says something to Grizz, too quiet for me to hear, that persuades her.

I try not to hear it, at any rate. I try not to hear the words "not long for this world."

I have a plan. I make my way down the tower steps from the belfry with the babies. I know what to do. How to give my daughter a good life, the kind of life I never had. It all depends on the woman next door, the woman with the gleam of gold at her wrists and stories of a baby missing from her arms.

MELA:

She comes in the very earliest moments of the morning, when the light is just starting to show its chill brilliance, little Lily with a bundle in her arms, to the back door.

When I open it, she stares up at me. There is fear in her face, but there is also desperation.

She says, "Miss Mela, you lost your baby, didn't you?"

Satisfaction flares in her eyes when I nod, and she holds the bundle out to me.

"Here," she says. "You take her. You'll give her something better, eh?"

My paws twitch, but I don't reach out for the bundle.

She tries again. "Think of your son."

When I do, when I remember the perfection of his pudgy paws, of the needle-sharp kitten teeth, of the milk and flesh smell of him, I reach out. The baby is heavier than I remember.

"You'll take care of her, won't ya?" the maid says. The anxious morning sunlight reveals her features. "You'll give her a good life. Better than mine."

It is, as always, easier not to reply. That is the way of my People. So she turns away, reassured, when she should have listened to what I did not say.

LILY:

After I've given her my baby, I go back to the attic and what I have there. The fairy baby and Mrs. Smith's big blue bottle. The baby looks at me with its dark eyes. Its skin looks older, withering.

I sing to it while everyone sleeps, down in the darkened house. I pretend it's my baby, that we will leave soon and go away to the country, to a little house, a little garden where there is sunshine and no soot. But even while I sing, I see it fading away.

Three drops, never more, never more, the doctor said. I put much more than that in the glass of water and drink it down.

On the bed, I curl up with the changeling, and pull the blanket and my coat around us in a nest of drowsy warmth. We lie there together, and I sing a song that sounds a little like Violet's and pretend it's my own baby there. The fairy baby doesn't breathe, although it watches me, its features fading, and slowly the darkness swallows me, and it, and we are gone.

MELA:

I take the baby to a gate I know, a doorway that is watched by the fairies, and pay the watchmen there. They eye the infant in my arms with covetous looks, but they do not dare meddle with me. I take it to the Queen of the Old Country, and there I trade it for what she has for me: a tiny key that will unlock a drawer, a drawer full of sunshine and memories.

I slide the drawer open. It is narrow, one of many making up the brass-bound apothecary's chest. The drawer's thick walls make the inner compartment, lined with golden foil, smaller still.

The interior shimmers with a memory: mid-afternoon sunlight filtered through acacia leaves. My cub and I lay on the mudflats near the water, the chalky blue and gray water. The air smelled of the shift between rainy season and drought, when the sun-warmed mud begins to dry and curl at the edges. A big-headed baby baboon perched nearby, high in a yellow acacia's canopy, picking at the bark to make it bleed sap—a sweet, sugary whiff on the wind.

We watched it because the pair of flat-headed basilisks that spent their days quarreling over the division of the tree's many-branched territory were working together for once. They were creeping up from two sides, and between them, they might be its match, if the nearby mother didn't notice what was happening soon enough.

But she did, she does. The baby is saved, and the two basilisks driven off with furious shrieks. All is well. All is well.

My hand trembles on the drawer's knob. It wants to slide shut again, now that the last of its sunlight is gone. I keep it open as long as I can, but when my fingers' strength fades, it closes and cannot be opened again.

The Fairy Queen held a black-haired, blue-eyed baby in her lap and sang to it. And when she had finished her song, she took it downstairs, for servants are scarce in the Old Country, and it was time for this one's tenure to begin.

A Twine of Flame

"A Twine of Flame" takes place in the same world as Tabat, but in the last days of the Shadow Wars, when sorcerers fought each other by any means available, including magical plagues such as the one Annie carries.

Annie dreamed of fire. Where once she would have feared the dancing flames or stretched out winter cold hands to catch their warmth, now she felt only weariness and resignation and disgust. She counted the flames and thought of numbers, wondering how many deaths were credited to her now.

When she woke, she found herself in fire as well. The sprites had once again worked themselves loose from under her skin, and they circled her as though the air were full of flaming feathers, shedding waves of heat like chickens being plucked. The grass, already dry as last year's noodles, smoked and smoldered. At the rock's edges, leaves of lamb's quarter succumbed to the heat, crumpling inward as they withered. Annie sighed and held her arms open.

The sprites flowed back into her like water, pouring along her wrists and elbows, wriggling in under the muscles like fading wisps. As always, she wondered at the sensation. She felt their movement, but not the heat that could have cooked her to the bone.

The sky overhead was autumn's chilly blue, but she did not know if winter would come, not in these years of mingled deaths and miracles. Along the deserted road, corruption splotched the fields with spots like blackened sores, fringed with icy mushrooms, as though someone had been raising the undead.

Annie had little to fear from the zombies that might rise from those dark clusters. The flames that companioned her would kill them long before they could touch her. Still, they were unpleasant company. Two weeks ago, she had been trailed along the road by a pack of them, an entire village's worth, it had looked like. After she'd killed two, the rest of them had the sense to stay back, but still they followed, staring at her and trying to talk. They expelled air from their rotting lungs, forcing it out in groans and phlegmy bubbles of single words. "Giiirrrlll." "Fiiiiiirrreee." "Please."

Once she had stretched and peed among the ditch grasses, she took the road again. She no longer carried anything. She was lucky the flame sprites allowed her any clothing at all.

Up ahead a hamlet huddled in the road's curve. The gates were closed, a good sign. They had not succumbed yet to the undead, but they might or might not welcome Annie. She was another hand against the encroaching monsters but she would be also another mouth to feed from ever-scantier supplies. And if they had heard of the Flame Plague, they would be watching her. It was risky, but there were so many lives there. Enough to free her? She didn't think so but it would put her closer, much closer.

She checked her clothing: intact for the most part and the only burns along one sleeve, easily torn away and discarded. Smoke curled from three chimneys to join together in a single, reaching pillar. Perhaps there would be soup, thick bean soup with cabbage and chunks of sausage. Her mouth watered.

Two teenagers, all knobby wrists and haunted eyes, guarded the gate. She tried to bear herself like an asset, something of use, not something that would drain their resources. They looked at her and shouted as she came up the road. One motioned her back while another ran to fetch a priest.

The holy man's hollow eyes were glittering pits set in a stubbled face. Townspeople leaned from the walls to watch. Their faces were like sooty, smudged fingerprints, hard to make out.

"Where are you from, girl?" the priest asked. His breath stank with starvation. He was denying himself for the sake of his flock. He saw himself as their savior, that was his weakness. Could she play the part of a message from God? She was not sure what God would have to say to these abandoned people. Or to her. Or even if God existed anymore. He might have been torn apart, like these lands, by the ever-warring sorcerers.

She bowed her head to him and stammered. "I ran away from bandits. They took my horse and pack."

"She'll lead them to us!" someone hissed, but the priest held up a hand.

"Where are you from, though?" he asked again.

"Canal du Midi, on the coast. My father sent me inland, to escape the storms."

He nodded. Everyone knew of the storms harrying the coast, none of them natural, leaving behind pools of tainted, murky water that poisoned everything that touched or drank from them. Wind elementals, twisted by sorcerers vying for power, drank the souls of those unwary enough to be caught outside at night or in storms.

The priest studied her. She dropped her eyes, trying to look subservient, meek. Unthreatening. She could see doubt warring with compassion on his face, and she let her head droop as though weary for a moment, hoping to touch his heart. At length he beckoned her inside.

They fed her onion soup and a single slice of black bread, full of grit that crunched between her teeth. Far fewer of them than she had guessed. Two dozen of them altogether, the youngest a babe in arms, the oldest a grandmother. Six able-bodied men.

After the meal, they told their stories. They took it in turns to patrol the walls and watch for zombies, four at a time. They had made it through months of hardship so far in this way. Every two hours they switched. She gathered that if she stayed, she would be a welcome addition to their ranks.

They laid out bedrolls in the common room and set no one to guard them while they slept. Convenient. She curled up with her eyes closed, feeling the sprites brewing beneath her skin. They were impatient. She let them wait until the next change of guards had passed and the two newcomers laid down to rest, their breathing become regular and rhythmic.

When she finally let the sprites loose, they flickered out into the darkness, each taking a separate person. She lay there, listening to the catch of breath each time a flame sank into its new host. They would not feel the building heat as anything other than an odd flutter, a touch of dizziness. The lucky would never know what had happened.

She pulled herself from her blankets and crept out, not bothering to close the door behind her.

The hungry flames would begin feeding soon. The bodies would lie slumbering, smoke tendrils curling from their nostrils, their ears, their eyes, their open and gaping mouths. Eventually some would collapse into ash. When the patrollers returned, when they stooped in horror and disbelief, the flames would rush them. This time they'd control their hosts better, to lurk for additional travelers or unwary refugees. Eventually, though, everyone in the village would burn, and her debt would be a little further along to being repaid.

Moonlight scrawled its impatient signature on the icy shingles. She didn't see the priest coming until he lunged out of the darkness near the gate.

"Fire-ridden!" His arm clamped over her throat, throttling her. Most of her flames were gone, she was weak, but the two she had left surged from her skin, flaring out to burn him. He released her and staggered back with a cry. Someone shouted in the distance.

She left him with the flames dancing in his eyes, blinding him, and darted down an alleyway. The gate was deserted—everyone was back tending to the priest or some other victim, no doubt. Her luck held—no zombies lurking close outside. The high moon shed a pure white light across the frosty landscape, but she slipped off the well-lit road and made her way to a huddle of haystacks. She curled into the farthest one, beneath a trio of beech trees.

By the time she roused in sunlight, the flames had returned to her. She pulled away from the haystack and let them dance in its depths. Within a few moments, the flames roared, reaching upward. A few raced off in other directions, wavering through the grass. She knew from experience eventually they would meet wall or brook and rebound to her, consuming what they could along the way.

She thought back about the tiny town. Two dozen souls, perhaps. So many, yet only a small portion of her obligation. So many flames to be fed still.

She continued along the road.

Annie neared the town of Barbaruile on sunset's heels, the sun gleaming over her left shoulder, sitting on the horizon like a fat egg of red flame. The narrow road's chalky stones led up towards the town through thickets of small, trees whose dark, waxy leaves rattled together in the wind, obscuring the upward view. The roadway wound back and forth, climbing the steep hill as best it could. She was panting hard by the time she was a third of the way up. Further on she sat down by the side of the road to rest, looking back over the landscape and its patchwork of small fields shaggy with untended growth.

The sun sank deeper and the dry leaves rattled like the clatter of rolling dice as her breathing slowed. The flames inside her leaped as though in recognition of some other presence and she cried out into the darkness as it advanced upon her, "Who's there? Come out now!" The power of the flames was in her voice.

As though summoned, two forms slowly, reluctantly stood from the ditch where they had been concealed. The two women's similarity of face and frame proclaimed them mother and daughter. They wore clothing like her own, worn and ragged, assembled from cast-offs and corpse-leavings.

"What are you doing here?" Annie demanded. She fought the flames back down. Not yet, not yet, despite their hungry, hot prodding. Two lives were very small when reckoned against the possibility of a village.

The older woman spoke, only the lips moving in her still white face, "We saw you coming and hid. We did not know what you might be."

The daughter nodded. It made sense to Annie. These were extraordinary times and monsters walked every night. She made her voice soothing, letting the flames caress the intonation's edges with power. "It's all right. I'm as human as you. Do you belong to the city up there? Will they give me shelter for the night?"

The two exchanged glances.

"We are strangers here as well," the daughter said. Her voice was a higher version of her mother's. "We will not know without asking."

Together, they progressed up the hill. They did not exchange names.

At the top, the town gate would not yield to their knocking. There was the flare of a torch on the other side of the wooden planks, but whoever was there did not speak, despite the pounding all three made on the wood. Annie beat at it till the heels of her hands ached, feeling the frustration build. She had thought three women would seem harmless, but perhaps she had erred. She cried out, "Please!"

Still no answer from the other side.

The daughter turned away and led them along a narrow path that companioned the wall for fifty paces or so before darting down among close-knit groves. They curled in the hollow of a grassy bank and built no fire. The mother and daughter wrapped their ragged cloaks around each other and fell asleep.

The leaves clattered and chattered, keeping Annie awake. The moon crept a hand span up the sky as she watched between slit eyes. Finally she heard the rustling from the other side of the hollow.

The daughter's cool hand was on her forehead, cold as ice, sweetly cold in a way she had not felt since the flames first touched her.

"She's hot," the girl whispered back over her shoulder.

The mother's breath hissed in, "Get away!" But it was too late. Flames raced along Annie's face, flowing from the confines of her breast to dance up along the girl's arm. She screamed, falling back, arms wheeling. Her voice was high and terrified. The flames took her hair and danced on her lips.

Her mother swept her cloak over the daughter's head, but the flames only licked at that greedily as well, reaching for her.

The two women screamed, burning candles in the night, as Annie watched. She could smell their flesh cooking. She wondered what the town thought of the screams. They'd never let her in now. Turning her face away, she sobbed herself to sleep.

In the morning their skeletons were rendered in black ash, showing their elongated skulls and their clawed hands. Not human after all, but sorcerer created, like the flames Annie carried. She kicked dirt over them and made her way around the town and northward.

A small, red-peaked tower capped each end of the Valentre Bridge near Cahors. Vines grew up along the brown stone sides, withered, and furred with frost. They wavered feebly despite the lack of wind as she passed and she felt eyes watching her, she presumed from the northern tower. But no one challenged her as she made her way across. The ice-glazed water ate her reflection when she looked down, making her shudder and withdraw.

The dragon waited at the other end.

It was small as far as dragons go. Two weeks ago, she had seen an immense one flap overhead, gleaming red against a cloudless blue sky. By contrast, this dragon was perhaps as long as she was tall, but by the reaction of the flames within her, it blazed brighter than she ever had.

Before she could speak or move, the flames boiled from her, pulled towards the dragon. It reared upward as they surrounded it, seething, and its wings flapped, although it appeared unharmed. She stood, feeling the wind's cold bite for the first time. Then as quick as thought, the flames left it and returned to her, somehow subdued and contemplative. The dragon blinked its golden eyes. Its forked tongue flickered out, sampling the air now vacant of flames.

"You're not like the other brief ones," it said. Its voice was smooth as honey, seductive as a spring night's whisper.

She swayed towards it, feeling her heart throb in syncopation to the syllables. The flames lurched and swayed, and flared in her loins. She blushed.

"Give me gold," it crooned, then laughed silently as she tried to pull away.

The flames roared in her and the attraction stopped as though burned to ash. The dragon's eyes narrowed into cat-fine crescent moons.

"Where are you going, whither do you wander, westward or northward, wickedest of women?"

She shook her throbbing head. Her clothing began to smolder, coils of smoke ribboning the air above her shoulders.

Its wings moved lazily, fanning the flames, and she felt them leap. It leaped into the air even as the fire reached for it, and hung there, wings moving too fast for perception. Her clothing tumbled away in burning fragments.

Just as suddenly, the dragon was gone. In the sky above her, the huge shadow was moving again. She ducked into the shadow of the tower and watched it pass. Half a mile further on, she found an abandoned cottage and blankets to wrap herself in.

Two days later, she had reclothed herself and reaped another eight souls but was less sure of her path. She thought that the flames under her skin might be subsiding, that she might need to return to the sorcerer to have her soul filled with them again. They replenished themselves more slowly the further north she went and the further into eternal winter the weather slid.

She wavered on the road, hesitating. She was again in zombie territory, but she was stronger than when she took the little town whose name she did not remember. She had slept last night in a deserted cottage, under clean sheets. In the morning the sprites had burned her outline onto the counterpane.

It had taken her three weeks to come this far from Canal du Midi, but she could find a faster way home. She knew the sorcerer was still there. She could feel him across the miles as keenly as though he had set barbed fishhooks in her soul.

She found a cart and a neglected pony, fat on the oats that had been left behind for him. She couldn't figure out why they would have left him, unless their horses were so fast that his stubby legs would have slowed them down. She lined the cart with wool blankets soaked in the cottage's well, sodden and hard to carry but also hard to set alight. There were two water tuns, so she filled them and rolled them onto the ramp to load them in the cart. The pony, a mild-faced beast with a black streak along his fuzzy brown nose, protested at first, but she let him take his own pace and she returned southward.

At night purple stars blazed and crackled overhead. She did not know whose emissaries they were. She slept in the cart, and when the flames insisted on being fed, she left the fire behind quickly, trundling on after renewing the water in her blankets.

The next day she came to a frozen pond so wide she could not see the opposite bank. She circled it rather than risk crossing. The pony shied away from the glittering crystals. She was willing to trust his instincts.

When she saw the church beside the road, she turned the pony's head. It was abandoned. She scavenged through the verger's hut for food, finding a gnawed flitch of bacon and a mold-ridden loaf.

The pony pushed its head against her shoulder until she climbed the pear tree in the cemetery to throw down an armload of the frozen yellow fruit. She took two of the mushy pears for herself and ate them sitting on a slate tombstone, its letters blurred by time and rain.

Motion caught her eye and she tossed the second core to the pony before she approached the wall, peering upward. She admired the cat-necked gargoyles that leaned out at right angles from the crenellated walls. The closest turned its head with a gritty, grinding sound to regard her.

She stared transfixed as it crawled spider limbed down the ivy-traced wall. The flames inside her did not react as it neared.

It came within reach and extended a stone-taloned paw. She raised her hand and it gripped her index finger with its otter's long digits. Its mouth worked soundlessly. It sniffed the air with a rasp of intake.

"He's not sure what to make of you," a voice said behind her. She turned her head, her hand still caught.

At first she thought him another priest, but as he emerged from the shadows, she saw that his robes did not have a clerical cut. He was her height, dapper and clean-shaven, his smile chilly and perfunctory.

"Leave it," he said to the gargoyle as he stepped closer. The creature released her hand just in time for the sorcerer to take it in turn.

He was younger than she would have expected, given the power radiating from him. Angry pimples marred his cheeks, and his goatee, waxed to make it shine, was sparse as her pony's tail.

"Who are you, girl?" he demanded. His arrogant eyes searched hers and she felt him plucking at her thoughts, fraying them into distraction so she swayed, almost dizzy. She tried to pull her hand free but he held her tight. The flames coiled like springs inside her, but she made them bate, waited to see what happened. Despite his power, she felt no menace in him.

"Where are you from?"

"Canal du Midi."

"I know it well. The plane trees are green beside the canals there." He studied her. Sliding creakily, the gargoyle climbed back to its original perch.

"They used to be, but they burned down months ago. What are you doing here?" she said.

He shrugged. "It seemed as good a place as any while I consider my next move."

She frowned. "Your next move?"

He shrugged like a child waiting to be picked at tag. "I am warring with the Conte de St. Jerome, who lives to the east. I assaulted his home a day ago with the trees that grew around it. He dug trenches around the place that drowned all I could throw against him."

He paused, sniffing, before he slid his arms around her like an old lover and leaned to nuzzle at her ear.

"Oh, you reek of power, like a rose dripping perfume," he breathed drunkenly, inhaling from her skin.

She pushed at him but he held her firmly.

"I carry sorceries of my own, beware!" she said, and he loosed her to hold her at arm's length.

"Whose pawn are you?" he said, his nostrils still flared as though to smell her better. "I'll pay whatever ransom he or she demands, and make you mine. You are cinnamon and cardamom, warm bread threaded with saffron. You are the very scent of love."

"I must pay ten-score lives to redeem mine and that of my sisters," she said.

"So few?" he laughed. He touched his lips to the inside of her wrist as though drinking from her pulse. "I will take them for you and lay them at your feet, as though you were a sorcerer yourself.

The flames boiled in her as though she were an iron kettle with its lid on too tight, furious steam building.

"Get back!" she gasped, and his grip tightened, pulled her close again.

Panic flared and the flames were loose. Like a blue film they closed over him. He pushed her away, screaming. The gargoyles far overhead roared with brass and granite voices and she ran pell mell, grabbing for the pony's reins, flames following in her wake. In the road she mounted the pony and rode him furiously southward until he groaned beneath her and she became aware of the burns on his sides.

Half sobbing, she reined him in and slipped from his back. As soon as her weight had left him, he reared and pulled away from her, then thundered away down the road. She did not see him again.

She knew she was close when she saw the towers of Capestang. The slate roofs of the towers gleamed blue in the late evening light. Southward smoke billowed, an immense impossibility of smoke.

There were two other people on the road.

She did not know how she sensed that they also carried flames under their skin, but she did, feeling a tremulous flicker when they were near. She fell in behind them, but did not join their camp that first night. At dawn, they all rose, leaving the smoldering outlines where they had slept.

They were traveling with each other but rarely spoke—they did not talk to her at all. She followed them, towards the billowing smoke.

At noon, they paused and she asked, "Excuse me, what is that?" She pointed at the billowing column.

"He summoned a volcano out of the water," the woman, a hard-faced blonde, said. The man resembled her and Annie wondered if they were brother and sister. He nodded, and they turned around to head southward again.

As they neared the immense black slope growing out of the beach, she saw other people. By the time they were trudging upward across the slick black glass, there were dozens.

Her captor hovered in the center of the volcano. She wondered why he floated there. Flames lashed upwards, caressing him, and he shuddered and writhed. Averting her eyes, she looked elsewhere.

There were hundreds of them, she realized. Lining the ledge of the volcano, staring inward at the sorcerer. She thought two hundred, and then two hundred again. And again. And again. How many lives had he claimed? How many would she claim for him? She trembled. Inside her the flames were building as she came closer to the sorcerer.

Around her on the lip of the volcano, the sorcerer's minions trembled, feeling their flames swell and multiply. Some had expressions that mimicked the glazed pleasure on the sorcerer's face, others looked merely horrified. Their flames replenished, they turned to stagger back down the slope and northward again, leaving burning footprints in the blackened grass. Refilled and ready to claim more lives in their master's name. Had it been worth it, to save her sister? She was very afraid that the answer was no.

She was the only one among the many that leaped, but no one noticed her, no one noticed the flames that floated away like handkerchiefs on the air to flow back towards the sorcerer. The tears that filled her eyes for an instant as she fell were just as quickly gone, and all that was left behind was a twine of flame and then, a moment of ash.

The Dead Girl's Wedding March

"The Dead Girl's Wedding March" was written in the fall of 2005, after Clarion West. It started with the initial image of the rat proposing to the girl, and what happens as a result. It is more of a fairy tale set in Tabat than a "real-life" history, but there is indeed a zombie city without a name far below Tabat, where part of the action of "The Bumblety's Marble," which appeared in the collection Paper Cities *in 2008, takes place. This story appeared in* Fantasy Magazine *in 2005.*

Once upon a time a dead girl lived with the other zombies in the caverns below the port of Tabat, in the city beneath that seaside town, the city that has no name. Thousands of years ago, the Wizard Sulooman plunged the city, buildings and all, into the depths of the earth, and removed its name, over some slight that no one but his ghost remembers. There life continues.

Some dead folk surrender to slumber, feeling that there is no point pretending an agenda. A few, though, pace out their days in the way they once paced out their lives.

The only actual living things in the City of the Dead are the sleek, silver-furred rats that slip through its streets like reversed shadows. On a day there like any other day, a rat addressed the dead girl.

Her name was Zuleika, and she was dark-haired, dark-eyed, and smelled only faintly of the grave, because every evening she bathed in the river that flowed silently beneath her window.

"Marry me," the rat said. It stood upright on its back legs, its tail curled neatly around its feet.

She was pretending to eat breakfast. A pot steamed on the table. She poured herself a deliberate cup of chocolate before speaking.

"Why should I marry you?"

The rat eyed her. "To be sure," it admitted. "There's more in it for me than for you. Having a bride of your stature would increase mine, so to speak." It chuckled, smoothing its whiskers with a paw.

"I fear I must decline," she said.

Leaving the rat to console itself with muffins, she went into the parlor where her father sat reading the same paper he read every morning, its pages black rectangles.

"I have had a marriage proposal," she told him.

He folded his paper and set it down, frowning. "From whom?"

"A rat, just now. At breakfast."

"What does he expect? A dowry of cheese?"

She remembered not liking her father very much when she was alive.

"I told him no," she said.

He reached for his paper again. "Of course you did. You've never been in love and never will be. There is no change in this city. Indeed, it would be the destruction of us all. Shut the door when you go out."

She went shopping, carrying a basket woven from the white reeds that line the river's banks.

Passing through a clutter of stalls, she fingered fabrics lying in drifts: sleepy soft velvet, watery charmeuse, suedes as tender as a mouse's ear. All in shades of black and gray, whites lying among them like discarded moonlight.

The rat sat on the table's edge.

"I can provide well for you," it said. "Fish guts from the docks of Tabat and spoiled meat from its alleyways. I would bring you the orchard's gleanings: squishy apricot and rotted peaches, apples brown as bone and flat as the withered breasts of a crone. I would bring you bits of ripe leather from the tannery, soaked in a soup of pigeon shit and water until it is soft as flesh."

"Why me?" she asked. "Have I given you reason to suspect I would accept your advances?"

It stroked its whiskers in embarrassment. "No," it admitted. "I witnessed you bathing in the river, and saw the touch of iridescence that gilds your limbs, like plump white cheeses floating in the water. I felt desire so strong that I pissed myself, as though my bones had turned to liquid and were flowing out of me. I *must* have you for my wife."

She looked around at the market she had visited each third day for as long as she had been dead. At the tables of wares that never changed but only endlessly rearranged their elements. Then back at the rat.

"You may walk with me," she said.

The rat hopped into the basket and they strolled along in silence. At length, he began to speak.

He told her of the rats of the city without a name, who have lived so long so close to magic that it has seeped into their skin, their eyes, and down into their very guts. How they have seen their civilizations rise and fall over the centuries, and their sorcerers and magicians have learned cunning magics, only to see them torn away each time they re-descended into savagery. How the white-furred rat matrons ruled their current society, sending their swains out to gather them food, eating more and more, in order to gain greater and greater social weight.

"That is what first drew me to this idea," he said. "A human bride would have more weight than any of them. But then when I saw you, it seemed a meaningless and stale calculation."

She felt a thrill of warmth somewhere in her chest. Upon reflection she realized that it was an emotion that she had not felt before she died. It was part interest, and part intrigue, and part vanity, and part something else: a twinge of affection for this rat that promised to make her his world.

"There is no question," her father said. "This would bring change to the City."

"And?"

"And! Do you wish to destroy this place? We are held by the Wizard's spell—fixed in a moment when, dying because we cannot change, we do not die because we cannot change."

Zuleika frowned. "That makes no sense."

"That's because you're young."

"You have only forty years more than my own five thousand, three hundred and twelve. Surely when one considers the years I have lived, I can be reckoned an adult."

"You would think so, if you overlooked the fact that you will always be fifteen."

She stamped her foot and pouted, but centuries can jade even the most indulgent parent. He sent for a Physician.

The Physician came with eager steps, for new cases were few and far between. He insisted on examining Zuleika from head to toe, and would have had her disrobe, save for her father's protest.

"She seems well enough to me," the Physician said in a disappointed tone.

"She believes she wishes to marry."

"Tut, tut," the Physician said in astonishment. "Well now. Love. And you wish this cured?"

"Before the contagion spreads any further or drives her to actions imperiling us all."

Zuleika said nothing. She was well aware she was not in love with the rat. But the idea of change had seized her like a fever.

The Physician overlaid her scalp with a netting of silver wire. Magnets hung like awkward beads amid crystals of midnight onyx and gray feldspar.

"It is a subtle stimulation," he murmured. "And certainly Love is not a subtle energy. But given sufficient time, it will work."

He directed that Zuleika sit in a chair in the parlor without disturbing the netting for three days.

The days passed slowly. Zuleika kept her eyes fixed on the window, which framed a cloudless, sunless, skyless world. She could feel the magnetic energies pulling her thoughts this way and that, but it seemed to her things remained much the same overall.

On the third day, the rat appeared.

"My beautiful fiancée," it said, gazing at where she sat. "What is that thing you wear?"

"It is a mechanism to remove Love," she said.

Its whiskers perked forward, and it looked pleased. "So you are in love?"

"No," she said. "But my father believes that I am."

"Hmmph," said the rat. "Tell me, what is the effect of such a mechanism if you are not in love?"

"I don't know."

It considered, absently flicking its tail.

"Perhaps it will have the opposite effect," it said.

"I have been thinking about that myself," she said. "Indeed, I feel fonder towards you with every passing moment."

"How much longer must you wear it?"

Her eyes sought the clock. "Another hour," she said.

"Then we must wait and see." The rat sniffed the air. "Did your family have muffins again this morning?"

"I've been sitting here for three days; I didn't have breakfast."

"Then I shall be back within a half hour or so," it said and withdrew.

At the hour, the door opened, and her father and the Physician entered. The rat, licking its chops, discreetly moved beneath her chair where, hidden by her skirts, it could not be seen.

"Well, my daughter," her father said, patting her on the back as the Physician removed the apparatus. "Do you feel restored?"

"Indeed I do," she said.

"Good, good!" He clapped the Physician's shoulder, looking pleased. "Good work, man. Shall we retire to discuss your fee?"

The Physician looked at Zuleika. "Perhaps another examination..." he ventured.

"No need," her father said briskly. "Love removed, everything's fixed. Our city can continue on as it has for the past millennium."

When they had gone, the rat crept out from beneath her chair, regarding her. "Well?" it said.

"I do not wish to be married down here."

"We can make our way to the surface and say our vows in Tabat," the rat said. "I know all the tunnels, and where they wind to."

And so she took a lantern from where it hung in the garden, shedding its dim light over the pale vegetation nourished there by sorcery rather than sunlight. They made their way to the first tunnel entrance, the rat riding on her shoulder, and started towards the surface. Behind them, there came a massive crash and crack.

"What was that?" the rat said.

"Nothing," Zuleika said. "Nothing at all, anymore."

She marched on and behind her, the City with No Name continued to fall.

Worm Within

"Worm Within" is a classic unreliable narrator, a robot who believes it is the only secret human being left, and which has grown so alienated from itself that it imagines its own brain is a parasite. The story was sparked by a Halloween contest held by the Codex Writers Group and based on a seed from Rachel Dryden. It appeared in Clarkesworld *in 2008.*

The LED bug kicks feebly, trying to push itself away from the wall. Its wings are rounds of mica, and the hole in its carapace where someone has tacked it to the graying boards reveals cogs and gears, almost microscopic in their dimensions. The light from its underside is the cobalt of distress.

It flutters there, sputtering out blue luminescence, caught between earth and air, between creature life and robot existence. Does it believe itself insect or mechanism? How can it be both at once?

I glide past, skirting the edge of the light it casts, keeping my hood up, watching fog tendrils curl and dissipate. A large street, then a smaller one, then smaller yet, in a deserted quarter that few, if any, occupy. Alleys curling into alleys, cursive scrawls of crumbling bricks and high wooden fences. My head down, I practice walking methodically, mechanically until I find a tiny house in the center of the maze. Mine. Another LED bug is tacked beside the entrance, but this one is long dead, legs dangling.

Once inside, I linger in the foyer, taking off my cloak, the clothes that drape my form as though I were some eccentric, an insistent Clothist, or anxious to preserve my limbs from rust or tarnish. Nude, I revel in my flesh, dancing in the hallway to feel the body's sway and bend. Curved shadows slide like knives over the crossworded tiles on the floor, perfect black and white squares. If there were a mirror I could see myself.

But after only a single pirouette, my inner tenant stirs. He plucks pizzicato at my spine, each painful twang reminding me of his presence, somewhere inside.

He says, *They'll find you soon enough TICK they'll hunt you down. They'll realize TICK what you are, a meat-puppet in a TICK robot world, all the shiny men and women and TICK in-betweens will cry out, knowing what you are. They'll find TICK you. They'll find you.*

I don't know where he lives in my body. Surely what feels like him winding, wormlike, many-footed and long-antennaed through the hallways of my lungs, the chambers of my heart, the slick sluiceway of my intestines—surely the sensation is him using his telekinetic palps to engage my nervous system. I think he must be curled, encysted, an ovoid somewhere between my shoulder blades, a lump below my left rib, a third ovary glimmering deep in my belly.

He says, *You could go out with TICK a bang, you could leap into TICK the heart of a furnace or dive TICK from a building's precipice, before they put you TICK in a zoo with a sign on the wall TICK, "Last Homo Sapiens." Last Fleshbag. Last Body.*

I do not reply. I gather my clothing back to myself and shrug my shoulders underneath the layers, hiding. He flows back and forth, like a scissoring centipede, driving himself along my veins.

In the kitchen, I stuff food in my mouth without thinking about it, wash it down with gulps of murky fluid from the decanter I fill each night from the river. The liquid glistens with oily putrefaction as it pours through my system.

He says, *You disgust me. There are TICK hairs growing inside your body, there TICK are lumps of yellow fat, there are TICK snot and blood clots and bits of refuse TICK. Why won't you die and set me free?*

If only I could wash him away, I'd wallow by the riverside, mouth agape in the shallows, swallowing, swallowing bits of gravel and rusted bolts and the tinny taste of antique tadpoles.

I can't, but even so he doesn't like the thought. He saws at the back of my skull with fingers like grimy glass, until the bare bulb shining above the kitchen table shatters, rains down in shards of migraine light, my vision splintering into headache.

When I sleep, I lie down on a shelf beneath the window on the upper floor. I don't know who used to live in this house—when I found it, the only closet was full of desiccated beetles and rows of blue jars. I fold the spectacles I wear– two circles of glass and brass that I found in a drawer. I set them on the windowsill with the drawing of a clock face I have made. I slide my eyelids closed.

Even asleep, I can feel my parasite whispering to himself, thoughts clicking and ticking away. Turning the circuitry and gears of my brain for his own use.

I dream that I am dreaming I'm not dreaming.

The morning sky unfolds in the window, mottled crimson and purple, like marbled bacon, speckled sausage. Brown clouds devour it to the sound of morning shuffling. I get up. I take the mass transit, I go to the store and buy replicas of food, the same pretense everyone else makes, mourning the regularities of a lost life. I stand on a street corner with a pack of robots, looking at a wall screen. A few are clothed, but most are bare, moisture beading on their chrome and brass forms. Some are sleek, some are retro. No one is like me.

I walk in the park. Where did all these robots come from? What do they want? They look like the people that built them, and they walk along the sidewalk, scuffed and marred by their heavy footsteps. They pretend. That's the only thing that saves me, the only thing that lets me walk among them pretending to be something that is pretending to be me.

I sit on a bench by the plaza's edge, a bend of concrete, splotched with lichen. Little sparrows hop along the back, nervous hops, turning their heads to look at me, one beady eye, then the other. I hold my hand out, palm upward. One hops closer.

Inside my ears, inside my lungs, vibrating inside my bones, I hear him whispering. He tells me where I could throw my body in front of a tram, where I could undermine a bridge, where I could leap in a shower of glass, where I could embrace a generator.

The sparrow lands popcorn-light on my palm. My fingers close over it. The other sparrows panic and fly away as my hand clenches tighter and tighter, latching my thumb over the cage my hand has become, feeling the crunch beneath the fluff.

My fingers spasm before my thumb swings away to let them open. Tiny gears fall and bounce on the concrete, and fans of broken plastic feathers flutter down. I stand and try to walk away, but he keeps talking and talking in my head.

You disgust me, he says, and then for once he is silent, as another presence intrudes, as something touches my arm. It is the creature that raised me, it is my mother robot, made of lengths of copper tubing and a tank swelling for a bosom. Carpet scraps are wrapped around its wrists and ankles. It says through the grillework, its beetle-like mouth hissing and crackling with static. *You are not well, you must come home with me, won't you come home with me? I worry about you.*

How can robots worry? I shake my skull, I turn away so it won't see the meat, the flesh, the body.

You don't know what you're doing, who you are, what you are, it says. The voice is flat, emotionless.

It pulls at me again, but I brace myself and it cannot budge me. It walks away and does not look back. It will come tomorrow and say the same words.

He begins in my head again and I make it only a few steps before crouching down in the middle of the plaza, feeling the passing robots stare at me. I must master this, must master him before the Proctors come and discover me.

I say to the insides of my wrists, the delicate organic bones of my wrists, clothed in blood and sinew, *Listen to me, listen to me. Let me get home, home to safety and I'll give you what you want, whatever you want.*

He releases his grip on my sanity and we walk home quietly. I eat and drink and say, *What do you want?*

Sleep, he says, and for once the voice is gentle. *That's all. Go to sleep. Things will be better in the morning.*

At half past midnight, I open my eyes. On the floor are legs torn from an LED bug, dried shells, silver scraps. I watch and he lifts one, then another, drifts and clicks so quiet I cannot hear them. One, then another, and then both. As though he was practicing. As though he was getting better. Stronger.

I didn't know he could use his telekinesis outside my body. As the last shell falls, I feel him lapse, exhausted, into his own simulacrum of sleep.

Downstairs there are no knives in the kitchen, but there is a piece of metal molding that I can peel away from the counter's edge. Slipping and sliding across the floor and the fungus growing on the ancient bits of food scattered there, I go into the living room, an empty box like every other room here, but here the walls are red, red as blood. The blood I imagine, over and over, in my veins.

I poise the knife before my belly and I say goodbye to my body, to the burps and the shit, to the unexpected moles and the cramps and the itches, and flakes of skin and hot sore pimples. To my good, hallucinatory-rich flesh. To my bones that have pretended to carry me for so long. To my delusive blood.

He wakes and says *What are you doing?* And *No.* Even as the length of metal slides into me, and I look down to see my foil skin sliding away, to reveal my secret's secret to the world, to show my gears and cogs and shining steaming lunatic wires, and in the midst of it, the clockwork centipede uncoiling, he is my brain seeing itself uncoiling and recoiling and discoiling, my mechanical, irrational brain saying *No* and *No* and *No* again.

Magnificent Pigs

I wrote "Magnificent Pigs" in the fall of 2005. It owes much of its inspiration to my classmate Kris Dikeman, who both suffered through a tattoo while I was watching (and was irritated that I was writing down the names of inks while she was in pain) and contributed the idea that Charlotte (and by extension Jilly) remains alive through fiction.

"Magnificent Pigs" originally appeared in Strange Horizons *in November 2006. It has been reprinted several times and appeared in audio form, read by Matthew Wayne Selznick, on* Podcastle.

The spring before it happened, I went upstairs and found my ten-year old sister Jilly crying. *Charlotte's Web*, which we'd been reading together at bedtime all that week, lay splayed on the floor where she'd thrown it.

"What's wrong?" I said, hovering in the doorway. As Jilly had gotten sicker I tried to offer her the illusion of her own space but remained ready in case big brotherly comfort was needed.

"I was reading ahead because I liked it so much—and Charlotte dies!" she managed to gasp between sobs.

The big brass bed creaked in protest as I sat down beside her. Gathering her into my arms, I rocked her back and forth. It was well past sunset and the full-faced moon washed into the room, spilling across the blue rag rug like milk and gleaming on the bed knobs so they looked like balls of icy light contending with the dim illumination of Jilly's bedside lamp.

"It's a book, Jilly, just a book," I said.

She shook her head, cheeks blotched red and wet with tears. "But, Aaron, Charlotte's dead!" she choked out again.

I retrieved the book from the middle of the room and set it in front of her. "Look," I said. "If we open the book up again at the beginning, Charlotte's alive. She'll always be alive in the book."

The sobs quieted to hiccups and she reached for the book, looking dubious. When she opened it to the first chapter, I began to read. "Where's Papa going with that ax?' said Fern to her mother as they were setting the table for breakfast. 'Out to the hoghouse,' replied Mrs. Arable. 'Some pigs were born last night.'"

Curling against me, she let me read the first two chapters. After she slipped away to sleep, I tucked the blanket around her then went downstairs to cry my own tears.

My father and mother were farmers. They were raised by farmers who had themselves been raised by farmers and so on back to Biblical days. They saw my talent for drawing as a hobby until the age of seventeen, when I proposed that my major in college be an uneasy mixture of art and agriculture. They were dubious but they were also good-natured sorts who only wanted the best for me. So they sent me, eldest of their two children, off to Indiana University. Jilly takes after them.

Jilly, a late arrival to the family, was six years old at the point I left. She consumed most of their attention, which I did not begrudge her. From day one she was a tiny, perfect addition to our household and I loved her.

Three years later on a rainy September afternoon my parents died in a car accident and I returned home to the farm to take care of Jilly. A few townfolk felt I shouldn't be allowed to raise her by myself but a year later when I hit twenty one, that magic number at which you apparently become an adult, they stopped fussing.

Since the other driver was not only drunk but driving a bus with faulty brakes that another company had failed to fix, the court settlement provided enough to live on. I supplemented it by raising pigs and apples in the way my parents always had and taking them to Indianapolis where the pigs were purchased by a plant that made organic bacon, pork, and sausage and the apples by a cider mill. I didn't mind the farm work. I'd get up in the morning, take care of things, and find myself a few hours in the afternoon to work in the studio I'd fixed in the attic.

A year ago Jilly started getting stomach aches so bad they had her doubled over, crying. When I first took her to the hospital, they diagnosed it as Crohn's disease. Six months later, after I'd learned the vocabulary of aminosalicylates and corticosteroids and immunomodulators, they switched to a simpler word: cancer.

Insurance covered the medical bills. It didn't cover much else so I laid aside my art and bought some more pigs. I had to hire a nurse to take care of Jilly whenever I couldn't—I wanted someone with her all the time. I didn't want her lonely or unable to help herself.

At first I hired a chilly but competent woman, Miss Andersen. She was expensive, but I figured she was worth it. I had a crazy idea that I'd use my talent to become a tattoo artist and make enough extra cash to pay her. A Superior mobile tattoo set from E-Bay cost me a hundred bucks and got me started. I named my enterprise Magnificent Pigs, in honor of Wilbur.

But tattoos aren't a high demand item in Traversville, and you need to practice a lot to get any good at it. Once I'd run out of old high school friends who were willing to let me work on them in the name of a free tattoo, I turned to the pigs.

It's not as cruel as it sounds, I swear. According to the vet, pig skin is tough as nails and has few nerve endings. He sells me cartons of a topical anesthetic lotion that I use beforehand, just in case.

The pigs have never objected. They're placid beasts—give them a bowl of mash and they don't care what you do. My dad believed in playing classical music to calm the animals so I crank Beethoven cello suites to hide the buzz of the needle, and go to town. The first time I took a tattooed pig to the slaughterhouse, they gave me odd looks when they saw where I'd inscribed, "Mother," "Semper Fi," and "Tattooing gets pretty boring after a while" in blue and red and black on the leathery white skin, but as long as it didn't mark the meat, it was okay.

I didn't achieve my dreams of becoming a brand name tattoo artist, no matter how many coiling koi and serpents I covered the pigs with. Southern Indiana is a conservative place—the KKK had its second rebirth nearby—and there is no room for much outside the mainstream designs like scorpions, the Confederate flag, and tribal symbols from no tribe that ever existed. I liked the business because it made me feel like an artist but few people came out for tattoos.

I had to let Miss Andersen go, promising I'd have her back wages for her within six months. She wasn't happy about it but had a good contract with the nursing home waiting so she let it slide.

Jilly was glad to see her depart but didn't tell me till weeks later about the meanness that had revealed itself when tending a hapless ten year old.

"She was just mean," Jilly said.

"She never touched you, did she?" I asked cautiously.

"No, not like that. She pinched me a few times but mostly she said mean things. Like what a shame it was that I was an orphan and how you'd probably get rid of me when you got married."

I looked at her but her face was clear and unworried.

"That didn't bother you, Jilly?" I asked.

"I knew you'll always take care of me."

Which was all fine and well but even so Miss Andersen's departure made it feel as though things were pressing in on all sides. Nightmares lapped at my sleep all that night.

The next day, strung out on caffeine and weariness, I stood in the cramped grocery store aisle looking at jams and sandwich spreads and couldn't decide between crunchy and smooth peanut butter. I literally couldn't remember which Jilly or I preferred. I must have stood there for ten minutes.

See, one of the side effects of the disease is nausea and loss of appetite. Peanut butter's one of the few things Jilly will eat, and it's high in protein. So it's important to bring home the right one.

There's a wide variety of peanut butter labels. I stood there, looking at Jif and Skippy and Peter Pan and Kroger brand, going through the same loop in my head over and over: "No I think I like crunchy and Jilly likes smooth, but maybe it's the other way around, and what other groceries do we need, but first—crunchy or smooth?" While this frenzied loop continued, I became aware that a woman and her cart had been circling me, going back and forth in the aisle and warding off other shoppers. The Muzak on the store intercom switched from one piano piece to another.

Finally she stopped beside me. "Buy them both," she advised. It broke the spell that had held me.

I turned. She was an elderly woman dressed in black, a blue and white scarf bound around her hair to hold it in place. She had a beaklike nose and bright black eyes that glittered at me as though daring me to rebuff her. It was Mrs. Huber, whose husband had died a few years before. I don't know why she stuck in Bedford. She had, and was an object of some curiosity, being the town's only Jew. Jilly and I are a step outside that, being people whose parents were born elsewhere as well as the family of the town invalid.

"Thank you," I said, and took down two jars. She stood beside me, and it didn't feel awkward at all. Like we were family who had happened to meet there and would see each other again at dinner.

She said, "The little girl needs a nurse, no?"

"Yeah, she does," I said. I gestured at the shelves. "It's okay, though. I just got a little side-tracked, that's all."

We stared at each other. My only other encounter with Mrs. Huber had been selling her salt water taffy when I was in sixth grade and trying to win a trip to Washington, D.C. in the school candy drive. I found out later she bought candy from every kid that approached her. With three grades selling, ten to fifteen kids in each class, that must have been a substantial pile of sweets.

She didn't look too much older now. The lines around her eyes were more defined and her lips drooped at a harsher angle. Finally she said, simply, "You need nurse too maybe?" and after that we came to an arrangement.

Jilly loved her like a mother. I got fond of her myself. There was a certain irony to a Jew living on a pig farm, particularly with a tattoo artist. She didn't keep kosher, so she ate with us each night, although she'd never touch pork. I cooked any pork chops, or sausage, or bacon, or other variants of pig meat. But most of the time I left it to her to cook. She coaxed Jilly's tender appetite with blintzes and rugelach, kugel and kreplach. The kitchen took on a simmer of cinnamon that was a pleasant change from TV dinners.

After supper we'd sit in the parlor, Jilly watching TV or reading while I studied up on farming or tattooing methods and Mrs. H. knitted. She turned out shawls, scarves, baby blankets, and a multitude of sweaters for Jilly, with patterns of pigs or flowers. Jilly's favorite was the one with her name knitted into the front. She'd scold me for working too hard and when I came in bone weary from a day of fretting about pig vaccines or Jilly's latest set of tests, she'd say in her harsh accent, "Worries go down better with soup."

Sometimes I thought that God had sent her by way of apology.

I don't want to make it sound like everything was fine. But it wasn't as bad as it could be, at least for a while.

I was practicing on one of the pigs, writing out words, when Jilly came into the barn and leaned on the bench near me. It was early spring warm. By now we were long past recognizing the smell of pig shit—sometimes I forgot that it clung like an invisible film to my clothing until I noticed people edging away from me in lines.

The other smells weren't hidden by the omnipresent odor: the sour redolence of corn mash, the tang of the straw underfoot, the distant sweetness of apple blossom coming in through the window.

"What are you doing?" Jilly asked.

"Practicing writing words," I said.

"What's that?" she said, pointing to a passage of text on the pig's rounded back.

"It's the first verse of 'Stairway to Heaven.'"

"Nice."

"It was the only poetry I could remember off the top of my head," I said.

She sat there watching me, so I started tattooing the words that Charlotte uses to describe Wilbur onto the pig's broad back. When I reached "Magnificent," she giggled, just as Mrs. H. called us to dinner. She went ahead while I cleaned off my needles.

She asked me at dinner, "Don't we have runts that we could keep? Like Wilbur?"

"Jilly, we can't afford to keep them as pets," I said. She couldn't have a cat or dog because of allergies, not to mention my own fears about compromising her immune system. She started to protest and I cut her off. "That's final."

But that night, after Jilly was asleep, Mrs. H. said to me, "Maybe you should give her a pig for a pet."

"We can't afford it."

She looked at me, her eyes sad. "I think she might be gone before the pig gets sent off."

"She's getting better," I said. "Look at how she chattered all through dinner."

But she was right, and we both knew it.

"When one must, one can," she said gently.

The next morning dawned hard and bright, and it seemed inevitable that after a long night's birthing, one of the pregnant sows had six perfect piglets surrounding her in the straw. I took Jilly out to look at them and told her to pick one.

"It has to be the runt," she said. And then, "But they're all the same size!"

I looked at her, leaning on the railing with her gawky bird-like arms, so thin that she could wear rubber bands for bracelets, and felt a hard lump in my throat.

"Take them all, Jilly," I said. "They'll all be your pigs."

She named them Celeste, Patience, Rutabaga, Bill, Princess Ozma, and (predictably) Wilbur. Jilly spent hours by the pen, wrapped in a blanket and watching the piglets with an expression of beatific joy. They came to know her and would come when she called. She spent enough time petting them that I got in the habit of spraying them down with a hose in the mornings and evenings, to cut down on the amount of pig smell that ended up clinging to her. The mother pig remained unmoved by Jilly's appreciation of her young, but when the piglets were napping, piled on each other like puppies, tiny tails swishing like sporadic windshield wipers, she and Jilly beamed down at them with identical expressions.

Mrs. H. professed to hate them. "Trafe!" she said, and spat whenever they were mentioned, but I noticed her assembling leftovers for Jilly to feed them.

The piglets grew fast, prancing around the yard like models in high heels, stealing bits of food from Jilly's hand. All the while my baby sister diminished, curled in on herself as though she were becoming a little old woman, as though each day the cancer claimed another morsel, scraping her from the inside, hollowing her out till she was light as air..

Jilly's pigs were fat and fine, sleek as colts and almost full grown when I came home one day to find her weeping even harder than she had for Charlotte, while Mrs. H. fussed around her.

"What happened?" I demanded. "Is she in pain?"

"That very bad woman," Mrs. H. said. "She came by to speak to you, Mr. Aaron, about her money. Such a tongue in her head should rot."

"What did she say?"

"It was Miss Andersen. I told her that I was going to school next year," Jilly said. She clung to me, and hot tears soaked my neck. "Because by then I would be better, and she laughed and said I'd be better when pigs grow wings and fly. Is it true, Aaron? Am I not going to get better? Am I going to die?"

"No, no," I said, clutching her to me. "No, Jilly, you are going to school next year."

Mrs. H regarded me. We'd had this argument before. She thought I should tell Jilly, but I wouldn't. I wouldn't let her know she was dying. That would make it too real.

"No," I said, and pressed a kiss onto the top of her head. "It's all right, Jilly. It will be all right."

She let herself be comforted, but all through that evening, I felt myself angrier and angrier at Miss Andersen's words. Going outside, I looked at Jilly's pigs. Fat and happy, while my sister lay inside wasting away.

I went inside and fetched my tattoo kit. I was tired, but too angry to sleep, and I could tell I'd be up for hours. Mrs. H. came out and waved goodbye to me as she revved her tiny Civic and drove away, her headlights cutting swaths in the darkness of the farm road. Overhead, the stars were bright and distinct in the fathomless sky. I opened the door to the pen and Jilly's tame pigs followed me into the barn.

I set up shop in an abandoned stall, and when I was finished with one pig, it would walk out to the others to be inspected proprietarily while another one came in.

I gave them wings.

It was the finest work I'd ever done. For Celeste, a phoenix's wings, flame bright, coiling red and yellow. Patience's skin displayed a dove's wings, muted in color, browns and grays that showed like bruises against the white hide. A blue jay's wings for Rutabaga, a vivid iridescent blue striped with black. Bill got green plumage like a parrot's, touched with scarlet and indigo at the tips. Princess Ozma's were gold and silver, a metallic sheen that reflected light and cast it across the pen.

And Wilbur had black wings, black as night. Black as death.

It took hours as they stood patiently beneath the buzzing needle, letting me etch the lines into their skin, wiping away the blood that welled up beneath the images. When I was done, I was so tired I could not stand. Instead, I sat there on my stool, looking at them.

One by one, they circled in front of me, like some ritual. The Inspection of the Pigs by the Artist, I thought. I debated going to sleep where I sat or somehow, impossibly, hauling myself up the stairs and into my own bed. The pigs shuffled around each other, and admired my bright-inked creations on their backs. And I found myself dreaming. I dreamed that I sat there watching while Wilbur went to the door and nosed it open, the pigs slipping out into the yard and making their way to the house, where Wilbur repeated his performance and one by one they slipped inside the door.

And then I shook myself awake, and stumbled to my feet. The door was wide open and the pigs were gone, so I scrambled out to the yard to see it empty as well. Up on Jilly's balcony, movement caught my eye and the French doors shuddered open. A shadow lifted from the balcony, an impossible boxy shadow that floated across the sky, blocking out the clouds that outlined it in pearly tones.

As the moonlight struck it, I saw what it was. Jilly's brass bed, the frame supported on either side by three flying pigs. Their wings beat the air in tandem while she sat upright, her face moonlight bright with wonder as she gazed forward.

Did she notice me, did she wave? I'm not sure, because clouds obscured the view as she rose higher and higher into the sky. I'd like to think she didn't—that she knew Mrs. H. and I would take care of each other, and that she didn't need to look back.

I like to think that every inch of her attention was focused on the journey, on that marvelous moment when we both learned that pigs could fly.

A Chronology of Tabat

The seaport of Tabat is a major seaport in the world in which many of my stories and the novel *The Moon's Accomplice* are set. It is located on the south-eastern coast of the New Continent, an area settled by refugees from the Old Continent, destroyed by wars between rival sorcerers, as detailed in "A Twine of Flame" and "Sugar."

I originally designed Tabat for a game that never came to fruition. I found, though, that I'd imagined it clearly enough—as I should have, having drawn out and described its major streets and landmarks—that I felt compelled to tell some of the stories taking place within it. I can say with assurance that it has plenty more to supply.

Paper Golem

LaVergne, TN USA
22 September 2010
198122LV00001B/142/P